When you recommend a book to a friend, you want to say, "This book is like this other book that you enjoy!" *The Mean Reds* is going to make you want to say, "This book is kind of Augusten Burroughs, but kind of Chuck Palahniuk, but kind of Christopher Moore, but kind of Kurt Vonnegut." You're going to want to say that because a) you WILL want to recommend it to your friends; and b) your brain will be wrestling with the truth: *The Mean Reds* isn't like anything you've ever read before. It's a truly unique debut novel, full of broken people and unreliable narration and cringe-inducing situations, all told in Bridges' distinctive, masterful prose. It's goddamned glorious.

    - Dr. Christopher Bell, Skydance Animation

Dale Bridges' debut novel is a hilarious bourbon-soaked, hash-toned slacker noir with an unforgettable, stumbling cinephile at its heart. Bridges is natural at crafting worlds and populating them with wild, endearing, outrageous, and utterly believed characters. Expect conspiracies, parties, drugs, and more classic movie references than you can shake a weed pipe at. Also expect the unexpected. This book will surprise you!

    - Owen Egerton, author of *Hollow* and the
    writer/director of *Mercy Black*

Packed with highly caffeinated observations on pop culture and classic film icons and an unreliably hungover writer protagonist, *The Mean Reds* announces Dale Bridges as a hip, smart, and wickedly funny writer.

    - Jesse Sublett III, author of *Last Gangster in Austin*

For more information:
Stephen F. Austin State University Press
P.O. Box 13007 SFA Station
Nacogdoches, Texas 75962
sfapress@sfasu.edu
www.sfasu.edu/sfapress

Managing Editor: Kimberly Verhines
Book design: Katt Noble
Cover Design: Katt Noble

Distributed by Texas A&M Consortium
www.tamupress.com

ISBN: 978-1-62288-925-9

THE MEAN REDS

a novel by

Dale Bridges

STEPHEN F. AUSTIN STATE UNIVERSITY PRESS

For Michelle. Barf.

Chapter 1: The Long Goodbye

THIS ALL STARTED BECAUSE MY EDITOR wanted me to write a story about a dead stripper. She left a message on my cell phone telling me to be at her office at nine o'clock sharp. I rolled out of bed at three-thirty in the afternoon with the mother of all hangovers and braced myself against the familiar nausea and vertigo that followed. The contents of my stomach pitched and moaned, but mercifully everything stayed where it belonged. Afterward, I found a cold slice of pepperoni in the fridge and a half-smoked joint on the coffee table, and decided perhaps I wasn't going to die after all.

While I sat cross-legged on my bed, eating breakfast and staring into the void of alcohol-soaked memories from the previous evening, Aubrey Hepburn began rubbing against my leg and purring accusingly, and I remembered I was supposed to pick up cat food from the store. Again. I pulled back the Marx Brothers blanket that was nailed to the wall in lieu of a curtain, and opened the window. Immediately, I regretted it. It was mid-January, and there wasn't a cloud in the sky. The sun's rays were like dirty syringes being shoved through my eye sockets and into my dehydrated brain. So far it had been the warmest winter in Colorado since the drought of '75. Temperatures had dropped below freezing on several occasions and there had been some snow flurries around Christmas, but nothing stuck. The ski season was a bust, and out on the prairie, farmers were already preparing for crop failure. Newscasters kept claiming we were due for a record-breaking blizzard, but as the weeks passed and even the mountaintops remained bone-dry, murmurs about where said newscasters could stick their predictions were growing louder and more creative.

Squinting into the glare, I put Audrey on the windowsill and said, "See if Doc will let you steal some of his Fancy Feast." There was a fat one-eyed Maine Coon that lived with a grad student across the street and he had a crush on Audrey. He was neutered so he couldn't knock her up, but that didn't stop the old eunuch from puffing out his tail and sniffing her ass whenever she happened by. Audrey wasn't interested, but she wasn't above letting him cop a feel if it meant a full belly. My landlord had an irrational aversion to cats, so Audrey came and went via a sick elm tree out back that had one thick, dead branch that conveniently scraped the side of the building next to my only window. She sniffed the air and looked at me indignantly. "I know, I know," I said. "I'll pick some up today. I *promise*." Finally, she hopped onto the branch and proceeded to the rooftop of the enormous, colonial fraternity house next door, and then onto the balcony and down a staircase. She shot me one last I'm-going-to-piss-on-your-favorite-shirt-while-you're-sleeping glare, flicked her tail, and then she was gone. I experienced the usual panicked heart-flutter of a protective father watching his only child cross the street alone for the first time, wanting to run after her and shower her with kisses, but the moment soon passed.

Behind the frat house there were two muscular boy-men wearing nothing but athletic shorts and backward-facing baseball hats with Greek letters embroidered on them. Despite the unseasonal weather, it was still winter on the Front Range and therefore too cold to go shirtless, a fact the hairless duo were studiously trying to ignore. They were shivering over a barbeque grill, sucking on vapes and clutching giant silver cans of Pabst. One of them spotted my head poking out of the window and yelled, "Chicken titty?"

"Excuse me?" I said.

He pulled the grill open, revealing half a dozen charred hamburgers, as many sausages, and several large chicken breasts smeared with red sauce. He pointed at one of the breasts with the spatula and giggled like a sixth grader. "You want a chicken titty? We have extras."

The smell of roasting flesh and cherry tobacco smoke filled my nostrils, causing my stomach to lurch, and I cursed the smooth-chested bastards.

"No, thanks," I said.

"Suit yourself, bro," he replied, somehow offended.

I belched and the tangy taste of bile burned the back of my tongue. The room began to spin once again. I banged the window closed and frantically kicked around a pile of laundry until I found my blue hoodie and a pair of moldy flip-flops. I put them on and shuffled as fast as possible across the hall to the bathroom.

My apartment building was a former sorority house located three blocks west of Mountainview University, which would have been my alma mater if I hadn't dropped out in the middle of my final semester six years ago. The building had no official name, but everyone who lived there called it The Trap, either because of the plethora of dead rodents and cockroaches decomposing within its sodden walls or because, like the house in Robert Wise's 1963 psychological thriller *The Haunting*, the structure had a tendency to ensnare its occupants, holding them in thrall for decades while it slowly drained their life force. It was an imposing slab of whitewashed brick and brown ivy with red plastic cups perpetually littering the dead front lawn. Rent was seven hundred dollars a month including utilities, the cheapest lodging in town by at least a hundred bucks. The residents were all harmless losers who needed temporary housing. Some of them had been recently released from jail on minor offenses—petty theft, disturbing the peace, that sort of thing. Others were mentally unstable but not crazy enough to be institutionalized. There were at least two drug dealers, three occupants with bipolar disorder, one Korean exchange student, and a schizophrenic in a pear tree. Most were alcoholics. They were all men, primarily in their thirties and forties, misfit Lost Boys who'd wandered away from Neverland and accidentally grown up. There was nowhere else for them to go in this increasingly expensive tourist paradise. My room was two hundred square feet of frayed carpet and peeling lead paint. There was just enough space for a mini fridge, a futon bed, a Goodwill couch, a coffee table, two bookcases filled with three thousand four hundred thirty-eight movies (including two hundred seventeen Criterions, thank you very much), and a seventy-five-inch flat-screen LED HDTV with built-in Wi-Fi and surround sound that took up the entire wall. The communal kitchen and bathroom were both across the hall, which made my frequent morning vomiting sessions a public performance.

As always, when I opened the bathroom door, the Mayor was standing in front of the wall-length mirror, shirtless, eyes red and glassy with manic fervor, clutching a green dry-erase marker in his hairy-knuckled right hand, his rotund gut resting on the sink as he leaned in to draw a rectangular box around the name "L.H. OSWALD," which had been scribbled on the mirror in child-like block letters, surrounded by the words "CIA," "G. SOROS," "DEEP STATE," "9/11," and "MKULTRA."

"Precisely, precisely," he mumbled as he drew an arrow connecting the green rectangle to a red triangle above it containing the name "WILLIAM CAMPBELL." He turned to me and waved the marker like a frantic conductor keeping time for an invisible orchestra. "Why didn't I see it before? It's so obvious. That's how The Beatles got the *White Album*. *White Album*...White House. 'Revolution 9'...nine Supreme Court Justices. It's so obvious."

The Mayor was the landlord of The Trap, as well as the resident conspiracy theorist, and he spent approximately six hours a day in the bathroom waiting for some poor schmuck to use the toilet so he could ambush them with his latest rant. I had been avoiding the restroom altogether for the last two weeks because I owed the man a considerable amount of money, but this was an emergency. Before he could ensnare me in a conversation, I turned my back on him and kicked open the nearest stall. Inside the porcelain bowl was an unflushable gumbo of toilet paper, feces, and cigarette butts. I backed out with my palm over my mouth. The next stall had a handmade out-of-order sign taped to the door in the same manic scrawl as the letters on the mirror. I belched again, and my lower jaw began to tingle. I started to panic.

Thankfully, the third toilet proved serviceable, and I fell to my knees in front of it just as a stream of pizza and whiskey shot fountain-like out of my mouth.

"Not feeling so good, huh?" said the Mayor. I tried to tell him to shut up, but all that came out was a whimper and another retching session. "You got in pretty late last night," he continued, the words sounding distant and hollow from inside the bowl, like the voice of God in a Cecil B. DeMille movie. "Two o'clock in the morning. I was listening to Alex Jones. Did you know there are chemicals in our drinking water that are turning frogs gay? Now, don't get me wrong, man, I got nothing against the homosexual community as such. My nephew is gay. I think. Or maybe he just likes eyeliner. You know how kids are these days. None of my affair. What one consenting adult does with another consenting adult inside the confines of his or her own domicile with various lubes and devices is none of my affair. But, you know, man, amphibians, Sam… *amphibians*, well, they got no choice in the matter. Uncle Sam decides to put fluoride in the water supposedly for dental hygiene reasons, but of course it doesn't stop there. Next thing you know they're testing out all kinds of drugs on the population. That's why these kids are maturing so quickly these days. Have you noticed that? Junior high girls with fully developed mammaries and eleven-year-old boys with mustaches. It's the hormones in the water, and believe you me, gay frogs are just the beginning. You don't usually stay out that late on Thursdays, but I guess you had a big date or something. Did you have a big date or something, Sam?"

The Mayor tracked the movements of all the residents in The Trap. His room was at the front of the house with a large bay window facing the street, and when he wasn't trying to solve the JFK assassination on the bathroom mirror or microwaving Hungry-Man dinners, that's where he sat, hour after hour, like Norman Bates' mother in *Psycho*, smoking weed and listening to alt-media podcasts on his laptop.

His real name was Kenneth Nostmann, but everyone called him the Mayor. He had once been the mayor of Mountainview, back in the mid-'70s, when the city was still a quaint little hippie hamlet, and Kenneth was a quaint little twenty-two-year-old hippie, fresh out of college, complete with long flowing blonde hair, paisley bell-bottoms, and patchy mutton chops. He ran for office on a lark, telling the newspaper he'd recently graduated with a philosophy degree and could not find suitable employment. When the primary Democratic candidate dropped out of the race because of a family emergency, Kenneth found himself facing off against a far-right dinosaur whose platform included segregated swimming pools and a crucifix on the front lawn of the post office. Kenneth's father was a prominent businessman who owned property all over the Front Range, and even though he didn't support his son's farcical campaign, the Nostmann name carried weight in the local community. Kenneth won by less than five hundred votes. To everyone's surprise, he took the position seriously and ended up occupying the mayor's office for two relatively uneventful years before he was ousted by a more traditional candidate in a three-piece suit. Unfortunately, Kenneth did not take the loss well. He claimed the election was rigged by "Nixon's plumbers," and despite his family's protests, he vowed to spend the rest of his life exposing the dark powers that had conspired to keep him out of public office. Kenneth's parents didn't disown him exactly, but they did choose to move out of the state shortly thereafter. The Nostmanns sold off all their assets and retired to Florida, leaving their son a single piece of property as his inheritance. Kenneth was supposed to hang on to The Trap for a few years and then sell it when the market was up, but instead he moved in and started renting out the rooms, dealing drugs to his borders when he needed extra cash.

Forty years and seven Grateful Dead songs later, here he remained, trapped in The Trap, trying to suss out how it all connected—Kennedy, Lennon, Malcolm X, the Bay of Pigs, and his failed political ideals. The property was probably worth a cool million by now. His blond hair had turned gray and abandoned the apex of his scalp, leaving a greasy horseshoe around the edges that he pulled back into a sad ponytail; his stomach had ballooned into a hairy mass reminiscent of a pregnant orangutan; and despite the thickness of his round wire-rimmed glasses, he could barely see ten feet in front of his face. He left the apartment to do laundry and buy groceries, but aside from that, he was here. Always.

"Last Thursday, you came home right before midnight, and you were with that girl. The one with the red hair. You didn't introduce me to her, man, so I don't know her name. I remember because I was watching the Zapruder film, and she looked a little like Jackie O. Not the hair so much, or the body, or the face, but there was something about her eyes. You ever notice how Jackie's eyes are set too far apart, like a deer or a rabbit? Prey animals have eyes on the sides of their heads for greater peripheral vision, while predators have eyes in front. Anyhow, the girl you brought home last Thursday…the one with the red hair…she had prey-animal eyes like Jackie. Did you notice that, man?"

My abdominal muscles were on fire. Throwing up was really the only form of physical exercise that I got. It wasn't a great cardiovascular workout, but I did have a flat stomach. I leaned my head against the side of the bowl for a short breather and then went back to work. Two more dry heaves to make sure I'd made a full deposit and I felt whole again. I flushed, wiped away the tears, and stood up, a full-fledged *homo erectus* once again. Meanwhile, the Mayor was still narrating fragments from my life like a bloated, balding Rod Serling setting up the premise for the most boring episode of *The Twilight Zone* ever made.

"And then last Friday, you didn't come home at all. I mean, you came home eventually, of course, but not that night. I asked you about that later and you said you slept over at a friend's house and I asked you what friend and you said that was none of my business and I said, 'You got that right.' Remember that, man?" He put the marker under his nostrils and inhaled deeply. "By the way, you owe me sixteen-hundred forty-seven dollars and thirty-five cents."

This was something the Mayor was particularly adept at. He would lull you into a false sense of security with blather about gay frogs and Trap gossip, and then, just when you thought he was a harmless addle-brained socialist, he'd ambush you with capitalist demands.

I rinsed my mouth out with water and spat in the sink. "Sixteen-hundred? That can't be right."

"Sixteen forty-seven and thirty-five cents." He pointed to the far corner of the mirror, which contained a row of numbers underneath the words "Sam D," and then he began listing my expenses. "Rent for November and December, plus that ounce you bought from me on New Year's Eve. Remember that? You came home with that blonde, knocked on my door at two in the morning, said you'd pay me in a week. That was sixteen days ago."

"Oh, right. I forgot about New Year's."

He put the cap back on the marker and set it on the sink. "I bet you did. And then October tenth you needed thirty-five cents for the laundromat. Said you had to do a load of whites. Emergency, you said. Never did get that back to me, man. Of course, these figures don't include the late penalties."

"Late what? Ah, come on."

"It's right there in the lease, man. If you don't pay by the third of the month, there's a hundred dollar fee and an additional penalty every subsequent week thereafter. We went over this last month." He inserted his index finger into the dark cavern of his bellybutton up to the second knuckle and began to rummage around in there thoughtfully. "That's the problem with your generation. Always looking for a handout. Never planning ahead. This isn't a charity house I'm running, man. I gotta eat too, you know."

It didn't look as though he had been skipping any meals recently, but I held my tongue.

"I told you I'd get you the money. I have a couple of checks I haven't cashed, and my editor called this morning with an assignment."

"Another movie review?" he sneered. "I don't think that's going to cover it, man."

"A cover story."

I had no intention of writing the article, but he didn't need to know that. Like most shut-ins, the Mayor loved gossip, especially if it involved city politics or law enforcement, hoping to one day uncover the poison pill he could force feed the Mountainview Illuminati and reinstate himself in the seat of power. He was incredibly well informed on local affairs for someone who never read a newspaper or went outside.

"Well, well. Look who's playing with the big boys," he said. "What's it about?"

"You know I can't tell you that. But it's a huge piece. It'll cover my debt and then some. You'll see."

"Yeah but…"

"Great. I'll let you know when the check comes in."

I exited the bathroom before he could stop me, rushed across the hall to my room, and bolted the door. I wasn't worried about the Mayor. He liked to talk big, but the man rarely followed through on any of his threats. He'd calm down if I gave him five-hundred dollars. Of course, I didn't have five-hundred dollars and I couldn't avoid the bathroom forever, but that was a problem for another day.

I pulled the blanket off the bed and wrapped myself in it again. I was already seven hours late for the meeting with my editor, so I figured one more wouldn't make a difference. The Mayor had disrupted my morning routine, and I needed to be centered if I was going to make it through what promised to be a challenging day.

I gargled with mouthwash and spat into a *Nosferatu* mug sitting on the windowsill. I plucked the joint off the coffee table and finished it off in three enormous hits. I put a kettle of water on the hotplate and fired up the DVD player. It felt like a Humphrey Bogart kind of day. I selected *The Maltese Falcon*. I didn't have time to watch the whole thing, so I skipped ahead to my favorite scene, the one at the end where Bogie, in a smashing pin-striped double-breasted suit, presents the bad guys with the coveted falcon statue the movie is named after, which turns out to be a fake, causing a perm-headed bow-tie-wearing Peter Lorre to shout obscenities at a fat dapper Sydney Greenstreet before falling into a chair and crying like a baby. When the criminals leave, Bogie immediately turns them in to the police before badgering a murder confession out of doe-eyed femme fatale Mary Astor, while simultaneously declaring his undying love for her. This all happens in the span of about four minutes.

The kettle began to whistle. I poured the hot water into a mug over an Earl Grey tea bag and dumped in three heaping spoons of sugar. I blew and sipped. I opened my laptop and logged onto my website. I wrote: *Watching* The Maltese Falcon *hungover and high, which is really the only way to watch* The Maltese Falcon, *methinks. I love how romantic relationships work in old movies. There's no dating, no casual sex, no moving in together to see if you're emotionally compatible, none of that half-assed postmodern crap they talk about in* Cosmo. *She walks into the room looking like a million bucks and, BAM, you both just know. So what if she turns out to be a ruthless sociopath who murdered your business partner and lied about it? Does that mean you dump her? Hell, no. You banter with her for a while, insult her, prove that you know just how dark her soul really is, and then, in the middle of an argument, you plant a kiss on her. But not one of those gross twenty-first century open-mouthed kisses. No way. It's got to be a classic-movie kiss, a black-and-white kiss. A kiss where you grab her roughly by the head and mash your face against hers while the violin music swells in the background. No tongues allowed. And even if she's a no-good deceitful devil woman and you're a hard-boiled detective with a secret sentimental streak and you have to send her to jail for twenty years, she knows you'll be right there waiting for her when she gets out. Because that's what love is, baby doll.*

I posted it on the usual social networking sites. The likes and lols immediately began rolling in. I closed the computer and started looking around for my coat and bus pass. Someone at the paper was bound to see that post and report it up the chain. Now I definitely had to get to work.

Chapter 2: His Girl Friday

THE *MOUNTAINVIEW CHRONICLE* WAS LOCATED on the far north end of town in a building so square and unimaginative, it could have been made out of Legos by a slow third grader. There was a garden conspicuously placed out front so everyone could see the publisher's daughter harvesting organic tomatoes in a bikini during the summer. Inside, the carpet was thin and brown and the walls were beige, and the entire space was divided up by cubicles like a cramped maze for over-caffeinated rats obsessed with the *AP Style Manual*. I had never actually taken a journalism class myself, so I simply wrote my reviews in my own style, much to the chagrin of the beleaguered editorial staff who had to correct them each week. There were three full-time editors and a dozen freelance writers who provided content. All were grotesquely underpaid. However, despite such a meager crew, they still managed to put out a quality paper every Wednesday, complete with local news, cultural commentary, music criticism, event listings, comics, restaurant reviews, and classifieds. I had no idea how they did it, nor did I want to find out.

When I entered the building, the receptionist, Chloe—"It rhymes with 'no'," she told me the first time we met—shook her sexy shaved head and stage-whispered, "Where have you been? You are like seven hours late."

I grinned. "Guilty. Listen, don't rat me out, okay? If Victoria asks, I was at a double feature with my phone turned off."

Chloe gave me a sideways look. "I am many things, Samuel Drift, but a snitch is not one of them."

"I knew I could count on you."

She winked a sparkly, florescent-green eyelid. "Just a sec," she said. "I've got something for you."

Her usual blasé delivery betrayed an uncharacteristic note of excitement. She bent over and opened the bottom drawer of a filing cabinet near her desk. While she was rummaging around, I leaned in to examine the six inches of exposed skin between her skirt and blouse, which was covered entirely with a colorful tattoo that appeared to be part of a scene from a Bosch painting. I'd always wanted to find out just how far up her torso that tattoo went, and whether or not it somehow connected to the lovely Japanese floral arrangement between her breasts. But, alas, it had never come to pass. Over the years our relationship had remained flirtatious but sexless, which was probably one of the reasons she still spoke to me. Chloe straightened up and handed over a manila envelope. "You really should check your office mailbox more often."

My bowels turned to ice when I saw the name above the return address, *Maggie Chase,* written in a familiar lascivious script, the *M* forming a pair of enormous breasts, the *g*'s practically humping one another, and the *i* dotted with a bullet hole. Maggie Chase was my ex-girlfriend from college, and the last person in the world I wanted to receive a mysterious envelope from. I opened my mouth to say something clever but for once nothing presented itself, so I closed it back up, tried again, nothing. Chloe watched in amusement as I gagged helplessly like a fish that had suddenly been yanked from its watery home. I wanted to turn and run, but my feet wouldn't move. I needed a drink. And some Valium. And possibly a plane ticket to Mexico.

"Aren't you going to open it?" she finally asked. She was like a bloodhound that had caught the scent of an escaped convict.

"Not now," I croaked.

"Why not?"

"I think it's expired."

"Huh?"

"I'm pretty sure milk and mail go bad after two weeks. In fact, all four-letter items that start with *m* should be consumed immediately for your own personal safety."

Not my best, but it would have to do.

Chloe was undeterred. We went directly to the lightning round.

"Who is Maggie Chase? Why is she writing you from Los Angeles? Why is she sending mail to your work instead of your apartment?"

She reached for the envelope, but I pulled it away. "No one. I mean, it's nothing. Thanks for the mail, Chloe. You're the best." I pointed toward the front door. "Oh my God! Is that John Waters making out with the late David Bowie?"

She ignored my brilliant attempt to divert her attention and prepared to continue the interrogation. Thankfully the phone on her desk rang at that moment, and the noise loosened the invisible shackles that had encased my legs. Chloe turned to put the caller on hold, and I dove inside Victoria's office and slammed the door behind me, my heart pounding out the baseline to a Bernard Herrmann score.

Victoria didn't bother to look up. She was typing so fast the noise coming off her keyboard sounded like a tap-dancing centipede. "Sit down, Sam," she said.

I moved a stack of files and took a seat on the couch next to Reyna Laurent, the managing editor of the newspaper and my secret crush since she started working here three years ago. The daughter of a French-Canadian dentist and a Guatemalan physicist, Reyna had her mother's Husky-blue eyes and her father's dark complexion. Her curly chestnut hair was cut short and flopped over to the side, like a bassist in an all-girl punk band, and when she was exasperated, she leaned her head back and blew a jet of of air toward her forehead, causing her bangs to do a little jig. Like most children of immigrant parents, she had an eye for truth and a nose for bullshit. She was smart, efficient, principled, and utterly relentless. In short, pretty much everything I was not.

"Hi, Reyna. You look good," I said. "I mean...not just good. Great. Really good and great. How have you been?"

"Hey, Sam." She acknowledged my presence with a dismissive nod of the head, and then turned her attention back to Victoria. "I have two sources in his office that confirm the affair, but neither of them will go on record."

"Then you don't have a story," replied Victoria.

"I know." Reyna fell back in the couch and made her bangs dance. She wore her usual winter uniform: a faded Bauhaus t-shirt underneath a brown cardigan missing all its buttons and worn blue jeans tucked into a pair of yellow galoshes. Somehow she made this outfit look great. "But I'm close. Just give me another week. I'm gonna nail this guy."

Victoria sighed. "One more week, but after that, I need you back at City Hall. Our freelance budget is already maxed out this month." She nodded at me. "We're lucky this stripper thing fell in our lap. No pun intended. Otherwise we wouldn't have a front page this week."

I had no idea what they were talking about, which was not unusual. Despite Victoria's best efforts to mentor me on journalism and local politics, most of the conversations at the *Chronicle* went over my head and under my attention span.

Reyna stood up and walked to the door. "I know, I know. I'll close it by Friday, I promise."

"Don't promise," said Victoria. "Do it. Because next week I need three-thousand words on the environmental bill they're pushing through city council. I think the yoga mafia is trying to sneak some new zoning regulations into it."

"You'll have it," Reyna said. She pulled a notebook out of her back pocket and wrote something down. In three years, I had never seen her without a notebook and pen. Once I ran into her at the supermarket, where she was purchasing enough instant ramen to feed a family of six, and in the top basket of the cart, where you're supposed to put a child, there they were, the ubiquitous pen and paper set, just in case a story broke in the produce aisle at two o'clock on a Sunday afternoon.

"Bye, Reyna," I said. "It was good to see you. We should grab a coffee..."

She shut the door without responding. I took a moment to regain my composure, and then I sprawled out on the coffee-stained couch in a faux faint, hand over forehead, palm out, like Susan Sarandon when she first meets Dr. Frank-N-Furter in *The Rocky Horror Picture Show*.

"Alone at last," I said. "You won't believe the day I've had."

Still typing Victoria replied, "Let me guess. You woke up hungover and then you watched some old movie and diddled around on your blog for a while instead of coming straight here like I asked you to."

I sat upright. "How *dare* you!"

She turned her head and looked at me over the top of her purple bifocals.

"*The Maltese Falcon* is not just 'some old movie.' It happens to be a classic John Huston film that defined the noir genre, thank you very much."

"Yeah, yeah. What's that?" She pointed a chipped blue fingernail at the envelope in my hand. Like all good journalists, Victoria had a sixth sense for controversy and uncomfortable questions.

"Nothing." I folded the envelope twice and shoved it in my back pocket. "Just some mail Chloe was supposed to give me weeks ago."

She raised a bullshit eyebrow but thankfully decided the truth wasn't worth the hassle. I bounced up and down a few times to make certain the envelope was nice and crushed.

While Victoria typed, I took a moment to marvel at the unholy chaos that was her office. Aside from a two-foot-wide path that led from the door to her desk, every inch of carpet was covered by precariously balanced piles of newspapers from all over the world dating back decades. If you picked up any one of them, you would find highlighting from one end to the other and red pen marks noting spelling and grammar errors. If the paper happened to have a crossword puzzle, it would be completed. Also in red ink. She just couldn't help herself. Her desk was a graveyard of to-go cups from various local coffee shops, and her walls were littered with journalism awards, often half covered by crappy kids' drawings and magazine clippings of Ian McKellen dressed as Gandalf the Grey. I had known her for almost five years, and I had never seen her outside this building. Not once. For all I knew, she lived here, surviving on flavored lattes and peanut M&Ms, which appeared to be her only source of protein. I bent down and picked a pen up off the floor. It was new, but it was supposed to look like an old-timey fountain pen, gold plated with an engraving on the side. I slipped it in my pocket.

Finally, she finished up her typing spree and turned her attention toward me. Victoria Wood was a tall, striking woman in her late-fifties with an unruly tangle of red fusilli-shaped hair streaked with gray. She was covered from aquiline nose to fetching ankle with freckles, and there were always dark bags under her Irish-blue eyes. Aside from being a full-time newspaper editor and single mother, she also wrote fantasy novels under the pen name Vicky Night. They were sexy bodice-rippers that took place in faraway kingdoms where Druid princesses battled armies of trolls and made out with centaurs on a fjord. Not my cup of whiskey, but I admit I did pick one up at the library once and finished it in three days. The woman definitely knew how to write an interspecies sex scene. She also participated in kickboxing tournaments around the state and spoke three languages. One of them was Elvish, but still.

Victoria was the one who hired me to write for the paper, against protests from the staff and despite the fact that I had never been published before. She shepherded me through those first rocky months when I didn't know a subtitle from a byline, and after I became a competent movie reviewer, she kept pushing me to finish my degree, to cut back on my drinking, to make dentist appointments, and, over and over again, to learn the numerous grammatical, stylistic, and ethical rules that governed traditional journalism. But all I wanted to do was watch movies.

"I would like you to write the stripper story," she said.

"No, thank you," I replied. I stood up and gave her a military salute. "I'm glad we had this little chat. We should do this again sometime…"

"Sit down." My salute took a nosedive, and I slumped back onto the couch. "Let me rephrase that sentence: Gerald *insists* that you write the stripper story."

"Why me?" I whined. "I'm not even supposed to be here today."

"What?"

"It's from *Clerks*."

She gave me a confused look.

"Kevin Smith?" I said. "Jay and Silent Bob? Classic indie raunch-com from the nineties? Never mind. I'm not a real journalist. You know that. I'm a freelance movie reviewer. I make snarky comments about mediocre Hollywood action flicks. That's my wheelhouse. Why don't you make Reyna do it?"

Victoria took off her glasses and let them dangle from the chain around her neck. "Reyna is working on an article about a sex scandal in the governor's office right now. Stay out of her way. And Gerald asked for you specifically. I already told him you're not a real journalist, and he doesn't care. He thinks your style will add color to the story."

She said the word "color" like a chef at a four-star restaurant would say the word "ketchup." This was an ongoing debate between Victoria and the publisher, Gerald Moore. Victoria insisted on an old-school approach to journalism that involved careful research, multiple sources, and objectivity, while Gerald saw dollar signs in the more controversial, attention-grabbing formats increasingly used by online news sources. Victoria had been winning the argument for almost three decades, as the paper's prosperity soared under her leadership through the end of the twentieth century and into the next millennium. But in recent years, with the proliferation of sensationalist internet news and the growing cynicism surrounding "mainstream media," circulation numbers had declined, even in small papers like the *Mountainview Chronicle*. The pressure to keep up with the twenty-four-hour news cycle had begun to chip away at her resolve, giving Gerald room to push the *Chronicle* in a more modern direction. Everyone in the editorial department despised Gerald, but I didn't think he was so bad. He had always been supportive of my writing.

"Listen, I don't like this any more than you do," said Victoria. She pointed to a manila folder on her desk. I opened the folder and looked at the first page, which contained a chart with a single red line going up and down like a cartoon mountain range. The end of the line was headed down. "That's the report from last quarter. Our circulation numbers are tanking, and you are our most popular writer at the moment, for reasons I'm not inclined to go into. You're the only one who has a sizeable online presence...whatever the hell that means. Gerald wants you to blog about this story and twat it."

"Tweet."

"I know what I said. Honestly, part of the reason I didn't put up a fight is because there's simply not much there. A dead stripper in a town like Mountainview is a sexy headline and it'll move some papers, but I've already spoken with the police department. The poor woman slipped on a patch of ice and hit her head. That's all. But he's right, we have to run *something*. You've written about the Pink Door in the past, so you have connections over there. Everyone else is tied up, and Gerald wants you. So it's you. I'm sorry."

It was true I wrote a story several years ago about the strip club at Victoria's behest. When the Pink Door first opened, the local citizens freaked out, primarily because it was located on the Pearl Street Mall, a beatific outdoor shopping area smack dab in the middle of the downtown business district and the center of tourism for the city. This was hallowed ground in Mountainview, a hipster oasis where four-star restaurants served vegan, gluten-free meals at exorbitant prices and trendy spas charged two hundred dollars an hour for organic mud baths. The Pink Door did not fit the wholesome, enlightened image the Pearl Street Mall was supposed to represent. When news of the club's location went public, feminist soccer moms wrote scathing letters to the editor about misogyny and the male gaze, and New Age yoga dads warned that the city would soon be flooded with criminals and drug addicts. Business owners near the Pink Door started a petition to close the club down, claiming its existence depreciated their property values. When that failed, they pressured the city into conducting multiple health and safety inspections, which the Pink Door passed with ease. I found the whole situation amusing, and when I proposed writing a pithy little opinion piece on it, Victoria jumped at the offer. It was a trap. She made me conduct dozens of interviews with lawyers, business owners, members of law enforcement, and politicians. She sent me to City Hall in search of obscure documents and mind-numbingly boring public records. Every fact had to be triple-checked, and every quote had to be on the record. It was a nightmare. Ten rewrites and two thousand words later, I barely recognized the article that was published with my name under the headline. It was the only serious news story I had ever written, and I had no desire to relive the torture.

"I really wish I could," I said. "But I just don't have time." I exhaled dramatically and brushed an invisible hair off my forehead, doing my best impression of Clark Gable in *It Happened One Night*. "The MIFF starts today, and I'll be swamped all week. But next time an exotic dancer dies in this fair city, give me a jingle. I'll be on it like white on a John Hughes movie."

The MIFF was the unfortunate acronym for the Mountainview International Film Festival, a mini Sundance that had grown exponentially in the past decade along with Mountainview's reputation as a fashionable tourist destination for affluent New Yorkers and Californians who wanted to get in touch with nature without actually touching nature. Along with hundreds of movies and documentaries showing all over the city, it was also an opportunity to throw extravagant parties, where minor celebrities sometimes showed up to rub elbows with the common folk. For cinema nerds like me, it was the Super Bowl, Christmas, and St. Patrick's Day all rolled into one. Plus, I got free drinks.

Unfortunately, Victoria was well versed in the goings on at the MIFF and easily thwarted my Gable with her own Claudette Colbert. "I know exactly what you do at that film festival," she said. "You drink too much free alcohol, schmooze with C-list celebrities, watch movies, and try to get laid. Well, you can do that while you're working on the Pink Door story. Everyone in town is going to be there, so you can kill two birds with one stone." She gave me another serious look. "Of course, you can't drink."

"*What!*"

She sighed. "This might not be much of a story, Sam, but it's not a movie review either. The information has to be accurate. You have to interview people and write down what they say and do some actual research. It's not an opinion piece. I know you don't take journalism seriously, but some of us do and I will not have you turn this paper into another buzzy webzine. Not while I'm the editor."

"Fine," I grumbled. "Is that all?"

"Actually, there's one more thing." She cleared her throat and her eyes started to glisten. This was nothing new. One rarely escaped Victoria's office without witnessing at least one decent crying jag. She was a woman of extremes, screaming in Latin one minute, calm as a frozen monk the next. It was like working for Gloria Swanson. You had to love her. "I'm stepping down as editor."

I rolled my eyes. "Yeah, right."

"I know I've said that before, but this time I mean it. My fantasy series is starting to take off, and I just signed a three-book deal. Tommy will be starting college next year, and I'll pay off my mortgage shortly after that. I turned in my resignation letter last week. I will stay on as editor through the transition, which might take a few months, but then I'm a free woman."

I looked at her closely to see if she was serious. Despite the tears, her face was placid, serene even. Usually she threatened to quit during the middle of a meltdown, and her reasons never involved financial practicalities. This was something different. My stomach felt queasy for the second time that day.

"But you love this job," I said.

She shook her head. "I do love it, but I'm burned out. In fact, I've been burned out for a while, and it's not fair to you guys. This paper deserves an editor who's willing to fight for it, and there are too many battles I just don't have the energy for these days."

"Is it because of him?" I pointed toward the floor above us where Gerald's office was located.

Victoria shrugged. "Yes and no. Gerald's an unethical prick with a Napoleon complex, but I've worked for publishers like him before. It's just my time." She paused and squinted her eyes in a manner that indicated she was unsure whether or not she should continue. Finally, she gave in. "I think Gerald is going to ask you to replace me."

My eyes widened. "What? That's insane. Why me? Why not Reyna? Or Mike? Or...anyone who's not me?"

She spread her arms wide in a gesture of wonder and martyrdom. "I recommended Reyna. He says he's considering her, but I think he's leaning toward you."

I looked at the Grand Canyon–sized furrow between her eyes. "And you don't think I can handle it, right?"

I didn't want the job, but I wanted her to want me to want the job.

"Honestly, I have my doubts," she said. "I think if you actually took it seriously, you could be a good reporter, but I don't believe you're ready for an editor position. But in the end, it's not my newspaper. Gerald makes the decisions. I just want you to think long and hard about why he wants you."

I dug my own canyon. "And why is that?"

"Just think about it," said Victoria. "And think about the job. I mean, seriously, my doubts aside, it could be a great opportunity for you. You'd have a steady paycheck, health insurance, a dental plan."

I shook my head. "Nope. No, ma'am. Absolutely not. I'm not going to think about it. Sorry, no. You want to know why I'm not going to think about it? Because you're not going to quit, that's why. You've been telling me you're going to quit from the first day I walked into this office. You're just going through a rough patch right now, but it'll get better. I'll keep writing movie reviews and you'll keep trying to mold me into a proper journalist and Gerald will keep making your life miserable and everything will be normal. You'll see."

Victoria frowned and put her glasses back on. "I am going to resign, Sam. And Gerald is going to offer you my job. Just be ready for it, that's all I ask. Prepare yourself. You're going to have to face reality sooner or later."

I stood up with as much indignation as I could muster and said, "I will *never* face reality." And then I stormed out of her office.

Chloe tried to flag me down, but I power-walked past her desk knowing she was just going to ask more questions about the envelope burning in my back pocket. As I passed through the front door, Victoria's ragged voice followed me into the street. "*And remember, no drinking on the job!*"

Chapter 3: The Cabinet of Dr. Caligari

THE OPENING CEREMONIES FOR THE MIFF were held at the Blue Dick, a gorgeous terra-cotta structure located at the far east end of the Pearl Street Mall, its cathedral-like, stained-glass windows staring down in disdain at the trendy boutiques and fusion restaurants that circled its foundation, like so many jackals yelping hungrily at the feet of an ancient bull elephant that had received a mortal wound. The theater was originally an opera house constructed in 1896, but when the popularity of people screaming at one another in song unexpectedly dwindled in the twentieth century, the owners were forced to sell it to a forward-thinking young businessman, who transformed it into Mountainview's first movie theater.

The new owner installed a fully equipped projection booth in the back of the house and paid a man from Louisville to redecorate the entire building in the art deco style that was all the rage at the time. For some reason, this included a thirty-foot-tall mosaic on the façade that featured a long blue shaft rising out of a green hummock into an explosion of orange and yellow stripes. Rumor had it the piece was supposed to depict a river flowing down a grassy hill with a sunrise in the background, but it looked unmistakably like a blue circumcised penis ejaculating fireworks into the ether. Whether or not this was the effect the Louisville designer was attempting to achieve, the building was declared a historic landmark in 1943, and therefore—much to the chagrin of successive owners and the delight of teenage boys—the enormous phallic symbol could never be removed. Since that time, the space had gone through a variety of changes, transforming into a community theater in the '50s, a disco tech in the '70s, a rock club in the '90s, and finally an event center rented out to the highest bidder—the real estate equivalent of an aging escort whose wardrobe was somewhat out of date but who still knew how to show a fella a good time—hosting artistic performances, high school reunions, corporate engagements, and, of course, international film festivals. With each new owner, there was a new name, but none of them stuck. Currently, there was a sign above the marquis that claimed, rather pompously, the building was to be called the Grande Theater, but locals still referred to it affectionately as the Blue Dick.

The streets were clogged with festival traffic, and the bus trip downtown took longer than usual. I sat in the belly of the petroleum-powered leviathan, on a cushion featuring turquoise trapezoids floating in a deep purple weave underneath two decades of mystery stains, trying to process the meeting with Victoria. On the one hand, it was disturbing to hear that she was abandoning me at a point in my life when I needed her guidance the most, but on the other hand, it was flattering to know that Gerald might want me for the job, despite the fact that I was not interested in the position. What did the editor of a newspaper actually do? I wondered. You told people to write stories, you read those stories, and then you told those people to rewrite those stories. There was probably some busy work, as well, but that was the gist of it, I supposed. Undoubtedly Victoria made the job more difficult by obsessing over grammatical and factual minutia and picking fights with Gerald about ethics, but if one approached the position from a more laissez-faire perspective, it probably wasn't too complicated. And Gerald was right about one thing—the *Chronicle* was woefully behind the times. The website was clunky, they had zero social media presence, and the writing was drier than a harem in the Sahara. I mean, seriously, who wants to read mundane articles about the byzantine details of local zoning laws or peruse a five-page interview with city officials about changes in the public school curriculum?

The more I thought about it the more it made sense that Gerald wanted me for the job. The other members of the staff worshipped Victoria and could not see past her outdated vision of print journalism, but Gerald needed someone from outside the system, a maverick, a rebel, a nontraditionalist who wasn't afraid to shake things up. Come to think of it, perhaps giving me this high-profile assignment was his way of testing me. Victoria kept insisting the stripper story was a simple slip-and-fall, but maybe there was more to it and Gerald needed someone with vision to see past Victoria's charts and facts to find the truth. And then there was the sad state of my finances to consider. I could handle the Mayor, of course, but he was right, in a couple of weeks rent was due again and I was going to owe him more than two grand. I didn't know exactly how much a newspaper editor made, but it had to be considerably more than what I was scraping together at the moment. It was a lot to process.

I shifted in my seat and winced at the sound of crinkled paper. I took Maggie's letter out of my back pocket and looked at the Los Angeles address. I turned it over. I held it up to the window and tried to see through the envelope. I put it to my nose and inhaled deeply, hoping to catch a whiff of her lavender perfume. Nothing. It was definitely her handwriting though. She had tracked down my work address and written both of our names on a blank envelope. She had purchased a stamp and placed it in a mailbox. These things took effort. Surely that meant something. It had been more than six years since she ran off to Hollywood with my best friend, leaving me here to rot by myself. Our breakup was the reason I dropped out of college and started drinking heavily. I had imagined our reunion a thousand times. Sometimes she came crawling back to me and I rejected her, sometimes she came crawling back to me and I forgave her, but the important part was the crawling back. While drunk and high in my crappy little apartment, I had recited a thousand dramatic monologues that began with, "How dare you..." or, "How could you..." But in the end, I had to admit to myself that she dared and she could, and after a few years, I lost hope that we would ever get back together. And now this. Was she writing to apologize for cheating on me? Did she want me to take her back? I pinched the top right corner between my thumb and index finger and began to tear it open. I got about a half inch into it when I started to hyperventilate. My breath came in deep, frantic gasps, I clutched my chest, and spots danced before my eyes. I couldn't do it. It was too painful. I wasn't ready to hear from her, not yet. I shoved the letter back into my pocket, and my breathing immediately returned to normal, my pulse regulated, and my vision cleared. I would throw the letter away. That's what I would do. As soon as I found a suitable trash receptacle, I would tear that infernal missive to pieces and be rid of Maggie Chase for good, or my name wasn't Sam Drift.

It was dusk when I arrived at the Blue Dick, and the festivities were already underway. There was a sad, trampled red carpet extending from the front door to the curb, where two small searchlights traced aimless patterns in the bruised evening sky, valiantly attempting and failing to give the impression of Hollywood opulence. The marquis read, "Mountainview International Film Festival Opening Nite!"

The volunteer working the ticket booth was a skinny, bearded young man perched high on a stool behind a glass partition, wearing a denim vest over a distressed *Repo Man* t-shirt with a name tag that said "FRANK" and sucking on a lime-green vape in a Freudian manner, periodically releasing a chemtrail of white fog that melted away almost immediately and left behind the odor of a flatulent skunk that had recently dined out on rotten strawberries. I showed him my press pass and he slid two drink tickets across the counter.

I picked up the drink tickets and fluttered them in front of my face like a geisha fan. "Any chance you got more of these back there?"

"We're only supposed to give out two per person," he said. "It's like a policy or something."

I nodded and leaned in conspiratorially. "Right. I get that, and I would never want to undermine a policy. But hear me out. It seems to me that everyone who's supposed to be in there is already in there and you probably have a plethora of drink tickets left over and it would be a shame if those tickets went to waste."

He blinked rapidly. "I'd like to help you out, but they're pretty, you know, fascist about the drink tickets."

"Absolutely. But we can't let fascism rule the day. Am I right? Fight the power!"

"Yeah, but the power gives me a free pass to the festival, and also it wouldn't be fair to everyone else."

"Sure, it's important to be fair." I tapped my chin with my index finger, desperately searching my THC-riddled brain for the right words. "So, okay, think of it like this. You have a litter of puppies and the animal shelter where you work says you can only give away two puppies per person. You follow me?"

"I don't work at an animal shelter."

"It's just a hypothetical, Frank. You seem like a philosophical thinker to me. A student of the mind. An admirer of Socrates and Plato. Am I right?"

He chewed on his vape. "More of an Aristotle guy."

"There you go! Aristotle! He liked thought experiments, correct?"

"I guess."

"Of course he did. So think of this as an Aristotelian thought experiment."

"I don't think you're using that word correctly."

I waved him off. "So according to this arbitrary policy, you're only allowed to give away two puppies per person, and if there are any puppies left over at the end of the day, you are required to kill them."

"Whoa, my man. That's heavy. How?"

"What do you mean?"

"How am I going to kill these hypothetical puppies?"

"With…an axe."

"An axe?"

"Uh huh."

"Like, they just keep an axe hanging on the wall at the animal shelter?"

"That's correct. At this particular shelter, any animal that doesn't find a forever home at the end of the day is cut in half with an axe that they hang on the wall. It's cruel, but that's their policy."

"I think that would be a health-code violation, my dude."

"They clean the axe thoroughly with disinfectant. There's a big laminated chart in the break room on how to clean the axe and dispose of the chopped up puppy parts. It's very sanitary."

"And I have to do this? Chop up the puppies?"

"It's not your favorite part of the job, but that's the policy. But hold on, we're not there yet. Because you're very good at your job. In fact, you're the best puppy-giver-awayer at this shelter, and you think you can find homes for all the puppies before the end of the day. You work hard, you give away a lot of puppies, but despite your best efforts there are still six furry spotted newborn puppies left over at the end of the day. Oh, no. Very sad. You start to take the axe off the wall. But then, wait a second, what's that? You hear the door jingle."

"The door jingles?"

"Yeah, they have one of those bell things on the door so every time it opens, it jingles."

"Just one big bell or is it one of those long strips with a lot of small bells attached to it?"

"Which do you prefer?"

"I like the strips. They sound like sleigh bells."

"Okay, so the door opens just before closing and the bell strip jingles and a man walks in. A handsome and clever and smart man. And this handsome, clever, smart man says he'll take the rest of the puppies to his large, sun-dappled farm, where they can go on little puppy walks in the pasture and take little puppy naps under the willow trees. No puppies have to get chopped in half today. Isn't that good news?"

He smiled and nodded.

"So here's the predicament. Do you follow this meaningless and immoral policy and only let the man have two puppies and chop the other four puppies in half with the axe according to the regulations described on the laminated chart in the break room? Or do you take a stand against your tyrannical overlords like the hero I know you are and save all of the puppies?" I straightened my posture and put my hand over my heart. "Save the puppies, Frank. Save those goddamn puppies."

He inhaled deeply and shook his head, as though waking up from a coma. He stood up, raised his arms to chest level, and began a slow clap. "That was the most ridiculous thing I've ever heard anyone say to get free booze, my dude. And both of my parents are alcoholics."

I took a bow. He reached under the counter and came out with six more drink tickets.

"Bring back two puppies for me."

"What's your breed?"

"Whiskey."

"I knew I liked you."

I grabbed the tickets and headed for the door.

Chapter 4: Sunset Boulevard

IF THE OUTSIDE OF THE THEATER WAS A PHALLIC PASTORAL SCENE, the inside was an Egyptian tomb designed by a race of decadent aliens obsessed with geometric patterns and gold paint. The stucco lobby walls were decorated with ornamental scarabs and mysterious cartouches, and the ceiling featured a recurring oyster-shell design that made the Vatican look understated. The floor was blanketed by a luxurious maroon and blue carpet that had been polished to a shine along the main traffic areas and led into the auditorium, a large open space with arabesques and pyramids and a fifty-foot-tall, barrel-vaulted ceiling, from which hung a gold chandelier that would have taken out at least fifty unknown directors, producers, and Ingmar Bergman fanatics if the bolted joists holding it in place gave way tonight. There were three bars—two on the main floor and one in the balcony—each made of polished cedar and surrounded by gleaming bronze stools. I made a beeline to the closest one and ordered two shots of whiskey and an Old Fashioned. I drained one of the shots immediately and set to work on the Old Fashioned.

Including the balcony, the Blue Dick seated a thousand, but if the chairs in the back were removed and the plebeians were required to stand, the capacity was closer to twelve hundred. Tonight there were ten rows of seats in the front for honored guests, prominent businessmen, and industry types, and the rest of us were crammed in the back, rising up on tiptoes, bobbing our heads from side to side in an effort to see what was happening on the large, wooden stage at the front of the house. Currently, it was occupied by a seventy-something-year-old woman wearing a blue silk scarf and a sequined evening gown with a scandalous neckline, her silver hair piled high on her head in an elaborate series of curls and knots. She was talking about...

"...old men's balls. You want a job in Hollywood? That's my advice to you. It don't matter if you're a man or woman, gay or straight, start getting used to the sight of wrinkled testicles dangling in front of your face. That's the movie business in a nutshell...pun intended." She paused here for a lung-rattling coughing fit. Her voice was deep and hard, an ancient Cadillac driving down a gravel road. When the coughing ended, she took a drink from a glass filled with brown liquid. "Sorry about that, folks," she said. "You get to be my age, you got to refuel more often."

The audience members in the reserved seating upfront chuckled nervously, while those of us in the back laughed and whistled encouragement.

The speaker squinted into the house lights. "Sounds like the real party is in the back of the room tonight." She glared at the people in the front row. "What's wrong with you guys? Got a bug up your ass or something?" She took another drink. "I know, I know, you thought you were getting some classy broad in her twilight years, like Sally Field or Helen Mirren. But I ain't classy. I don't have a charity to support or some kind of social justice project I'm going to babble on about. I'm just an old drunk who doesn't give a shit anymore. Guess you'll have to deal with that. Or not. Makes no difference to me."

The cheers from the back of the theater increased.

Every year, the MIFF managed to entice a real-life Hollywood celebrity to the event with free airfare, a weeklong ski vacation for the whole family, a gift basket that could feed a middle-class family for a month, and the presentation of a lifetime achievement award. The award itself was a large piece of polished glass that weighed almost ten pounds. It was supposed to be molded in the shape of an eternity symbol, but it just looked like the number 8 lying on its side with the recipient's name carved into the base.

This year the committee had outdone itself. The guest of honor was a former scream queen—you know this person, but we'll call her V. just to be safe—who started her acting career just ten months out of the womb, appearing in a series of commercials for Beech-Nut® baby food in the 1950s, which featured her sitting in a high chair, waving her arms and legs spastically while a tall woman with a towering bouffant hairdo spooned apple sauce into her mouth and a disembodied male voice said, "Beech-Nut® apple sauce tastes *extra* good because the apples are cooked in their skins for *extra* flavor."

After that, young V. bounced around the children's advertising circuit for a while—cereal, toys, clothes—until finally, at the age of nine, she landed her first starring role on a family sitcom called *Li'l Lilly*, NBCs answer to *Leave It to Beaver* and *Dennis the Menace*. Lilly Foster was a precocious tomboy who lived in a large, nondescript house in a small, nondescript suburb with her attractive, nondescript parents. Each episode featured a banal moral problem created by Lilly and her circle of neighborhood friends that then had to be solved by the adults in the final four minutes of the program. She broke her mother's favorite lamp or brought home a stray dog or painted her blonde pigtails black with shoe polish in order to look like an "Injun." At the end of the day, when order had been restored to middle-class America and the square-jawed father asked Lilly if she'd learned her lesson, she would stomp her tiny foot and say her catchphrase: "Gimme a break!"

The ratings were middling, but the show managed to hang on for three seasons, until Li'l Lilly turned thirteen and, almost overnight, she wasn't so li'l anymore. In particular, there were a few specific anatomical areas that had grown. Suddenly, the pigtails and lacy dresses appealed to a new demographic. Rumors began to circulate about V. and the actor who played her father on the show. *Gimme a break!* NBC pulled the plug immediately.

After that, V. wandered Hollywood's halls of adolescent purgatory for a few years, too old for purity and too young for objectification, until finally a famously sleazy B-movie horror director spotted the curvaceous sixteen-year-old blonde lying on a towel at Newport Beach, a pair of heart-shaped Lolita glasses hiding her suspicious blue eyes. Without even a reading, he cast her as the scantily clad heroine/victim in his next movie, *The Beast With No Face*, a low-budget schlock fest about a high school chemistry teacher who, while conducting an after-hours experiment in the school laboratory, accidentally splashes acid all over his face, causing his eyes, nose, and mouth to melt together in a disgusting Picasso-esque fashion. For reasons that are never explained, he blames the accident on his students, specifically the flirtatious young blonde played by V., and attempts to murder them one by one. V. is chased through the woods, losing pieces of clothing along the way, until finally, half naked and breathing heavily, she is trapped against a rock. In the end, she is saved by a kindly huntsman, but before this happens, the creature reveals himself to her up-close for the first time, and when she sees his horrible casserole of a puss, she lets loose a scream so loud and shrill and terrifying that it spawned a whole new career.

Over the next three decades, V. went on to appear in more than forty horror and sci-fi movies, most of them just as tasteless and ludicrous as *The Beast with No Face*. Generations of teenagers watched her large breasts heave on the big screen, their eyes wide and their hearts racing whenever the monster ripped a piece of her dress and V. released her trademark shriek.

When I was growing up, my mother's extensive VHS collection included a movie called *Beach Creatures* about a race of crab men that live beneath the sand in Southern California and, following an earthquake, surface to snatch attractive young women sunbathing in bikinis. V. plays the part of a naïve newlywed on her honeymoon who is captured by the crab men and taken to their underground lair, where she is subjected to a variety of pseudo-sexual torture methods before being saved by her cleft-chinned marine biologist husband. When I was fifteen, I defiled an entire drawer of gym socks while watching a shackled V. writhe and shiver in her flimsy swimsuit.

And now here she was, in Mountainview, drunk, bawdy, pushing eighty but still sexy as hell, scandalizing the audience with her foul mouth and razor wit.

"*Anyhow,* I better get off the stage before I say something really crass," she said, looking down at her empty glass. "Also, I need a refill. Thank you for this award thingie. I'm an old lady, so I'm not going to even try and pick it up. One of those young boys running around here can haul it out to my car later on. I know you're only giving it to me because you couldn't get a real celebrity to come out here. That's alright. I'm only accepting it because I wanted to get the hell out of the retirement home my family locked me in. Also, I assume numerous attractive young men and women are going to buy me drinks after this is over. So there's that."

She paused for a moment and stared fiercely into the audience, as though she was deciding whether or not she should continue. At first, there was some giggling and whispering, but eventually the room became completely still.

"I'll just say one last thing. I love movies. I've always loved movies. When I was a little girl, I wanted to be just like Bette Davis. I wanted to be on a big screen. I wanted people to see me. To really see me. There's nothing wrong with that. I'm sure there are plenty of actors in this room who want to be seen. Follow your dreams, chickadees. Just don't equate Hollywood with movies. Don't ever do that. The movies are the fantasy and we all love a good fantasy, but Hollywood is real and it will grind you down. I don't regret getting into the movie business, but I do regret some of the things I did to stay there. Being a fantasy has a price, and that price keeps going up the longer you stay. Don't lose sight of what's important. I don't know if people believe in the soul anymore. I ain't talking about religion or any of that New Age hippie shit. I'm talking about human value. Self-worth. A conscious mind connected to a feeling heart. That's the thing that audiences want to see. Sex, sure. Charisma, yes. But more than that, people want to see their own humanity in you. They want to see the better angels of their nature. You can't fake that. There's no special effects for empathy, no CGI that will replicate the soul. That's the one thing you don't want to lose. Because if you lose it, you'll never get it back again. Trust me on that one." She saluted the audience with her glass. "Now someone come up here and help me off this goddamn stage, or I'm going to fall and break my hip."

When the speech was over, there was a raucous round of applause and then a mad rush for the bar. I managed to get two more refills before the deluge hit and then swam salmon-like against the river of thirsty humanity, my drinks raised over my head to protect their precious contents, until I broke through the crowd and found the spawning ground on the dance floor.

Festival workers were already busy clearing away the chairs, and a hipstery bluegrass band had materialized on stage with two banjos, one upright bass, a fiddle, and four pairs of red suspenders, launching directly into a technically impressive but ultimately cringe-inducing cover of Bob Marley's "Buffalo Soldier."

Mountainview had a strange obsession with bluegrass music that predated the recent trend that had swept through the rest of the country. You could walk into any bar or coffee shop in town and find an attractive young man in his mid-twenties wearing a pageboy cap and five days of carefully groomed stubble, plucking a mandolin and singing about riding the rails and drinking dandelion wine. It probably had something to do with being a mountain town, but since the real mountain men of Mountainview had long since been forced out by tech companies and real estate agents, it seemed particularly cruel to see their lives so earnestly plagiarized by a generation of trust-fund kids.

I moved away from the dance floor and found a shadowy corner behind a thick, embroidered curtain, where I could observe the festivities unnoticed, like Lon Chaney Sr. in *Phantom of the Opera*. I tried to sip my drink in a sociable manner but soon discovered my third Old Fashioned gone. No matter. I felt fine. That was another thing Victoria was wrong about. Sure, it was important to be professional, in a sense, but there was no reason I couldn't have a few drops on the job as long as I didn't get carried away. I flagged down a passing waiter and ordered another round.

The crowd's thirst was now satiated, and people began to wander back toward the dance floor, smiley and glassy-eyed, elbows ready to be rubbed and asses ready to be kissed. The attendees quickly divided themselves into two groups, like nervous participants in a junior-high dance, the industry representatives and advertising sponsors on one side of the theater in carefully tailored Zegna and Dior, talking loudly and drinking top-shelf liquor, and the artists on the other side, dressed in ratty scarves and oversized corduroy blazers, mumbling under their breath while clutching sweaty cans of craft beer. Each group was watching the other, wondering who was going to make the first move. It was a game of networking chicken, and it was important not to blink first.

Finally, a shy writer-director of some renown in the indie world broke from the ranks and crossed into no man's land, shuffling her feet Snoopy-like as she made her way toward a gaggle of industry types. The writer-director was known for making beautiful, personal horror movies about anxiety and body-image issues, usually involving a sad/creepy piano score (composed, played, and recorded by the writer-director) and a weirdly sexualized cooking scenes with dead animals being skinned and butchered in excruciating detail. She was hailed as a genius by critics in the blogosphere, but she couldn't seem to break into the mainstream and rumor had it that she was currently living in her parents' basement with a dozen maxed-out credit cards. She needed funding and she needed it bad. Hence, the current path into a social interaction that she clearly did not want to have.

She took a few tentative steps forward, paused, turned around, and began talking to herself, gesturing with her hands in a chastising manner, perhaps psyching herself up. She took a drink from the glass in her hand, and then another. She turned around and started toward the suits again.

This process repeated itself several times until she was within five feet of her intended goal. Just as she was about to lean forward and introduce herself to a group of people who could change her life forever, a guy with a man-bun and a yellow scarf swooped in front of her, speaking loudly and making large arm movements in the manner of an alpha male attempting to ingratiate himself to a group. He said something and slapped one of the suits on the shoulder, and the group erupted with laughter. The writer-director whirled around and ran for cover.

It wasn't always like this. In the beginning, the festival had been an insular affair created by and for filmmakers who had no access to the larger machinations of the industry and just wanted to see their movies on a big screen. Hopeless directors flew to Mountainview from around the world for the opportunity to view their creations in front of a live audience and then sit at a foldout table afterward answering inane questions about budgets and scene locations. The movies they screened back then were rough, sometimes even downright amateurish, but no one complained. There was an almost child-like glee to the event. Sure, people from Hollywood showed up from time to time, mostly industry gawkers and hipster cinephiles, venturing out into the wilderness of Middle America in the hopes of discovering the next *Sling Blade* or at least *Napoleon Dynamite*, but no one took them seriously.

It didn't start getting tawdry until five years ago when a small documentary that premiered at the MIFF, by some astonishing twist of fate, went on to win an Oscar, and the director thanked the town of Mountainview in her acceptance speech. The year after that the History Channel sent an intern to the festival, and they poached a Scandinavian writer-director to work on a mini-series about Norse mythology. After that, they kept coming—young men and women with expensive haircuts and suits, passing out cherished cards with promises printed on them: Netflix, Amazon, A&E, Hulu. The big cable channels never showed up and the big studios didn't even know we existed, but it was enough to fire the imagination of every small-time director and actor at the festival, and it transformed the event from a naïve, joyful affair into a game of cut-throat competition. As always, there was a rumor that this was the year HBO would send a representative with a golden ticket to make one little orphan filmmaker's dreams come true. It was almost surely false, but the chum was already in the water.

I finished my drink and took out my phone, noticing the battery was almost out of juice. I signed in to my blog and made a post.

Ah, opening night at the MIFF! Group orgies are always fun, especially when half the participants are virgins. It's the usual suspects here tonight. Liars and drunkards and bastards and thieves. And that's just the staff!

As usual, I'll be attending all the festival events, both official and unofficial, and I will be reporting the sordid details right here. So far the highlight of the evening has been a delightfully vulgar speech by the festival's delightfully vulgar guest of honor. Gimme a break! I won't mention any names, but if you see a sexy septuagenarian wandering the streets of Mountainview wearing a flashy evening gown featuring cleavage that would have made Liz Taylor look like a cloistered nun, buy her a drink. She deserves it.

By the by, my soon-to-be-retired editor at the Mountainview Chronicle *has commanded me to work on a local story about a dead stripper, so my inebriated movie posts will be slightly less frequent (but no less inebriated) while I delve into this mystery. My editor insists there's no foul play afoot, but I am not convinced. Maybe the dame in question was doing a private dance for some prominent politician who happened to be in town. Perhaps things got a little dicey and his goons put cement boots on her. Now the stripper's swimmin' with the fishes, see. A political figure like that would have a lot of juice with the police department, as well. This could be a conspiracy that goes all the way to City Hall! Or maybe the stripper just slipped on a patch of ice. Tune in next week to find out...*

I added several hashtags, a link to the Pink Door's webpage, some keywords for the Google bots, and posted it. Victoria wouldn't like the part about her retirement or the fact that I was mixing the MIFF blogs with the stripper story, but then again she didn't understand the fine art of mass communication in the internet age.

After doing all that hard work, I felt I'd earned a drink, so I pinballed my way through the drunken mob until I reached the bar. I had achieved the perfect level of inebriation: light, warm, and confident, with only a mild slurring of the speech and dexterity impairment. My skin buzzed with anticipation, and my head floated several inches above my neck. I had been drinking long enough to know that this would be the pinnacle of the evening. Right now, everything was perfect. I had achieved absolute balance between the sober yin and the drunken yang. I could walk in a straight line and talk in complete sentences. The world sparkled and blurred around the edges, as though the scene was being shot on a lens smeared with Vaseline, making every lame joke a hilarious witticism and each intolerable bore a vivid conversationalist. If I kept drinking, it would all fall apart. The sparkles would catch fire and explode, and the easy confidence that I now felt would grow dark, devolving into anxiety and self-loathing that would eventually force me to consume more alcohol to reverse the downward spiral and turn the night into a series of poor decisions that would result in an embarrassing montage in my head tomorrow morning, forcing me to consume even more alcohol. I would start obsessing about the diseased roots of my family tree and how everyone I had ever loved in my life had abandoned me when I needed them most and how I would almost certainly die alone, friendless and forgotten, with no one to mourn my passing except my beloved Audrey, if she hadn't perished from neglect. Of course, if I didn't drink more, this perfect feeling would fade away, eventually leaving me sober and ordinary and alone. The world would become normal, real, and I would be forced to look at it through rational, indefensible eyes, and I might see my life for what it really was and finally face the absurdity of my own existence and take responsibility for my actions and start making choices that would lead me down a path of accountability and renewal.

I ordered an Old Fashioned and a shot.

"Is that Sam Drift I see?"

The question was carried over the din of the crowd and the noise of the band ("Sexual Healing"—it just kept getting worse) by the flat, elongated vowels of East Coast money, and I turned in time to see an attractive middle-aged woman approaching at a determined pace, her thin, spotted arms open as though preparing herself for crucifixion. I took a step backward but before I could make a run for it, I was enveloped in white silk and expensive perfume. She pulled me close and did that European thing where you pretend to kiss someone on the cheek but instead kiss the air near the cheek. Her neck smelled like lavender, coconut, and something musky and exotic underneath.

"It's been a long time, Sam," she breathed in my ear in a husky voice, stirring the hair on my neck and sending a confusing tremor through my loins. I tried to pull out of the embrace, but she held me fast. She was surprisingly strong for such a small woman, no doubt the result of yoga, kale, and the blood of gluten-free babies. "I have information for you. We need to speak privately."

Liliane Easton was a local businesswoman and one of the MIFF's top sponsors. She owned a high-class spa on the Pearl Street Mall called Nirvana & You, which just happened to be located right next to the Pink Door. She was one of the business owners who led the attack on the strip club when it first opened, and she had not been happy with the article I wrote about it. The last time I saw her she threw a rolled-up newspaper at my head and said she was going to sue me for libel. The lawsuit never came, but I'd made a point to steer clear of her since then, which wasn't too difficult considering I didn't normally run in the same social circles as millionaire divorcees from Manhattan.

Liliane had been a permanent resident of Mountainview for all of five years. Before that she'd lived in New York with her husband, Samuel Easton, the eighteenth wealthiest real estate mogul in the country according to *Forbes*, and a blatant philanderer. If the internet was correct, he had a penchant for cocaine and blonde supermodels. Their divorce had been a nasty, public affair, and when it was over, Liliane walked away with an undisclosed sum of money and a postmodern plantation home in Mountainview, where she ensconced herself in the local political and social networks with frightening tenacity. She was one of those city people who believed small towns were inherently pure, and their residents something like naïve redneck angels. Not dumb, exactly, just too innocent for their own good. In New York, her fairytale marriage had been upturned by sex and drugs, and the media had hounded her relentlessly. She'd traded in that high-profile lifestyle for a simpler existence, and she was not about to allow her *Green Acres* fantasy to be disturbed by the sordid elements that had ruined her previous life.

Finally, she turned me loose, and I tried to step backwards but ended up tripping over my numb feet instead and grabbing onto Liliane's rock-hard shoulder (Jesus, did this woman have any fat on her at all?).

"How have you been, Liliane? Long time no see."

She stepped into my clumsy embrace and put her hand around my waist, guiding me into a waltz-like position, her taking the lead, of course, and danced me into a dark abandoned corner of the room, where my flesh pressed up against the rough stucco wall.

"I can't talk right now," I sputtered. "I'm supposed to write an article about the... But we should get together soon. Do breakfast, maybe, or lunch. Hell, let's split the difference and get brunch. More alcohol for that meal anyhow. Why is that? People think you're an alcoholic if you drink bourbon at noon, but if you eat pancakes at eleven on Sunday, you can suck down as many mimosas as you want. Weird, right?"

"Shut up, you fool," she said and covered my face with her hand, which was as soft and fragrant as a flower petal on a dewy morning. "Put your arms around me."

"Excuse me?" I said. At least, that was what I meant to say. With her tiny palm smothering my mouth, it came out more like, "Scuz ma?"

"Like this." She grabbed my hands and put them on her warm, toned hips, while simultaneously pushing her warm, toned torso against me. She was very warm and toned. Her dress was like some kind of fancy bedsheet, with folds of excessive material wrapped around her in a manner that somehow managed to be both loose and clingy at the same time, and pressing up against her like that started to feel good. A little too good. The feathers on her dreamcatcher earring tickled my nose, and I pushed my face into her neck to keep from sneezing all over her. However, she apparently mistook the intention of my action. "Yes, that's it," she crooned. "It's a party. Everyone is drinking. Things are getting a bit salacious. It is not uncommon for a man and woman to share a private moment in a dark corner under these circumstances. Am I right?"

I tried to respond but ended up just licking her neck. It tasted minty.

It was true that opening night at the MIFF often turned carnal as the evening wore on and connections were sometimes made that were not of the business variety, but it was early in the evening and the festivities were fairly tame so far. Furthermore, no one was paying any attention to us at all, and there was no reason to believe that we couldn't simply talk privately in the corner of the room without appearing that we were in the throes of a drunken make-out session. On the other hand, Liliane's thighs were warm and toned, and those last two drinks finally hit me, dropping my defenses and turning my skin all soft and melty.

"I have information about the story you're working on," she said. "But I can't give it to you here. It's not safe."

"What story?"

"The story about the girl murdered at that awful club. What else?"

"How do you know about that?"

Instead of answering, she leaned her head back and shook out her hair, an act of sexy exasperation. She had long wavy hair that had been teased and blown out to look like she'd just finished having intercourse in a convertible while it was going ninety miles an hour. It was jet black, except for a single streak of white like the line separating the lanes on a deserted highway.

"Wait. Murder? I thought she slipped and hit her head."

Liliane sighed. She had the perfect face for sighing, thin and noble and aggrieved, a fan of concerned crow's feet around her eyes where the Botox couldn't reach. "Oh, Sam. You cannot possibly be this naïve. A young female dancing naked in an underground facility owned by known drug dealers. Do you think it is a coincidence she turned up dead in an alley in the middle of the night?"

"I don't know. I was told the police report said—"

Another sigh. "The Mountainview Police Department is not equipped for this type of criminal activity. They are accustomed to doling out traffic tickets and arresting frat boys streaking across the football field. They are in over their heads. That is why it is up to the honest citizens of this town to expose the truth of the matter." She paused here to look furtively over her shoulder. I had never actually seen someone look furtively before, and it was just as thrilling as I had hoped. "I have said too much already. It is not safe here. Will you meet me tomorrow morning at my place of business? Say you will, Sam. I need you."

"I guess," I said. "If you have information about…"

But she was already gone. She whirled around with a dramatic flourish that almost knocked over a passing waitress, the folds of her white dress billowing around her body in silken waves, making her departure look like a ghost scene from a Terence Fisher movie. As I watched her fade into the crowd, I took a deep breath and thought about what had just happened. That was a damsel and she was in distress. Therefore, a damsel in distress had just asked me for help! And the distress involved murder! And drugs…maybe. I didn't really understand that part. Also, there was no actual evidence as far as I knew that the stripper in question was murdered. But still, damsel in distress. That was certain.

My phone buzzed in my pocket. It was a text from Victoria. "Damnit, Sam, take that post down now!"

I finished my drink in three long swallows and headed back to the bar. I was all out of tickets and also a tiny bit broke, but I could not risk sobering up now. There were too many things happening, and if I allowed my brain to return to such an unfamiliar state, it was very possible that it would all fly apart and I would lose the tenuous thread connecting these unlikely events. Victoria was quitting; I was being offered a promotion; the death I'd been writing about for the paper just turned into a murder; and there was a mysterious letter from my ex-girlfriend in my back pocket. I was going to throw that away. Yes, I was definitely going to do that. This was no time for abstinence. With this in mind, I grabbed three half-empty glasses on the bar next to me, dumped them all together and drained the contents while the bartender looked on in horror. Someone behind me said, "Hey, I was still drinking that."

I was about to apologize and make up a clever excuse when, across the bar, inside a crowd of young men, a high-pitched screaming laugh broke through the noise of the room and landed on my ears. I froze. I knew that laugh. I had heard that laugh in crowded parties and in private bedrooms. There was a point in my life when I would have done anything, absolutely anything to be the cause of that laugh. As I watched, the crowd of young men parted and standing at their center appeared the back of a woman's head, the back of a head that I'd woken up next to dozens of times, the back of a head that I knew as well as the sound of that laugh. It was Maggie. It had to be. Soon she would turn around and confirm this fact. In two seconds, she would rotate her head to speak to someone next to her or excuse herself to go to the restroom or ask the bartender for another drink, and when that happened, it would all be over. She would see me there staring at her, and she would wave, and she would come over, and we would talk. There was only one thing to do.

I turned and ran.

Chapter 5: Bride of Frankenstein

I CRASHED THROUGH A DOOR MARKED FIRE EXIT and found myself in the alley behind the theater, underneath a streetlight that cast a sepia glow on everything it touched, transforming the brick walls and rusted dumpsters into a familiar noir scene. I braced myself for the caterwaul of a fire alarm, but the night was quiet except for the distant sigh of passing cars and the babble of drunken humanity around the corner on Pearl Street. I took a deep breath and tried to convince my heartbeat to slow down.

"Who you running from, kid?"

I whirled around and saw V. leaning casually against the side of the building, cigarette in one hand, drink in the other. A frizzy fur coat that had seen better days covered her glittering dress, and her enormous award sat at her feet like an obedient glass dog waiting for a treat. Up close she looked less like a glamorous silver-screen beauty that had once captured the sexual imagination of a generation and more like an exhausted old lady who didn't want to socialize with a bunch of ass-kissing strangers. Still, there was something of the old starlet about her—the relaxed, regal angle of the hand holding the cigarette, the sensual way she slouched against the wall, the practiced smirk that did not look practiced at all. I experienced a moment of psychological vertigo, a metaphysical hiccup, like the onscreen jump of an old reel that has been cut together poorly. Fantasy and reality blurred together in my drunken brain, and I shook my head in an effort to separate them again.

"You're, um... I mean, I've seen you... That is, I used to..."

That was all I could manage.

She rolled her eyes like Bette Davis in *Whatever Happened to Baby Jane?* and waved her cigarette in the air like a magic wand, the white smoke standing in for the glittery trails of Disney fairy dust.

"Yeah, yeah. You've seen my movies. You used to butter your corn every time the villain ripped off my clothes, yadda-yadda. I've heard it all before, kid. So why don't we skip the stuttering confessions and the weird fanboy shit. I came out here to get away from all that crap. Trying to breathe some of this fresh mountain air that no one will shut up about."

She took another long drag on her cigarette. I shifted my weight from one foot to the other like a child doing the pee-pee dance, barely able to contain my excitement. I was talking to an *actual* movie star, a woman whose name appeared on large screens, a woman who had an affair with Richard Burton when he was married to Liz Taylor. She looked at me and gave a long-suffering sigh.

"Well, go ahead, Zippy. Tell me all the movies I've been in. You know you want to."

"You were in *Attack of the Dog Men!*" I squealed.

"*Attack of the Handsy Director* is more like it. That was a steaming pile of dog shit if you ask me. Got paid half what the male lead made, did twice the work, and got my ass groped by the director every goddamned take. What was his name? Skinny guy, face like a scabby meatball."

"Sam Fielding."

"Yeah, that's the one." She made the same face her character in *Deathland II* made when the villagers offered her a sandwich made from raccoon meat right before they were attacked by the mutant hordes. "His breath! Ugh. It was like something died in his mouth. I still have nightmares." She shuddered.

"You were so great in *She Evil*!" I couldn't stop myself now. The adulation was spewing out of me like vomit from the little girl in *The Exorcist*. "And *Call of the Night Widow*, *The Thing from Red Lake*, *Die Again III*..."

"So you really are going to list all my movies. Wonderful."

"I'm sorry," I said, trying to catch my breath. I was hyperventilating slightly and possibly hopping up and down. "It's just that I never expected to meet the woman who bit the head off a cat in *Revenge of Vengeance*. How did they do that? It looked so real?"

"It *was* real." I gave her a sideways look, and she laughed. "Taxidermied kitten with the head taped on and an enema bulb inside the body filled with ketchup. One of the prop guys rigged it up on his day off. We did it in two takes. Here's a bit of trivia for you: the cat belonged to the producer's daughter. He said it died after swallowing a sponge, but I think that old sociopath probably strangled it. He was a cold-blooded one."

"Jesus." I clutched my hand to my chest and fell against the wall. "This is the greatest moment of my life."

She laughed. "Well, shit, you make it sound like I cut the cat open myself. You're a sick little bastard. Why are you out here, kid? You should be inside enjoying the party."

"I'm, ah, running away from my ex," I said.

Out loud like that, it sounded absurd. The room had been dark and I was drunk. Maggie was on my mind because of that letter in my pocket. To be completely honest, I imagined seeing Maggie approximately once a week. It was embarrassing.

V. raised a penciled eyebrow. "Well, alright then. Now we're getting somewhere. Is the ex a boy or girl? Animal, mineral, or vegetable? Don't worry, Mama doesn't judge."

"Animal," I said. "I mean, um, girl...female...woman."

The answer seemed to disappoint her. Her eyebrow dropped and the twirling cigarette went back into her crimson mouth. There were several long seconds as I watched her take a drag and then release the smoke in a bored sigh.

"So what's the story?" she said. "Are you a lying cheater or a cheating liar?"

She drained the remainder of her glass, a solid two inches of straight alcohol, with the nonchalance of a lifelong drinker, and then stared regretfully at the empty receptacle.

"What?" I said. "Neither. She's the cheater. She left me. She left me for my best friend after he stole my movie script. I haven't spoken to either of them since. She just got on a bus and... I don't know why I'm even telling you this."

"Me neither, kid. You're turning into a real blabbermouth. Do you have any drugs on you?"

The abrupt subject change threw me off balance, and my hands immediately covered my coat pocket. "What?"

"You heard me. Drugs. Dope, horse, snow, acid, shrooms, bennies, ice. You know, things that make you high. Jesus, what the hell do you kids call it nowadays?"

"Um, we call it drugs."

I rummaged around in my coat until I produced a sad old joint.

V.'s eyes lit up, and she dropped her cigarette. It landed on top of her award with a spray of fiery ash. "That's what I'm talking about. Bring that skunk titty to Mama."

She placed the joint tenderly between her ruby lips and, as if by magic, produced a lighter out of thin air and fired up the end. She held the smoke in her lungs for a solid thirty-second count, and then exhaled with a relieved moan.

"Oh, you got the good stuff down here, baby."

She took another greedy puff and then handed it back to me. I took a drag on the joint, thinking the entire time, "This was just inside her mouth."

We passed the joint back and forth in silence for several minutes, letting the THC sink into our bloodstream, settle into our bones, chase away the psychological ghosts and ghouls that haunted our sober lives, until there was nothing left but sad little twist of paper that burned my fingertips, causing me to drop it on the concrete.

"How'd you get here?" V. asked.

"What?"

"Why do you keep saying that every time I ask a question? Am I not *ee-nun-cee-ate-ing* my words properly? Pay attention, kid. How did you get here? Did you walk, drive, astral projection?"

"I took the bus."

"Do you know how to drive?"

"Sure, but I can't go anywhere right now. My ex-girlfriend…"

"Yeah, yeah, you already told me about that. Girlfriend left you for your best friend. It was boring the first time, kid, and it's not getting any more interesting. I've got to get out of here quick."

"I don't know," I said. "Do you want a ride somewhere?"

"Somewhere, anywhere, I don't care. I haven't been out of the house in five years. That's the only reason I agreed to come to this ridiculous festival. You think I give a shit about awards at my age? Well, of course, I do, but not ones from… Where the hell are we?"

"Mountain—"

"I don't give a shit. The point is Mama doesn't get out much anymore, understand? I got a bad heart, a heartless family, and a nursing home in San Diego with padlocks on the doors. This might be my last chance for a good time before I do the Reaper mambo."

"I don't know. Maybe they're right. It's pretty late, and you've had a lot to drink. Maybe you should call it a night."

She groaned. "Why is your generation such a bunch of spineless prudes? What are you afraid of?"

"I'm not a prude," I said. "I've done…things."

"Listen to me. I'm serious about this. I want you to really hear me out. You kids are all a bunch of pussies. I'm not trying to be funny. It's a problem. You're waiting for something, but you don't know what. The past, the future, you don't know which way to turn. Half of you want to live in the '70s, the other half think life was perfect in the '80s. Your parents have you convinced the world ended when they were teenagers. There's nothing left to accomplish, nothing left to hope for. If they're the Greatest Generation, what does that make you, right? Well, it's all bullshit, kid. They were nothing. They knew nothing. They fought Nazis because a bunch of bureaucrats told them to fight Nazis. They protested Vietnam because they were afraid of getting drafted. Ninety percent of the movies made during the fucking Golden Age of Hollywood sucked King Kong's cock. You didn't miss out on anything. You have nothing to apologize for and everything to contribute. This moment, this moment right here, is all that there is. The future is yours. Take it, kid."

"Right," I said, biting my lip. "That makes sense. I see your point. But maybe we should just turn in for the night."

She raised her hand, and I thought she was going to slap me across the face, like she slapped her boyfriend/space alien mob boss in *Gangster Planet*, but instead she brought it down gently on my shoulder. "I have never said this unsarcastically to anyone before, but I pity you. You are a sad sad boy."

Before I could respond, the fire door swung open, and V.'s gentle hand on my shoulder turned into a vice grip. She was a lot stronger than she looked.

"You keep your mouth shut," she hissed. "Let me do the talking."

A gorgeous woman in her early twenties stepped into the alley and flashed a radiant smile. "There you are," she said. "I've been looking all over for you."

She was a stunning example of human perfection. Her hair was blond and shiny like the mane of a show horse, her teeth were dazzling white pearls inside pillowy lips, her eyes were large and crystal blue, and her body managed to be both thin and curvaceous at the same time. She was wearing a clingy green dress with a slit down the left side that, when she angled her hip in a come-hither manner, showed about five inches of toned, tan thigh.

"Well, hello," she said, directing all of her radiance toward me, rendering me red and mute. "And who is this handsome man entertaining my grandmother?"

I grinned like a fool and said, "Bah."

V. rolled her eyes. "He's no one, Nina. He doesn't work in the industry, so you can retract your fangs."

Nina's thigh disappeared.

"Where the hell have you been?" she growled. "You left me alone with two hundred drunk rednecks. One of them tried to touch my hair. People have been asking about you."

"People like who?" asked V. in a bored manner. "Not that guy from HBO?"

At the mention of those three magical letters, Nina's body went tense, like a bird dog that had caught the scent of a nearby quail.

"HBO? What guy from HBO?"

V. shrugged. "I don't know. Miller or Mailer or something like that. His daughter is in some crappy art film they're showing tomorrow, and he's here to scout a location for a series they're going to shoot about the Donner party."

Nina's jaw dropped. "And you're just telling me about this *now*. What's he look like? Where can I find him?"

"How the hell should I know? He's in his fifties, gray hair, blue jacket. He's probably hanging out on the balcony with all the other VIP assholes."

Nina closed her eyes and her head shot like a rocket toward the ground. For a split second, I thought she'd fainted and was falling at a peculiar angle, but the descent stopped when she was bent over as far as humanly possible at the waist, her forehead now level with her knees. She clawed desperately at her hair for several seconds—brushing, volumizing—and then she snapped back up as if pulled by an invisible string. A wave of curly blonde hair shot over her head and cascaded down her back in glittery waterfall, her face pink with the rush of blood.

"How do I look?" she asked in a breathy voice.

I blinked twice and said, "Bah."

She smiled. "Good enough. Look after the old woman until I get back. I am not kidding, asshole. If she has so much as a cold, I will hurt you…and not in a way that you'll enjoy."

She slammed the door on her way back inside.

"Who was that?" I asked, my voice finally returning.

"She has been known by many names throughout history," said V., staring at the door. "The Greeks called her Medusa. In Medieval Europe she would have been named Vampire. Today we call her kind 'Influencers.'" This one just happens to be my daughter's only child, God help us. She is beautiful and clever but completely talentless. Every time I get invited to one of these things, she handcuffs herself to me in the hopes of meeting some producer or director who will turn her into the next Marilyn Monroe...or at least Pamela Anderson."

"Why do you bring her along?" I asked.

She shrugged. "It's the only way they would let me out. I need a chaperone to leave, and she's the most incompetent adult I know. You do the math."

"If your heart's that bad, maybe they're right. Maybe you should stay at home."

"My heart is fine. There was an...incident."

"What kind of incident?"

She rolled her eyes and let loose a truly magnificent belch. "I was at home, minding my own business, drinking a fifth of vodka, and I fell down a teeny little flight of stairs." She massaged the meat of her left leg. "No big deal, but my half-wit son-in-law decides it's time to put me in a home, and when I refuse, he gets a court order. Now I'm spending all my time with prune drinkers. Got it?"

"Got it."

"Good. Listen, kid, we've got about fifteen minutes until the banshee in there tears the head off of every fifty-year-old man in a blue jacket and discovers there's no one from HBO inside. Then she's going to come back here looking for blood. I don't know about you, but I don't want to be here."

I thought about Nina's curvaceous body and the threats she had made if any harm came to her grandmother, and then I thought about the marijuana I had just smoked with said grandmother. "But I'm supposed to be working on this story about a stripper."

V.'s eyes lit up and she smiled in a lascivious manner. "Now you're talking Mama's language. Booze, sex, naked ladies. Why didn't you tell me this before? Shut up, it was a rhetorical question. Where is this house of ill repute?"

"It's just a few blocks west of here. But I probably shouldn't go. My editor wouldn't like it because of, you know, ethics and stuff."

V. ignored me and turned around in a circle looking at the sky. "Help me out here, kid. Which way is west in this hellhole?"

I pointed with my thumb. "The mountains are always west."

"Maybe where you come from." She patted her leg and then tightened the coat around her neck. "Okay then. Let's hit the road."

"Haven't you been listening? I shouldn't go."

She shook her head. "Yeah, I've been listening to your whining. God, you are such a bore. Did your editor say that you couldn't go to this strip club?"

"Well, no. Actually, she told me to interview the club owner, but I don't think—"

"There you go. Not only is it okay for you to go to the strip club, you are required to go for your job."

"But I really don't think that's what she meant."

"Okay then. You stay here." Without a backward glance, V. started walking down the alley, swinging her hips in a manner that did not at all coincide with her age.

"Hey, wait."

"I've done all the rationalizing I'm going to do, kid," she said over her shoulder. "I'm getting older by the second. Either you're coming or you're not. Make up your mind."

"What about your award thingie?" I said, looking at the large glass prize sitting forlornly on the pavement covered in cigarette ash.

"Leave it. We don't need awards where we're going."

She was almost at the end of the alley. In thirty seconds, she would be gone, and I would be standing here by myself when her sexy, pissed-off granddaughter came looking for her. I really had no choice. I picked up the award, tucked it under my arm like a football, and ran after the woman who was surely going to lead me down a path of destruction.

Chapter 6: The Innocents

ACCORDING TO MY FATHER, THE FIRST MOVIE I ever saw was *Breakfast at Tiffany's*.

"Well, technically, you only saw the second half," he'd say, his eyes foggy with pharmacological nostalgia and his mouth crooked in a secretive grin, as if the information he was about to divulge hadn't been repeated every day of my life since I was a toddler.

When the movie started, I was still inside my mother's basketball-shaped belly as she lay sprawled out on the sticky, popcorn-littered floor of a revival house on the seedy side of Denver called Play It Again. They were hosting a Hepburn marathon that day, and my mother had never seen Audrey or Katharine on the big screen. My father tried to talk her out of it, reasonably insisting she stay in bed just in case they had to rush to the hospital, but my parents' television was broken at the time and my mother was bored out of her mind. "If I'm going to lie around all day like a prize pig," she reportedly said, "I want to be entertained." So my father drove her to the theater and talked the mustachioed Slovakian owner into letting her lie down on the floor at the front of the house, her dainty dandelion head propped up on my father's rolled-up winter coat so she could see the screen without straining her neck. My father sank into the seat behind her and immediately fell asleep.

There were six movies on the schedule that day, and the contractions started during the opening credits for *Bringing Up Baby*. At first, my mother thought it was gas and ignored the discomfort. "She said she didn't want to wake me if it was a false alarm," my father explained. "But I think she didn't want to miss Cary Grant." The pain increased steadily during *Adam's Rib*, but my mother was too engrossed in Spencer Tracy's wry smirk to leave the theater. "And *The African Queen* was next. She had a thing for Bogie, too." When her water finally broke in the middle of *Roman Holiday*, she reached back and pulled on my father's pant leg. By that time, it was too late for the hospital.

Fortunately, the owner of the theater knew a retired midwife who lived down the block, and the rat-faced teenager who ran the ticket booth was dispatched to fetch her. Clean towels were procured from the custodial closet and bowls of water were boiled in the microwave behind the concession stand. No one knew what to do with the boiled water—"They do it in all the movies!"—so the steaming bowls were placed at my mother's feet like offerings to an angry fertility goddess. The projectionist wanted to stop the reel and turn on the house lights, but my mother wouldn't hear of it.

"We paid for six movies, sir," she said. "And I expect to see six movies today."

The midwife looked like a Shakespearean witch—hunched back, nose wart, chin hair—but she had a gentle touch and knew her profession well. It was an easy labor, all things considered. My mother's cervix reached eight centimeters during *Funny Face*, and she started pushing as Audrey emerged from a taxi on Fifth Avenue in the iconic opening scene of *Breakfast at Tiffany's*. I made my appearance about an hour later. If you trust my father's memory—and I would not—I screamed twice, opened my eyes, saw Audrey Hepburn's enormous gazelle-like face staring down at me from the glowing screen above, and fell silent. I spent the rest of the movie cradled against my mother's bosom watching Audrey and George pursue their troubled romance to a swelling Henry Mancini score.

Three years later, to the day, my mother chased a bottle of prescription antidepressants with a bottle of Johnny Walker Black and died in an ambulance on the way to St. Luke's Medical Center. Consequently, I have very few memories of her that aren't somehow clouded by my father's revisionist storytelling or wrapped up in a Technicolor fog of Hollywood's Golden Age.

Like Holly Golightly, my mother suffered from "the mean reds." She was a freelance seamstress and part-time costume designer for a small theater that specialized in popular musicals and period pieces. Our little brick rental was perpetually littered with powdered wigs, saloon-girl corsets, and Confederate soldier uniforms. When she was working for the theater, she was happy, but whenever a show closed and she was forced to hem pants and tailor business suits for money, she would sink into a deep depression. There were crying jags, fits of anger, and weeks when she couldn't manage to get out of bed.

My father was a computer programmer with a dreamy romantic streak that was peculiar for someone in his line of work. He spent his weekdays in an office with a Dilbert calendar, hunched over a keyboard, masticating lines of code for Hewlett Packard, but on the weekends he wore tweed jackets and browsed antique stores. He loved Jane Austen novels, jazz music, and old Ford Mustangs that he couldn't keep running. Most of all he loved my mother. She was beautiful in the manner of a silent-movie actress—dramatic and fragile and ethereal. She had Loretta Young's nose, Lillian Gish's tiny heart-shaped mouth, and Colleen Moore's yearning eyes.

A man of even temperament and wistful optimism, my father could never understand my mother's self-destructive nature. Following her suicide, he had a breakdown. He wasn't hospitalized or anything like that; he just sort of fell out of touch with reality. He quit his job at HP and became a freelance programmer, clacking away endlessly on his office computer, writing code from home for a variety of small companies for a fraction of his former salary. He started drinking heavily and seldom ate. His discarded wine bottles chattered endlessly in our recycling bin. At the insistence of a friend, he went to see a psychiatrist and, in a cruel twist of irony, was prescribed the very same antidepressants my mother used to end her life. They eased the pain but made him glassy-eyed and forgetful, a melancholy specter wandering from room to room in our house, touching old photographs, telling misremembered stories of my mother. He refused to throw out anything that had once belonged to her, including bottles of coconut-scented hand lotion in the medicine cabinet and an empty can of Sunkist sitting on the nightstand with a smear of pink lipstick on the rim. The clothes in the bedroom closet still smelled faintly of her lavender perfume, and there were three large, oak bookcases in the study filled with VHS tapes, which my mother used to purchase by the boxful at garage sales and secondhand stores. She had all the classics—*Casablanca, Citizen Kane, My Fair Lady, The Wizard of Oz, King Kong, Laura, The Third Man, Singin' In the Rain, Sunset Boulevard, Rear Window, Twelve Angry Men, On the Waterfront, Some Like It Hot, All About Eve, The Red Shoes, The Great Dictator, Cool Hand Luke, Auntie Mame, To Catch a Thief, Duck Soup, Charade*—and every day my father would feed a different tape to our large silver VCR, press play, and go about his business. When the movie finished, he would rewind it and install the next one. Over and over again.

It was a confusing time for me. My mother was gone, but our house was still filled with her things, her smells, her presence, and while my father was physically with me, he seemed more the ghost, drifting through my life, haunting our home. Whenever I asked him what had happened to my mother, he would sweep his arm around the room and say, in an addict's romantic slur, "She's in these walls. She's in these tables and chairs and books. She's in these old movies. She's always with us." And then he would usher me into my parents' bedroom, and we would curl up on their king-sized four-poster and watch *Breakfast at Tiffany's,* while my father told the story of my birth, his eyes blurry with tears and his lips stained purple by the cheap red wine in his coffee mug.

One of the few absolute, indisputable, non-drug-related facts I knew about my mother was that she grew up in Mountainview, so when it came time for me to choose a college, I picked MU without hesitation. I don't know if I was trying to stay close to her or understand why she had committed suicide or what. In any case, it didn't work. My college years were just as lonely and confusing as my childhood. After I moved out of the house, my father's health continued to decline, and he finally passed away during my sophomore year. The coroner's report said the cause of death was "complications of the heart." Think about that. You spend your whole life trying to figure out what it all means, and when it's over, a stranger examines your cold, naked body and sums up your existence perfectly in four words.

They're both buried in an old cemetery on the outskirts of Mountainview. I've never visited them.

Chapter 7: Bringing Up Baby

I WOKE THE NEXT MORNING to the sound of Buddhist monks chanting on a mountaintop in Tibet. Actually, they could have been Presbyterian plumbers mumbling in a cornfield in Iowa for all I knew. The noise was coming from downstairs. This was important information. Wherever I was, there was a downstairs. The bed I was lying on was enormous and soft and the sheets were the kind that had a thread count. I was completely naked except for one sock on my right foot. My penis was flaccid and resting on my thigh. It gazed up at me with a look of familiar purplish-pink disappointment. We had been in this position before, and we both knew it was my fault. It was a fine penis, neat, circumcised, reasonably sized without trying to show off, a gentle upward curve when erect that I imagined in my more confident moments provided extra gratification to its female counterparts, a small beauty mark just below the head that had unfortunately on two occasions been mistaken for venereal disease, but altogether a serviceable and trustworthy companion to have in the bedroom. My only complaint was the foliage surrounding the area, of which there was very little. It was like peach fuzz or the soft fluff on the back of a newly hatched duckling. In fact, the hair on my entire body was so fine and blonde that when naked I looked almost pre-pubescent. This was why I preferred sex in the dark and had in college refused all spring break invitations that involved the beach. Even now, the sight of my pale, hairless body inspired depression, and I pulled the sheets up to my chin to avoid looking at it.

There was a quiet scratching sound coming from the foot of the bed, like a child whispering or a small animal scuttling across butcher paper. I strained to hear it better, but it stopped immediately, almost as though whatever was causing the noise could sense my interest. I inhaled deeply through the nostrils and detected a somewhat-alluring combination of incense, perfume, dirty laundry, really good pot, and something sinister underneath it all that was musky and alive and familiar. My nose itched but I resisted the urge to sneeze. It was important to remain motionless, like an opossum. I needed more information before it was safe to officially wake up. I pretended to be dead. The pain in my head made me almost wish it were true. Slowly, almost imperceptibly, with my eyes still closed, I stretched and while doing so explored the rest of the bed with my hands and feet. Nothing. I was alone. This was good.

I tried to recall how I got here, but as usual, the director in my head had cut the most important scenes. I remembered talking to V. in the alley and then walking to the Pink Door. I remembered entering the strip club and ordering shots. After we sat down, someone at the bar recognized V. and the deejay stopped the music to announce her presence. She took a bow and signed some autographs. Then a group of strippers came over to our table and pulled her onto the dance floor. There were more shots and V. said something to the deejay and then Joe Cocker was singing "You Can Leave Your Hat On" and V. was doing a slow, sexy spin around a metal pole. When that scene ended, my hangover escalated from thundering ache to lightning anguish, and the screen went blank. I couldn't remember if I left V. at the club or got her a cab or walked her to her hotel. Surely, I'd made arrangements for her to get home safely. In any case, she was a grown woman. She could take care of herself.

Carefully I opened my eyes just enough to see through the gossamer curtains of lashes. There was a vast landscape of expensive clothing. Mountains of Nordstrom sweaters, valleys of Gucci sandals, Versace rivers cutting through Prada canyons. It was like waking up on a colorful planet made of fine-spun silk and handcrafted leather. Not seeing anyone else, I opened my eyes completely and took a good look around. Textbooks, cosmetic supplies, dreamcatchers, ski equipment, Buddha statues, paintbrushes, scented candles, hula hoops, and takeout containers were scattered throughout the fashionable terrain. Light trickled in through a large French window, which displayed a breathtaking view of Pike's Peak. It was morning, early, before eight if I had to guess, and the sky was a rich pallet of vivid pinks and subtle oranges. There was a single black cloud smeared across an otherwise pristine horizon, like a smudge of ink on the front of a new prom dress. The ceiling of the room was vaulted and lined with some kind of gorgeous stained wood, possibly pine. The walls were covered with…well, I guess it was art. There was paint involved, in any case, and canvases and shapes. One particular piece had a dark green background with a hazy, slightly lighter green square in the middle and a hazy, slightly lighter green square in the middle of that green square. It was called, inexplicably, "Earth Mother's Daughter." To the right was a yellow canvas with a red circle in the bottom left corner titled "Time Forever Stopped," and next to that was a painting of different shades of blue, darker at the top and progressively lighter as it moved down. It was called "Blue."

At last, I knew where I was. I groaned.

I drew back the blanket and eased myself into a sitting position, enjoying the delicious rush of oxygen to the brain, accompanied by spermy little spots of daydream neon wriggling across my field of vision in search of ova nightmares to impregnate. Out of the corner of my eye, I saw a flash of movement—something long and dark and toothed—but when I swung around to catch it, there was nothing there but shadows and lies. I tried to write it off to an overactive imagination and a paranoid hungover brain, but I couldn't shake the feeling that I was being watched.

The pain was really starting to pulse now as it moved from the back of my head right to the front. There was no nausea this time, so that was a small victory. All I had to do was find some pot and a plate of greasy food and I'd be all right. But first I needed clothes.

After a lengthy search among the laundry dunes, I managed to find my pants draped over what was probably a desk and my left shoe under the bed. My phone was still in the front pocket of my jeans, its screen funereal black. I spent a few frantic seconds stabbing at it with my index finger in the hope of resuscitating it. Nothing. There was no charger in sight, so I slid the phone into my front pocket and forged ahead. I still needed a sock, a right shoe, a shirt, and a coat. The underwear I could live without. Fortunately, there was a wide selection of garments available. I started picking through the piles again. A striped rainbow sock fit on the first try, and after a few failed T-shirt attempts I found a snazzy white Armani button-up with gray pinstripes and just one small mustard stain on the collar that fit disturbingly well, considering it had been made for a woman. The shoes were a bit more difficult, but in the end, I traded my one beat-up sneaker for a pair of black-and-white leather 1920s-style wingtips that I uncovered in the back of the closet, no doubt left there by an old boyfriend or one-night stand. The closet itself was a thing of excess and wonder, an enormous walk-in half the size of my entire apartment, and I spent a few minutes browsing its many hangers and shelves and drawers and shoeboxes, until I came upon an old, green belted trench coat in the back, probably a Goodwill purchase made as a joke for a Halloween costume or themed frat party. In any case, I couldn't resist.

I had a long history of petty theft. I never took money and had no interest in stealing from retailers, but I had a compulsion for picking up small, personal items and slipping them in my pockets—coasters, lighters, pens, hair ties. I mostly stole from lovers and friends, and the habit increased exponentially the closer I got to the end of a relationship. I'd never been caught, possibly because the items I took had no real value, except as nostalgic talismans that I could fixate on for short periods of time until I lost them among the alcohol bottles and pizza boxes of my own apartment.

Outside the closet, I stopped to take a look at my new costume in front of an oblong cheval mirror. Not bad, actually. The trench coat was old, worn at the elbows, smelled like an ashtray, and there was a fairly large hole in the right armpit, but with the collar up it had a sort of dignified-homeless-man quality to it. The shirt fit like it was made for me, and the shoes were so ridiculously out of place they made the rest of it work. My dry dishwater hair was a hideous mess, as usual, plastered flat against my skull in front, sticking up in back like the tail of a dying pheasant. I attacked it with my fingers but only managed to rearrange the geography of the chaos.

I stood in front of that mirror for ten minutes, trench coat open, collar upturned, pushing my hair up and down and back and forth, teasing it, pulling it, cursing it, trying yet again to make the end result look debonair, heroic. He was in there somewhere, that leading man, I just needed to find the right part.

Then I spotted the solution across the room, perched on a stack of cashmere sweaters like an exotic bird guarding a two-thousand dollar nest: a black fedora with a small brown feather sticking out of its powder-blue band. I approached it carefully, as though it might take flight at any moment. This was not one of those flimsy straw hats you buy during a weeklong vacation in the Bahamas. This hat was hand-stitched beaver pelt, and it had substance. A wide brim snapped down in the front, up in the back, silk lining on the inside, creased lengthwise down the crown and then pinched at the front to form the shape of a teardrop if viewed from above. When I slid it on my head, it seemed to hover for a second before settling perfectly over my temples, snuggling in, providing both disguise and armor. It was, of course, part of the hipster fashion trend that had recently swept through the country, but all I could think of was Sam Spade and Philip Marlowe.

I pulled the brim down a little further over my right eye and grinned. Feeling finally like a hardboiled journalist in pursuit of the truth, I made a cursory search for Maggie's letter but gave up quickly. I assumed I'd lost it at the theater or during the debauchery that followed, and I felt relief at not having to face whatever horrible memories it promised to dredge up.

I made my way to the bathroom and rummaged through the medicine cabinet for some aspirin. There were dozens of small apothecary-like vials with printed white labels that read *witch hazel, tea tree oil, St. John's wort*, etc., but nothing a normal human being would use in the twenty-first century. Finally, in the back of the towel closet, hidden away like a stack of fetish porn, I found several orange prescription bottles labeled Valium, Vicodin, and OxyContin. The date on the labels said the pills had been prescribed more than a year ago, so I figured the owner probably wouldn't miss them. I swallowed two Vicodin and pocketed everything else. I stuck my mouth under the faucet and drank until my belly felt like it would pop. Then I took off the hat and soaked my head. Afterward, I toweled off and felt better. I put the hat back on and looked at myself in the mirror. I looked good. Really good. Like leading-man good.

I gave the brim of the hat a playful tug and then swaggered to the bedroom door, which was slightly ajar. I poked my head through and looked at the scene below. I immediately dropped to my knees and crawled into the hall. I inched my way to the railing and peeked over the edge. Below, there was a twenty–two-year-old female sitting in the lotus position in front of a large canvas, the chanting monks reverberating from an expensive sound system behind her. All the furniture and detritus of the room had been pushed against the walls, leaving an empty crop circle in the middle. There were painting supplies strewn everywhere, and the beautiful hardwood floors were streaked with a rainbow of droppings. The artist responsible for the mess sat absolutely still, eyes closed, back ramrod straight, chest thrust forward, breasts perky, nipples erect and pencil-eraser pink, long blonde hair straight and parted down the middle like a 1970s Sissy Spacek, toasted brown legs folded on top of one another, the backs of her hands resting on her knees with manicured index fingers gently kissing thumbs, her vagina shaved to within an inch of its life, mouth slightly pinched, a look of concentrated boredom on her Disney-princess face.

I shuddered. How the hell was I going to get out of here?

I FIRST MET RIVER MOORE TWO YEARS AGO at an art opening downtown. She was there for the postmodern abstract expressionism, and I was there for the free drinks. One thing led to another, as the poets say, and we ended up back at her apartment, pulling at zippers, fumbling with buttons, having the type of pure, leg-trembling sex that can only be had between two strangers that share a bone-deep biological attraction but know nothing whatsoever about one another on an emotional or intellectual level.

It wasn't until the next morning that I discovered River was the daughter of Gerald Moore, the tyrannical publisher of the newspaper I worked for, and by then it was too late. Neither River nor I had the courage to confront Gerald on the subject. I didn't want to lose my job, and River was worried about her father's disapproval, which I came to learn over time was the foundation of their relationship. Besides, it was far too much fun sneaking around behind his back, sending coded text messages, whispering conspiracies in the dark, pretending our love was forbidden. This faux Romeo-and-Juliet routine got us through the first two months, but eventually it became apparent we had little in common, aside from the enjoyment of mind-altering substances and a mutual flare for the dramatic. It all ended abruptly and badly, as it had been destined to from the beginning, and since that time, we'd slept together on and off when we were between relationships and feeling particularly desperate. The sex was good; everything else was predictably bad. The last time I saw River she was preparing for the Moore's annual Christmas vacation ("holiday self-care" was what she called it) at some private resort in India that charged wealthy white Americans exorbitant fees to eat organic chickpeas with their hands and fetishize Buddhist culture. We had sex, fought, had more sex, and then agreed never to speak to one another again. Obviously, that plan had worked out well.

I BELLY-CRAWLED TO THE STAIRS and started to ease my way down, scooting on my ass like a toddler to make less noise. The staircase was a winding wooden

DNA strand that dropped to the floor about twenty feet in front of River and her canvas. This made descending risky business. On the other side of the stairs, there was a short hallway leading into a space that was probably meant to be a study but had been turned into a meditation room/coat closet, and on the other side of that was the back door and freedom. I made my way slowly, keeping an eye on River the whole time. The shoes were particularly tricky, as the soles were like glass, designed to make tap-dancing noises as they crossed a ballroom floor or some such thing, so I had to slide along on just the heels to keep them quiet. The chanting monks helped muffle any noise. The thrusting motion on the stairs combined with River's exposed breasts caused a partial erection to form, and I had to stop halfway down to adjust myself. Still, despite the distractions, I made it most of the way without being detected.

I was about to congratulate myself on my stealth skills when something warm and wriggly and hairless launched itself at me from behind, landed in my lap, and began aggressively licking the bulge in my crotch. I only saw it for a split second, but that was all it took to determine the beast was evil incarnate and had to be destroyed. I leaped to my feet and emitted a shameless high-pitched scream that would have made V. jealous. The creature emitted its own terrified squeal as it flew through the air, twisting and turning in an effort to regain its balance, before hitting the floor with a kind of comical grace, sliding several feet across the shiny wooden surface, regaining its footing, and then scampering into the kitchen.

"*Rothko!*" came the cry from the living room.

A blur of nipple and vagina streaked past me. I clambered back up the stairs wanting to put as much distance as possible between myself and the unholy creature that had just molested me. I waited at the top, clutching the banister and listening to a series of cooing and kissing noises coming from the kitchen. The Vicodin was starting to hit my bloodstream now, making me feel sort of lethargic and itchy.

Finally, River emerged, now wrapped in a colorful, silk sari, a look of anger on her face and a long gray dildo cradled in her arms. She picked up a remote from the coffee table, turned off the stereo, and then crossed the room. The dildo looked at me and growled.

"Now, Sammy, I want you to apologize to Rothko *this* instant," said River. "He was just trying to make *friends* and you treated him *horrendously.*"

Among the many things we fought about was River's insistence on calling me Sammy, a silly infantile version of my name that reminded me of a trained circus seal in a children's book from my youth, but at the moment I was too caught up in trying to identify the species of the creature I was supposed to be making an apology to. I took a few steps down the stairs, squinting to get a better look.

"Is that… Is it a dog?" I asked.

River exhaled sharply and tilted her head at a certain angle to indicate she was offended. "Of *course,* he's a dog." She buried her face in its spotted gray skin and affected a baby-talk voice that she had used in the bedroom with me on more than one occasion despite my protests. "This is my wittle puppy wuppy. Aren't yew? Yes, yew are. Yes, yew are my wittle puppy."

I descended the stairs quickly now, my courage returning as the Vicodin began an old, familiar dance. "What's wrong with it?" I said, genuinely interested.

River's eyes almost rolled out of her head. "Nothing! He's *perfect!*"

As I got closer, it became apparent that it was a malnourished wiener dog that had been shaved from neck to tail by a veterinarian. Its long stomach was practically concave and its ribs were sucked up tight against its splotchy skin. There was some sort of festering wound about the size of a nickel on its right flank that had been treated with sticky salve. Its floppy ears were ragged and lumpy from flea bites and brawls, and there was some kind of wart-like growth on its snout. Altogether it was one of the ugliest specimens of the canine persuasion that I had ever seen in my life.

I reached out to pet it, but the little shit snapped at my hand, missing by mere millimeters and prompting River to giggle and say, "Rothko! You naughty *naughty* boy!"

"Where did you find it?" I asked, rubbing my undamaged fingers. Obviously the phallic demon spawn had not been purchased from a breeder.

"*Him.* Where did I find *him?*" River corrected. She flipped the mutt over on his back and cradled it in the crook of her arm like an infant. Upside down it was even more hideous. Its belly was a Rorschach test of scars and spots and tick bites. Between its legs was a hairy penis nub and below that what looked like a couple of walnuts in a furry brown bag. Great, it wasn't even fixed. As if reading my thoughts, the animal bared its teeth and produced a strange buzzing sound that was halfway between a purr and a growl, all the while glaring at me with jaundiced eyes. Ignoring this, River began to rub little Rothko's disgusting tummy as she explained how she'd come to possess this tube-shaped Cujo. "Oh em gee! So! We were at Club Mahindra, of *course,* but we couldn't get our *usual* cabana because some icky Euro-trash doctor was, like, living there for a month because his wife just died or *something* and he refused to move out even though everyone *knows* we stay in that cabana every year because it's close to the meditation center and it's the *only* one that has three full-sized bathrooms and Gerald told Mahesh we would pay *extra* because it's, like, our family tradition and it would totally *ruin* the holiday season if we had to hike all the way down the beach every morning for yoga and then Gerald got mad and started *yelling* but I told him that he should just, you know, accept it as a gift from the Universe and…"

This was how she spoke, in long run-on sentences, staring at a spot just behind your head, without pausing for air or thought. Perhaps it was all that meditation—clear mind, circular breathing. She had this way of talking fast through her nose and emphasizing random words, as though she was a stage actress from the '40s delivering a monologue to an adoring crowd that was hanging on her every word. In any case, I'd learned long ago that trying to follow the entire storyline was maddening and interrupting was useless. It was best to stare at her blankly, nod, and listen for the relevant details. When we were dating, I got to be quite good at this. Sometimes on the phone I would put her on speaker and let her go for twenty or thirty minutes while I watched movies on mute or wrote reviews.

"…and the new cabana was next to the front gate, which is was just *awful*, of course, because of all the car fumes, so we told Mahesh that it just would not *do* and he moved us to the other side, which was much improved, except it was next to a *public* beach and these villagers kept coming over to sell us fruit and the security guard Naveen—he has such a crush on me—Naveen kept *running* them off and then this little angel ran right up to me and started licking my feet and Naveen yelled at him and tried to kick him and I said, 'Don't you *dare!*' and then…"

She went on for some time afterward, but that was the bones of the story. Apparently, there was a pack of stray dogs that lived near the resort where the Moores were vacationing, and the bravest ones would slip under the fence and steal food from the garbage. The dachshund was a particular nuisance, and the security staff had been attempting to catch it for months. If River hadn't been there, Rothko would have certainly met a painful end that day. But River fell in love with the filthy animal and, despite the numerous legal and medical obstacles involved in transporting an undocumented canine from India to the United States, insisted on taking it home. It had been shaved to get rid of fleas and inoculated for every disease known to man and dewormed and deloused and poked and prodded and disinfected, and somehow the lucky bastard made it through all that with its balls intact.

"…and there are *so* many other dogs down there, Sammy, and we have to do something about them because they're just sick and abused and they eat *garbage*, which is why I'm starting a charity to bring them here because the Dalai Lama says—"

"Wait," I said. "What was that?"

"The Dalai Lama *says* that in order to carry a positive action—"

"No, not that. The other thing. The charity thing."

River's face brightened. "I'm starting a charity to bring homeless dogs from India to Mountainview so they can be adopted by loving families. Isn't that a *great* idea? Gerald's lawyer is going to help me set it up and then we're going to have a *story* in the paper. Maybe you can write it."

I pinched the bridge of my nose between my thumb and index finger. The headache was fighting through the Vicodin. "Doesn't our Humane Society already have a bunch of dogs that need to be adopted?"

There was a pause. "Well, sure, but not *Indian* dogs."

"Right. But there are already dogs that need adoption here, and you're just going to import a bunch of foreign dogs that don't have homes. Shouldn't we find homes for the animals here first?"

"Listen to you. *Foreign* dogs. They're not going to *rape* our women and *steal* our jobs, Sammy. You're such a reactionary."

"That's not the point I was trying to—"

But River wasn't interested in the point. "You can be so *provincial* sometimes. I mean, good goddess, what could you possibly have against helping defenseless animals? The Dalai Lama says, 'In order to carry a *positive* action, we must develop here a *positive* vision,' and that's what I'm attempting to do, develop a *positive* vision, and I do not need all your negative energy right now."

"Okay, okay," I said, throwing up my hands. "I give up. You win. Flying a bunch of flea-bitten animals halfway across the world so they can be adopted by bored white people who need to ease their liberal guilt sounds like a magnificent way to spend your time and money. Well done."

River put Rothko on the floor and gave me a look of intense pity, a look that involved inclining her head ever so slightly, furrowing her brow, and poking out her bottom lip. "Oh, my poor Sammy," she said, throwing her arms around my neck. "I apologize for being impatient with you. Sometimes I forget the *conditions* you were raised in. I've had so many privileges that you were denied. It's no wonder you turned out cynical and close-minded." She pulled me closer and began to coo in my ear.

River lived to rescue things—animals, clothing, people, it made no difference as long as they had been cast out by society. Her pattern was to find the forsaken item, bring it back to her expensive apartment, shower it with affection, money, and moral superiority, and then release it back into the world when she grew bored. In this way, she managed to assuage her liberal guilt without making any substantive changes to her lifestyle. When we first began seeing one another, I couldn't bear to tell her what had actually happened to my parents, knowing I would be reduced to tears in the process and River would drown me in pity I did not want. Instead, hoping to stave off further questions, I told her that my parents were small-town conservatives, and I was no longer on good terms with them. From there, and with no help from me, River had constructed an elaborate Dickensian background for me that involved poverty, ignorance, and possible violence. For some reason, the thought of me abused and neglected always turned her on.

She ran her hands over my chest and said in a husky voice, "I like your new clothes, Sammy. I always *said* you would look handsome if you tried. You have so much potential."

"Hmmm," I answered.

Not only did she have no idea the clothes were hers, apparently she hadn't noticed what I was wearing last night when I knocked on her door. This was not surprising. However, since I couldn't even remember where I was when I woke up this morning, I didn't have much room to complain.

She continued to hug me, purring in my ear and rubbing that sari back and forth across my body. She started to say something, but I couldn't stand the thought of listening to her again, so I did what I always did in these occasions and shoved my tongue down her throat. She moaned and we spent a few moments wrestling with one another, each trying to gain some sort of psychosexual advantage. The fingernails on her right hand dug into the back of my neck, while her left hand reached down to cup my crotch, which was now fully aroused. I slid my hand beneath the kimono and found a silky torso that led lower and lower, until my fingers discovered the soft wet opening between her legs. River threw her head back and gasped. Like everything else, she was overly dramatic about sex, which was exciting at first but quickly grew dull when I realized her cries and contortions had little to do with me. It was all part of a performance piece. She pretended to be an extremely sexual person, but in reality there was only one thing that truly excited her. Pain. Mine, to be exact.

I took a step backward and stumbled on the stairs, going down hard, banging my tailbone on a sharp corner and tearing off River's kimono in the process. I cried out and River mistook this as an act of animal passion. The pain was excruciating, but before I could recover, she was pulling my pants off, biting my thighs, pinching my nipples, and then taking me in her mouth. I leaned back and moaned, partly from ecstasy and partly from the electric sting that was shooting up my ass. She climbed on top of me, knocked my hat off, and grabbed a fistful of my hair. I did not enjoy this, so I reached up and returned the favor. She didn't seem to like it either, and we both just sat there for a second, glaring at one another, and yanking each other's hair. And then I was inside her, and we were writhing together, slamming hips and shins into wood, pulling hair, feeding on each other's pain, riding out the weird hostile chemistry between us that made a relationship impossible but sex amazing.

When it was over, I started getting dressed, but River remained naked. She went to the window and made a big production of stretching, taking long exaggerated breaths while she did so. *Inhale*...arms raised out in a wide circle until palms touched above her head. *Exhale*....lowered prayer hands between her breasts. Repeat.

"Such a blessed morning," she said. "What are we *going* to do with it?"

"I can't stay." I slid my pants on and carefully tucked my penis inside before pulling up the zipper. "I have a deadline."

She gave me an indulgent smile. "That's wonderful, Sammy. I love reading your little movie reviews. They're *so* idiosyncratic."

"This isn't a movie review," I said, buttoning my shirt. "It's a front-page article about a murder."

River's eyes widened. "*Mon dieu*! Murder? Here in Mountainview?"

"Why? You don't think murder can happen here?" I snorted. "I got news for you, doll face. Murder happens wherever men lay their hats."

River cocked her head and gave me a curious look. Then she burst out laughing.

"What's so funny?" I said.

"Doll face?" she gasped. "Sammy, why are you *talking* like that?"

"I'm not talking like anything. Stop it. The murder of a stripper is nothing to giggle about."

She picked up her sari and wrapped it around her body in a single graceful motion.

"Are you talking about that *poor* woman at the Pink Door? Such a shame. But that was no *murder*, Sammy. You're always so dramatic about everything."

I threw my trench coat on and looked around for my hat. It had disappeared. "I am not dramatic. And how do you know anything about it anyhow? It just happened yesterday. Where the hell is my hat?"

River picked up a paintbrush and began picking at it. "Oh, Gerald was talking about it last night." She mimicked her father arguing with someone on the phone. " '*If an exotic dancer dies in my city, it's news. We have to print something. I have no choice.*'" River rolled her eyes. "Honestly, I don't know why he grovels to that woman?"

"What woman?"

"I can't." River pointed the paint brush at me in an accusatory manner. "Gerald has *forbidden* me to discuss it, Sammy, so don't even try to force it out of me."

I shrugged. "Okay."

"He would be absolutely *livid*. You know how he can get when it comes to his little secrets."

"Fine. We won't talk about it."

"He is my *father*, Sammy." She threw the paintbrush to the floor. "I would never betray his confidence."

"Jesus Christ. I don't care."

"Good," she said, smiling and squeezing my arm. "Thank you for respecting my boundaries."

"No problem," I said. I scanned the living room. "Where's my hat?"

She dipped her toe in an open can of paint and absently smeared it around the floor. "She's such a hypocrite."

"Who is?" I walked around the staircase thinking River might have thrown the hat in the corner, but there was nothing.

"Everyone in town is lining up to kiss her ass, *including* Gerald, but she's a total phony." Her toe painting had taken the form of a bird in flight. She was a better artist with her feet. "*All* that crap about spirituality and environmentalism. You know that spa she runs is supposed to be so green, but it's totally not. My friend Jenna *used* to work for her, and you won't believe what she does in that alley…"

"River," I said. "I don't have time for this."

I looked under the couch and found Rothko there gnawing on the brim of the fedora. I grabbed the other side, and managed to extricate it from his jaws after a brief tug of war. The top had been dented, and there were now teeth marks along the brim, but it was still serviceable. If anything it looked more like the hat of an intrepid reporter than ever.

"I have to go."

"Nonsense," River replied. She put the lid on the paint and headed for the stairs. "We are *going* to have brunch. Just let me take a shower and put my face on. You entertain Rothko. I'll be down in *no* time."

"Fine," I said. "You win. But make it quick. I seriously have to get to work."

She kissed me on the cheek and headed up the stairs. She was a marathon showerer, always spending at least thirty minutes in there doing God knows what. I put my hat on and slipped into the kitchen in search of weed. Rothko followed me, growling under his breath and nipping at my heels. With River out of the room, I was no longer forced to make nice, so I picked up a spatula and took a swing at him. I missed by almost two feet, but he got the hint and high-tailed it out of the room. I opened a bunch of drawers, checked the freezer, looked in the Shiva statue where she usually kept an eighth of primo sativa for parties, all the places she normally hid her stash, but there was nothing. This was unusual. River didn't smoke that much herself, but she had to maintain her image of being a relaxed, bohemian artist, so she always had at least an ounce of really good mountain bud around. Of course, she also dated the type of artsy losers prone to steal weed from their girlfriend and then resell it.

I was about to give up when I noticed a familiar envelope on the kitchen table under a pile of junk mail. I pulled it out and, sure enough, it was addressed to me. Also, it had been opened. My face went hot with anger. It was just like River to open my mail. We weren't dating or even seeing one another on a friendly basis, but it didn't matter. River Moore assumed everything was hers. Forget the fact that it had someone else's name on it. This behavior wasn't exclusive to me. She was like this with everyone, listening to other people's conversations without permission, going through filing cabinets, checking phone records. Once I opened my apartment door and found her on my couch looking at my email, and the thing that galled me most was that she wasn't even embarrassed about it. "The door was unlocked," she said when I asked how she got in. "And your laptop was open." I explained that it was rude to enter someone's apartment and look at their private messages, and she just blinked at me, legitimately confused.

The more I thought about it the more it pissed me off. That was a private letter, perhaps the most private letter I had ever received in my life. I hadn't heard from Maggie in more than three years, primarily because I changed my phone number and deleted my old email account and blocked her on Facebook during a drunken bout of self-pity. I wanted to forget about Maggie Chase. I wanted to edit her completely out of my movie. Now, after all this time she was sending me mysterious letters, letters I didn't want to open, letters that could only contain heartache. River knew about Maggie. I'd told her the story, albeit the revised version that made me seem like less of a pathetic loser. She knew this was a sensitive topic for me, but she just went right ahead and opened the letter. This was truly the most infuriating thing she had ever done, which was saying a lot.

I shoved the letter in my pocket. I wanted to pay River back, but as I looked around, I realized there was nothing she really cared about all that much. Since she bought everything with her father's credit card, she had no regard for material items, and she simply did not believe in privacy. I couldn't steal her favorite sweater or read her diary. She wouldn't even notice.

And then inspiration struck.

I opened the refrigerator and rummaged around among the cruelty-free salads and organic apples. Finally, I found what I was looking for—a package of vegan sausage from a local grocery store that specialized in charging ten times the going rate for items you could get at the gas station. I grabbed it and headed into the living room.

"Look what I've got, Rothko," I said.

He growled and backed away from me, but when he saw the sausage dangling in the air, he became instantly hypnotized.

"You want to help me leave a surprise?"

He followed me to the middle of the room, where River had been doing her naked meditation. I looked at her painting. It was a large canvas, nearly five-feet tall and just as wide, and it was pink. That was it, just pink. There was some darker pink on one side and some lighter pink on the other, and the pink in the middle was sort of swirled in a circle. But ultimately it was just a bunch of pink. I found a can of red paint and dumped half of it out on the floor.

"Come here, Rothko," I said. "Get over here, you ugly little disease sponge."

Rothko kept his eyes fixed on the sausage as it dangled right over the red puddle. He barely noticed when he stepped in the paint, and when I twirled the sausage around, he followed it, turning around in circles, pushing himself up on his hind legs to snap at it, coating his feet and his belly and his tail in fire-engine red.

"Good boy," I said. "Oh, that's a good boy. Now go get it!"

I tossed the sausage across the room and Rothko lunged for it, splattering red carnage everywhere along the way. The sausage bounced off the side of the couch and skittered across the floor with Rothko chasing it, slipping and sliding on his paint-covered feet, leaving red paw prints and skid marks all over the place. Somehow the runaway link managed to roll underneath the easel the pink painting was on, and the wiener dog charged headlong after it before I could stop him. The whole thing came crashing to the floor on top of the dog. The noise was deafening. I stood there in silence for several long seconds. I was certain Rothko was dead. I projected the image of his small lifeless body on the movie screen in my mind, his head flat, his little paws still twitching. I imagined River's screams when she saw him and the story in the newspaper that would follow, the headline reading "Movie Reviewer Slaughters Dog, Two Thumbs Down."

But then a small hole emerged in the middle of the canvas, precisely at the center of the pinkish swirl, followed by a filthy red paw and then a snout carrying a brown, oblong piece of fake meat. Rothko pushed his way through the painting, looking like a bloody, disfigured alien emerging from an enormous vagina, gave me a triumphant look, and waddled off into the kitchen to enjoy his prize.

I looked at the carnage around me. Red everywhere, a ripped and mutilated canvas, a dog that looked like he had been dipped in blood. This was not what I'd had in mind. I had wanted a few red paw prints on the floor that could be easily mopped up by River's maid. This looked like a scene from *The Shining*.

I picked the painting up and put it back on the easel. This did not help. If anything, it made the whole thing worse. Now it looked like an ex-boyfriend had stabbed a family pet and then purposefully wrecked his lover's artwork in order to make a point. When River saw the mess, she was bound to think the red paint was blood, and then she'd find Rothko covered in red and she would think he'd been injured. She would be scared and then angry. She might call the police. I had seen enough courtroom dramas to know that my side of the story would not be convincing in front of a jury. But what could I do? There wasn't enough time to clean up the mess. There was no way to take it back. I stood there cringing and biting my lip.

In the end, I dipped my finger into the can of paint and wrote on what remained of the mangled canvas: "Sorry. I didn't mean for it to happen."

This will surely be the epithet on my gravestone.

Here lies Samuel Drift. He didn't mean for it to happen.

I wiped my hands off on a paint-splattered rag, tiptoed across the room, and slipped out the front door.

Chapter 8: Kiss Me Deadly

IT WAS A BEAUTIFUL MORNING. The black cloud on the horizon had vanished like a cynical joke, and the new sky was as crisp and clean as the winter air. I inhaled deeply and blew out a white fog that twisted and spiraled around my face. In a nearby evergreen, a confused sparrow trilled a summer love song and was accompanied by the spasmodic rhythm section of a woodpecker in the distance. Several squirrels chased one another over a telephone line and then down the drainpipe of a mock Tudor. I strolled in a westerly direction and munched on cold vegan sausages that tasted like spicy shoe rubber while the drugs dissolved in my system, the incident in River's apartment already being cut and edited into an amusing slapstick scene by the trusty director in my head.

There was no one on the street. I was on the outskirts of one of Mountainview's newer neighborhoods, the wealthy part of town, although that didn't really narrow it down anymore. Everywhere you looked there were enormous houses, some of them designed to resemble log cabins on steroids, others straight out of a trendsetters issue of *Architectural Digest*. Sloped fiberglass ceilings and L-shaped greenhouses and solar-panel teepees and round adobe huts painted turquoise for no apparent reason. Salvador Dali structures clashing uncomfortably with the Ansel Adams scenery. Most were second homes belonging to wealthy Californians and New Yorkers who liked to spend a few months every winter skiing and smoking legal pot. If you looked hard enough, you could still find a few stubborn little shacks with lawn gnomes out front and beat-up VW vans parked in the dirt driveways, the bumper stickers pleading impotently to KEEP MOUNTAINVIEW WEIRD, but like the aging hippies inside, these prosaic structures were slowly dying off. Local residents were being priced out of their own city.

Once upon a flashback, Mountainview had been a sleepy little college town nestled at the base of the Flatirons like a baby tucked into a mother's bosom. For several decades, the large green sign welcoming visitors had declared the city's population to be just under twenty thousand. In those days, the university focused primarily on agricultural studies, and the tourists who trickled through were mostly bearded men with checkered hats and rubber boots pulled up to their testicles as they prepared to fish the Colorado River. It was just a town. A nice town, a pretty town, but just a town.

And then it happened. In the fall of 1965, a beatnik poet of some renown was hitchhiking his way across the country and happened to land in Mountainview just as the aspen leaves were transforming the Rockies into a flaming botanical wonderland. Enchanted by the landscape and schmoozed by the MU faculty, he decided to cut his travels short. He ended up staying through the winter, guest-lecturing at the university, partaking of Colorado's homegrown herb, wandering the many idyllic hiking trails, and bedding various cherub-cheeked lit majors who gathered to hear his halting charismatic readings in dimly lit coffee shops. This all became fodder for his slim poetry collection, *Gone Forever Now*, a nostalgic elegy to the American Dream, in which Mountainview served as the backdrop for everything that was once great about the fallen empire known as the United States of America. It was arguably the last book of poetry that captured the nation's attention, if only for a moment. Conservatives fawned over the almost-pornographic descriptions of their beloved American West, liberals snickered gleefully about the deadpan irony between the lines, and academics fought over the postmodern structure of the stanzas. Borrowed passages from the book were used in a sappy, chart-topping folk song, and an entire generation of jaded teenage idealists learned that paradise was "a bad cup of coffee with a girl named Amy Sue, the pink sun rising over Mountainview."

At first, residents were flattered by the attention and amused by the long-haired teenagers who began camping out in the park in front of the library, bathing in the river and pounding on bongo drums until two in the morning. Mountainview had always had an eccentric streak and more than its fair share of local pride. This introduction to the cultural zeitgeist simply confirmed that they were special, something the locals had suspected all along. John Denver played a show at the high school. The university announced plans to launch a creative writing program. Businesses profited from the added tourism and college enrollment doubled in less than a decade. The sign welcoming visitors finally topped twenty thousand, then thirty thousand, then fifty. Now it was threatening six figures, and those kids with the bongo drums were launching startup companies from their five-million dollar chateaus and bulldozing mom-and-pop shops to make way for hot yoga studios and upscale grocery stores. The tech industry had taken over the economy, and the average blue-collar worker had been pushed to smaller cities further out on the prairie. There was still a solid core of homeless poets and neo-hippie street performers, but they had been reduced to jesters, their rainbow dreadlocks and old-timey banjo music part of a nostalgic liberal Passion Play to entertain the new landlords.

As I PASSED A GEOMETRICALLY IRONIC HOUSE that looked like it had been designed by a third grader on acid, a middle-aged woman stepped out the front door in a silk robe that barely covered her naughty bits. She was carrying a shiny bowl with something brown inside. "Here Priscilla!" she called out in a scream-whisper. "Mommy has food! Pss-pss-pss!" She caught me watching her and gave me a pinched smile, one hand clutching the front of her robe as though I had planned my walk specifically to sneak a glimpse of her reconstructed cleavage. She started to set the container down on the front step but realized that she couldn't bend over in the tiny robe without exposing herself on one side or the other. After several failed attempts, she did a sort of formal curtsey, dropped the bowl on the way down, and hurried back inside.

I continued walking for another block and then circled back around through the alley. I snuck around the side of the house to the front step, where I found an enormous smoke-colored Persian crunching away at the food.

"Hello, Priscilla," I cooed. "Nice kitty. I just need to borrow some of your breakfast. It's for a friend."

I reached out slowly, making the requisite purring and kissing noises, but Priscilla wasn't having it. She flattened her ears and took a swipe, producing a deep red furrow down the back of my right hand. "Fuck!" I cried. I stuck the injury in my mouth and kicked Priscilla in the butt. She yowled and scrambled up the nearest tree. Inside the house, there were footsteps and the wheeze of a door. I picked up the bowl of cat food with my non-bloodied hand, shoved it in my pocket, and then took off running, my new wingtips banging so loud against the pavement the echoes sounded like gunfire.

When I was certain I was safe, I found a hiding spot behind a tall wooden fence, took off my hat, and put my head between my legs. I stood there for five minutes, sweating and moaning and dry-heaving. Like many men with high metabolism and no exercise routine, I was thin but horribly horribly out of shape. Anything more vigorous than a brisk walk left my lungs burning and my legs shaking from exertion. As always, I vowed to go to the gym the next day, and I quietly sang "My Favorite Things" to distract myself from puking.

While I was bent over mumbling about warm woolen mittens, the damn envelope dropped out of my coat pocket and landed in the dirt. I kicked it, and the contents spilled across the ground. The first thing I saw was a headshot of Maggie inscribed to me. *Dear Sam. Can you believe it? We finally got our movie made! See you soon. Love, Maggie.*

My legs went out from under me, and I sat down hard on the dirt, which caused a lightning bolt of pain to flash through my sore tailbone. I writhed around in the dirt for several seconds moaning and clutching my buttocks. When the throbbing finally passed, I returned to the letter. There were so many implications in those five lines that my head began to spin. I started with the most intriguing. "Love"? What did she mean by that? Was it just a figure of speech? A salutation? Or did she still have feelings for me? When people wrote "Sincerely" at the end of letters were they really sincere?

Probably not. But she didn't write "Sincerely," did she? She could have easily written "Sincerely" or "Best wishes" or "Platonically yours," but she didn't. She wrote "Love." She wrote a note to me that contained my name and her name and the word "Love."

Also, movie? What movie? *Our* movie? As in my movie and her movie? We didn't have a movie. I mean, once upon a time we made a few short films together, but that was in college, so what could she be talking about? I hadn't written a script in seven years, and I certainly had not been on a movie set in that time. I was not the most observant person in the world, but I would have noticed if I'd made a movie.

And finally: "See you soon." This one had to be a figure of speech. I was not going to see Maggie Chase soon. I could not see Maggie Chase soon. There was nothing in the known physical or existential universe that could force me to see Maggie Chase soon.

I was so stunned by this that it took several minutes to realize there was another piece of paper in the envelope.

It was a press release. No letter. No note. Just a press release. "Local writer/director Eric Cross will premiere his first full-length movie, *THE BIG CHECKOUT*, at the Mountainview International Film Festival. Mountainview University alum Maggie Chase plays a starring role in this modern indie noir." There was a date, location, and time, and a list of cast members. The movie was showing today at four o'clock.

THE LAST TIME I SAW MAGGIE CHASE SHE WAS STANDING at the bus station wearing a pair of cracked red cowboy boots and a sleeveless summer dress with tiny chickens printed all over it, the yellow plastic buttons on the front shaped like baby chicks. She'd found the dress while shopping for theater costumes at a vintage clothing store. The top button had gone missing during a drunken wrap party, so she used a safety pin to hold it together. I loved that dress. Her long honey-colored hair was pulled back haphazardly in preparation for the ride, a few missed curls framing her soft ingénue features, making her look more than a little like Katharine Ross at the end of *The Graduate*. She held a ticket for a seat next to Eric on a Greyhound headed to Hollywood. I was not invited. It was spring. Morning. I was wearing my lucky jeans and a black T-shirt featuring Lon Cheney Jr. dressed as the Wolf Man. I had recently shaved my head for reasons I can no longer recall. It was not a good look for me. Also, I was drunk. Also, I was crying. Eric was already on the bus. I glared at him. He looked away. There was a small audience composed of the bus driver, a dozen impatient passengers, several homeless men, and the elderly Chinese lady who ran the concession stand. We had already rehearsed the scene many times in preparation for the big event, so we both knew our lines well. I begged Maggie to stay. She told me she had to go. The irritated bus driver leaned on the horn. I moved in for one last kiss, and she let me have it, a sloppy, close-mouthed, tear-stained embrace that was extremely uncinematic.

And then she left me.

The bus pulled away in a cloud of gaseous fumes, and as it rounded the corner, I could have sworn I saw Eric turn for one last look back, his thin mouth pulled up in a triumphant smirk.

It was that smirk as much as the safety pin holding together Maggie's chicken dress that haunted my dreams.

We'd been a hot filmmaking trio in college. I was the writer, Eric was the director, and Maggie was our muse and leading lady. Technically she was my girlfriend, but our friendship was so close that passions were sometimes fluid. Our student films were the usual melodramatic/naïve/wonderful cinematic abominations that only clueless twenty-year-olds can produce. There was an undeniable artistic magic between us, a creative partnership that just worked somehow and none of us questioned why. At the end of our junior year, we swept the MU film awards, and Eric decided it was time to move on to something bigger. He had this ridiculous scheme to sneak into Miramax, show them one of our shorts, and demand they green-light us for a feature film. It was like the plot of the worst misfit comedy ever made.

I had an idea for a low-budget psychological thriller. Nothing fancy, just a full-length movie with a small cast and a twisted plot. Eric and I spent hours in coffee shops arguing over finer points of the narrative. He wanted to take it in a more artsy David Lynch direction, but I just wanted to make something entertaining and personal. Eric kept pushing me to finish the script, but I needed more time. I wanted to wait until graduation, polish up the screenplay, and get some local backers together so we could make it ourselves. Eric didn't want to wait that long.

I begged Maggie not to go, but Eric had filled her head with promises of wild evenings at the Viper Room and star-studded cast parties in Beverly Hills. She swore she'd keep in touch. I got a dozen emails from her about acting workshops and auditions, and then I deleted my account.

Of course, I continued to stalk them both online. Eric tried his Miramax scheme and was banned for life before he even made it through the front gate. Undeterred, he found part-time work as a grip and cameraman at a minor studio before creating his own filmmaking business, CrossRoads, which produced several low-budget shorts that made the film-festival rounds without much success. He made most of his money doing freelance editing for larger companies. Maggie began performing with a sketch-comedy troupe and landed a minor role as a feisty New Age barista on a sitcom that was cancelled before the pilot even aired. After that, she was cast in an internet commercial for an antidepressant. It was one of those advertisements that looks sort of like a recruitment video for a well-funded cult. Maggie's ecstatic face was featured in a series of short clips: laughing at a dinner party, playing fetch with a golden retriever in the park, running on the beach with a lavender scarf trailing behind her, etc.

Meanwhile, a breezy female voice described the benefits of the drug, while the list of possible side effects scrolled across the bottom of the screen in tiny print. "This medication may cause headaches, diarrhea, urinary tract infections, rashes, ovary inflammation, leg spasms, and death. If you experience a tingling sensation on the right side of your body at any time while taking this antidepressant, please consult a physician immediately." I must have watched that video a thousand times before the company took the commercial off their website and replaced it with an even creepier advertisement featuring an animated blob that lived alone on an island with an umbrella.

I admit it gave me some satisfaction knowing Maggie and Eric had not taken Hollywood by storm as they'd hoped, but I was still bitter about their betrayal. After they left, I stopped writing screenplays and started writing angsty poetry about disloyal women. I read my poems in halting, affected style at open-mics around town, where I met and slept with dozens of equally untalented female poets who had also been dumped by their partners and wanted to wallow in the righteous bliss of romantic injustice. I drank too much, stopped going to class, and eventually received a letter of dismissal. I told myself it would be a short sabbatical. I'd take a year off, write a new screenplay, maybe backpack through Europe, and then I would finish up my degree in grand style. But it never happened. Instead, I moved into The Trap and sold weed to students around the neighborhood to pay the rent. I started writing reviews for the *Mountainview Chronicle* for beer money and free movie tickets. Eventually, a local web developer approached me with a blogging offer that was just enough to cover rent, drugs, Hot Pockets, and cat food. I accepted on a temporary basis, making sure to let everyone know that I would be returning to academia soon and/or finishing my Oscar-worthy screenplay—and then I was done with this little mountain town! That was five years ago.

Chapter 9: The Third Man

I SHOVED THE CONTENTS OF THE LETTER into the dark recesses of my new trench coat and started walking. It was important to keep moving. This was too much to process all at once. I needed to distract myself from the gritty breakup montage that was playing on a loop inside my head. I dug around in my pocket until I found the orange bottle of Oxy and popped two in my mouth. I couldn't afford to wait for my stomach acid to dissolve them so I bit down hard, gagged on the bitter tree-bark taste, and then crunched repeatedly until I had reduced the tablets to a gummy paste that I then swallowed. My mouth was numb and my stomach felt awful, but I knew my head would soon be improved.

I had no idea where I was going at first, but then I remembered I was on the job. Somewhere in the sleazy underbelly of this sleepy little mountain town there was a killer roaming the streets in search of their next victim. Well, actually, it was pretty early, so the killer was probably just waking up, stumbling into the kitchen for that first cup of coffee, heating up a breakfast burrito, wondering whether or not they had time for a shower before heading out, deciding how many of layers of clothing to put on, feeding the dog, and *then* wandering the streets in search of their next victim. They probably thought they'd gotten away with murder, but they didn't know the intrepid journalist Sam Drift was on the case and would not stop until the fiend was brought to justice. I turned around and headed for the Pearl Street Mall.

The Pink Door would be closed at this early hour, but the owner—a small, bombastic woman known as Mouth—often stayed up all night drinking single-malt scotch and playing poker with the bouncers. I'd been invited to join them on several occasions, but always declined because the only card game I knew was UNO. If I was lucky, she'd still be there, and I could file my interview before noon. That would show Victoria who was a real journalist.

Mouth's real name was Monica Larkman, and aside from the Pink Door, her family owned several liquor stores, a bar, some fireworks stands, a tobacco shop, and a half dozen marijuana dispensaries along the Front Range. Unlike the many wealthy out-of-state transplants that had overtaken the rest of the Pearl Street Mall, the Larkmans had deep roots in Mountainview, dating all the way back to its settlement in the mid-1800s. In those days, they were poor sharecroppers who mostly kept to themselves. Aside from the occasional wedding announcement and obituary, their names didn't show up in the local newspapers until 1931, when Mouth's great-great grandfather, Albert Larkman, made headlines by opening a speakeasy on an Arapaho Indian reservation just outside the city limits. The Mountainview chapter of the American Temperance Society tried to shut it down, but they got wrapped up in a legal battle with the Arapaho tribe over jurisdiction. By the time the case was settled, the Eighteenth Amendment had been repealed and Prohibition was over.

Albert's exploits turned out to be a eureka moment for the Larkman clan. They discovered they enjoyed enterprise and controversy a lot more than farming and poverty. Since that time, they had become both the bane of Mountainview and its most ardent cheerleaders. They started investing heavily in what economic moralists call the "sin industry." Alcohol, tobacco, gambling, drugs, and sex. Even though their businesses were legal, they caused consternation in the small, quiet community. Their actions stirred up controversy; controversy brought newspaper reporters; newspaper reporters brought free publicity. Their businesses thrived.

But the Larkmans had a soft side, too. They served on city council, attended the Unitarian Universalist Church, sponsored Little League teams, donated to charities, harassed referees at every high school football game, and ran the local chapter of the Odd Fellows. They also got arrested for public drunkenness at least once a month, grew marijuana in their backyard before it was legal to do so, organized a Halloween event known as the Naked Pumpkin Run, and periodically defaced the bronze statues of Mountainview's prominent political figures in front of the courthouse with spray paint and dildos. All of this information was happily volunteered to me when I wrote the story about the Pink Door two years ago.

For the most part, the Larkmans were viewed as minor nuisances by local authorities and loveable mascots by longtime residents, who grew up on tales of their exploits and antics. However, with the recent population boom, the Larkmans' reputation had started to evolve into something more sinister. The new class of Mountainview residents was not accustomed to the culture of a small town, where all members of the community were forced to interact with one another despite political and social differences. Unlike New York and Los Angeles, if you didn't like your neighbors in Mountainview, you couldn't simply move to the suburbs. Therefore, unable to put physical distance between themselves and the Larkmans, the business owners on Pearl Street had opted to construct clear social boundaries. The Larkmans were thugs, pimps, gangsters. The gossip was all the more ugly because there seemed to be a glimmer of truth to it. There was even a rumor around town the Larkmans were connected to the Smaldones, an Italian-American crime family in Denver that served as a go-between for the mob bosses in New York and the underlings who ran their Vegas casinos. The head of the family, Anthony Smaldone, had recently been indicted for fraud and racketeering, and according to some, he had passed some of their business on to the Larkmans in order to divert attention away from his family. I'd always considered this idea preposterous, but perhaps it was time to take the Larkmans more seriously. Mouth had always been nice to me, but maybe she was just buttering up a member of the press so I wouldn't start asking questions. After all, this was a family that had been in and out of trouble with the law for almost a century. They sold drugs and convinced young women to take off their clothes for money. They vandalized government property. These were known facts. Obviously, they had little regard for authority. Would it be such a shock to discover they finally decided to take the plunge into real criminal activity? And as novice criminals in over their heads, wasn't it conceivable they might let some information about their illicit activities slip to an exotic dancer working at one of their clubs? And, just for the sake of argument, was it really such a stretch that an exotic dancer might decide to blackmail a wealthy family with said information in order to, for instance, feed her heroin addiction? Wasn't that motive for murder?

Not yet, obviously, since there wasn't a shred of evidence that any of this was true. But what if I found evidence? What if I managed to dig underneath the lovable, eccentric façade of the Larkmans and locate their ugly secrets? What if I broke one of the biggest crime stories in Colorado history? This story had everything: sex, drugs, violence, a lone underdog journalist asking the tough questions no one else wanted to ask. There would be calls, interviews. CNN, NBC, ABC, CBS, FOX. My name would be in all the newspapers. Agents and publishers would come knocking. Someone was bound to offer me a book deal. And if the book became a bestseller, Hollywood producers would start calling. Victoria would beg me to take that editor job at the *Chronicle*, but I would have to refuse, what with a national book tour coming up and a screenplay to write. I could just imagine Maggie calling me after all these years, hemming and hawing and finally breaking down, apologizing for running off with Eric, begging me for a part in the movie, a minor role, a walk-on, anything I could do for her, for old times, please, Sam, please. And who would play me in the movie? Not some vapid pretty boy, obviously. Not Keanu or Brad. Leonardo wasn't right for the part. Someone with some stage experience, someone with grit. Jake Gyllenhaal maybe. Or Ryan Gosling. Yeah, Gosling, with that lopsided grin, and those sad, uneven eyes, like someone had made his face out of Play-Doh and accidentally squashed one side. There was something real about him, something that hinted at complicated motivations and inner depth.

The more I thought about it, the more real it seemed. Why not? Stranger things had happened.

THE ENTRANCE TO THE PINK DOOR WAS AN ACTUAL PINK DOOR located in an alley behind the Pearl Street Mall. There was no sign, just a Pepto-Bismol–colored rectangle with hundreds of crushed cigarette butts in front of it, most of them smeared with red lipstick. I had never seen the alley in the light of day, and it was decidedly less exotic than it appeared at night, with the gutter water reflecting the moonlight and my bloodstream diluted with equal parts alcohol and anticipation. However, the knowledge that this was now an official crime scene sent a small, morbid jolt of electricity though the cynical muscle in my chest, and I soon found myself bent over circling the pavement. Looking for what? A shotgun shell? A bloody axe? It didn't matter. I had never investigated a crime scene before.

To be honest, it was somewhat disappointing. It just looked like a normal alley. At the very least, I expected to find the chalk outline of a body or some yellow police tape, but there was nothing aside from the usual human detritus that accumulates in dark corners away from the public view. I found four empty beer bottles, a Burger King bag, an unused condom still in the wrapper (Ribbed for Her Pleasure!), a single size-ten sneaker with no laces, a bicentennial quarter, and the headless torso of a small, naked doll. I put the quarter and doll torso in my pocket and widened my search.

The Pink Door was bordered on one side by an artisanal bakery and on the other by Liliane Easton's spa, Nirvana & You.

The section of the alley behind spa was spotless. Even their dumpster appeared to have been recently polished. I lifted the dumpster's lid and poked my head inside. Empty. I closed the lid and circled around behind it. It was strangely clean for an alley, almost like someone had scrubbed down the pavement with soap and water, but aside from that there was nothing out of the ordinary. No bullet casings on the ground, no bloody handprints on the side of the wall. Just a boring old alley. I decided to end my search.

I planted the toe of my right foot and prepared to make a quick, authoritative turn. The next thing I knew my feet were flying out from under me, and I had that slow-motion weightless feeling of falling. My body made a series of unconscious adjustments, feet backpedaling in silent-movie fashion, arms reeling in wide circles to maintain balance. I grabbed the side of the dumpster with both hands and somehow managed to stay upright. After taking a few moments to catch my breath, I knelt down to examine the pavement. I wiped my finger across a storm drain and discovered it was covered in some kind of slippery substance. I rubbed it between my thumb and index finger, and then put it to my nose. It smelled, not unpleasantly, like coconut. *How could I know that murder can sometimes smell like sunscreen?* Gingerly, I stepped around the puddle of slick material and scraped the bottom of my shoe along the pavement in an effort to wipe off the grease.

And that's when I spotted it.

Inside the storm drain, half covered by dead leaves and muck, was the plastic end of a medical syringe. There was just enough room for me to squeeze my flattened hand through the iron bars of the drain guard, and I managed to scissor the end of the syringe between my middle and index fingers, careful not to jab myself with a used needle in the process or smudge any fingerprints that might have been left. When it was clear of the drain, I laid it on the cement and examined it closely. It was filthy, of course, but I didn't want to risk wiping it clean. The needle had been broken off, so it was just the plastic tube and plunger. There appeared to be a tiny bit of brownish liquid still inside. My skin began buzzing and my blood pounded in my ears. It was a clue! An honest-to-God clue! This could have been used by the victim. Maybe she was in the alley shooting up heroin when the murder took place. Or perhaps the killer injected the exotic dancer with a drug first to incapacitate her and then committed the crime at his leisure. The only way to know for sure was to have its contents tested in a lab and then attempt to get a usable fingerprint. I fished around inside the trench coat and found a clean, white handkerchief. I picked up the syringe using the handkerchief and carefully deposited it in one of the coat's many inside pockets. When it was safe, I felt better. Confident. This was happening. I was going to solve this thing.

"Good morning!"

The greeting came from behind me, and literally knocked me off my feet. There was still a thin layer of mystery grease on the bottom of my shoes, and when I whirled around to see who was there, my feet once again flew out from under me, but this time I was not able to break the fall. My tailbone hit the pavement at precisely the same moment the back of my head slammed against the side of the empty dumpster, creating an ominous *BONG*, like the death knell in the bell tower at the end of *Vertigo*. *Give me your hand! Give me your hand!*

For one blissful moment, everything was peaceful and white, like falling asleep on a pile of cotton. My body felt warm and numb, my fingers tingled not unpleasantly.

This did not last long. When the shock passed, the throbbing began.

"The pain is all in your head."

I opened my eyes and saw Liliane leaning over me wearing bamboo hoop earrings, numerous silver bracelets, and a cream-colored alpaca poncho with tribal images on it. Her hair was pulled back in a tight bun held in place by a pair of ivory chopsticks.

"That's what my yogi used to say." She was staring at me with unnerving intensity, and she had a strange smile on her face. Not amused or mean-spirited, just sort of indifferent, like she could read my thoughts and was unimpressed by what she saw. "The physical world is an illusion designed to distract us from our spiritual natures. Pain is all in the head."

I rubbed the back of my skull. "I couldn't agree more."

"You poor boy." She held out her hands like a mother beckoning her child into her arms. I took her hands in mine and stood up. "I am glad you came to see me. I didn't know if you would make it. You were terribly intoxicated last night."

"Oh, no," I said, breathing in her aroma, something rich and sexy, a smell so familiar it almost knocked me down again. How did I know that perfume? "I never drink on the job. I was just distracted, that's all. You said you had some information for me."

"Whatever do you mean?"

"Last night. At the theater. You said you had some information about, you know, possible illegal, um, criminal…stuff…connected to the demise of the vic."

"Vick? Was that her name?"

"No, Vic is short for victim. It's just a term we use in the business. Never mind. I don't know her name."

"Oh, my. Shouldn't you learn that, dear?" Liliane hooked her arm through mine and turned us in the direction of the spa. "Perhaps we should speak about this inside."

"That's a good idea," I said, scanning the alley. "Wouldn't want to tip off the perp."

My eyes were accustomed to the true light of the sun, and it took a minute for my dilated pupils to adjust to the soft luminescence of energy-efficient bulbs. Entering the spa through the alley door was like walking through a portal into another dimension. A dimension filled with Enya and expensive marble. Attractive young women in white uniforms scurried silently around us, carrying towels, pushing carts, wiping counters. They were all in their early twenties, tall, blonde, and thin, as though they had been cloned from a single source of feminine beauty that was at the same time unattainable and pedestrian. Even though the spa wasn't officially open yet, they smiled aggressively and greeted us in practiced customer-service/cult-member voices. Liliane ignored them the way a plantation owner would ignore the house slaves, gliding through the blinding white hallways with her poncho trailing behind like a cape, waving those expressive hands, tossing out orders with each flick of her ivory wrists. "Refill that lotion. Change the music. That plant is not feng shui." The employees followed after her like sexy obedient ducklings, breaking from the group one at a time to complete the tasks.

She led me through a lobby, a reception area, a sauna, and another lobby. The sterile, white theme continued throughout the building, broken up occasionally by stark postmodern furniture resembling large insects frozen in black glass and long, rectangular pots filled with precise rows of bamboo. On the walls hung a variety of enormous black-and-white photographs of female body parts taken in extreme close-up. Here was the gentle slope of a woman's neck, there was the elegant curve of a naked thigh. It took a moment to connect the dots, but eventually I realized all the photos were of Liliane. It was an impressive display. I imagined putting the individual images together like a giant puzzle and producing a fifty-foot-tall nude portrait of my host.

As we walked, Liliane kept up a constant chatter that was part tour guide and part gossip about spa regulars. Did I know the mayor's wife had corns on her feet the size of quarters? Was I aware that a certain CEO of a certain multi-million-dollar software company requested a full-body wax once a week? I responded to these informational morsels with the requisite head nods and guttural noises.

When we finally stopped walking, we were in a private room with more white marble walls, a black obsidian floor, a sink in the corner with a gold-plated faucet, a tiny potted bonsai tree on a wooden stand next to the sink, multiple cupboards, a small refrigerator, a large flat-screen television with mounted speakers, and a brown leather massage table at the center of it all.

"Remove your clothes," Liliane said.

"Oh, no thank you," I replied, thinking of the scene in *Eyes Wide Shut* when Tom Cruise sneaks into the orgy mansion. "That's not... I mean, I probably shouldn't. Professionalism and all. It would compromise the, um... But thank you. Very kind of you to offer."

She closed the door and touched a knob on the wall. Immediately the lights dimmed and the television turned on, showing a video of a gurgling river flowing through a lush wooded area, the faint sound of wind chimes in the background.

She took a step toward me. "Have you ever experienced reiki, Samuel?"

I backed away until I bumped into a wall. "No, but I tried kale once. Didn't care for it. Too bitter."

"There is a universal energy called qi that flows through all living matter." She opened a cupboard next to me and pulled out a white sheet and a robe. She handed the robe to me and spread the sheet over the table. "A reiki master can focus their energy through their palms and pass their qi into another person to activate spiritual and physical healing. I trained with reiki master David Lu of Brooklyn. He taught me how to block the negative energy from the world and purify my qi."

"That's great," I said. "Maybe we can do some reiki later. Right now, I'm working on this story about the Pink Door."

Liliane sighed and put her hands together in a prayer pose in front of her mouth. "Yes, that poor girl. I tried to warn them, you know. Please take off your hat and coat. We won't do a full session today, but I need to cleanse your qi. You are quite unbalanced."

I thought about this for a moment. While it probably was not professional to receive naked massage sessions from potential sources, playing along with Liliane might get her to open up about the insider information she claimed to possess. I took off my hat and coat.

"Lay down on the table. Do it now. This is important."

I climbed up on the table and lay on my back. It was quite comfortable, actually. The table looked like it would be hard, but it was soft and supportive in all the right places. Liliane stood above me with her eyes closed and her hands hovering over my stomach. "Just relax," she said. "Let your mind go. Clear your brain of all conscious, inorganic thoughts. Breathe in through your nose, exhale through the mouth. Release your ego into the cosmic void."

She produced a quiet humming noise through her nose and lowered her hands until her palms were mere centimeters from my stomach. My skin tightened and broke out in goosebumps. She had lovely hands, soft and sensual, and I could not help but imagine what they might feel like on my torso, caressing my body, holding me to her warm bosom. She was doing some kind of strange circular breathing that caused her throat to convulse rapidly as she expelled a steady stream of air from her flared nostrils, and her warm breath washed over me, adding a new sensation to her non-touch, creating a feeling so dense and powerful that even though she was not touching me, I felt the weight of her entire body on mine, pushing me down, covering me, soaking into my flesh. In the alley, her fragrance had been difficult to pick up, but in this small room, her aroma filled the space completely, adding yet another layer of her ethereal presence to the experience, filling up my nose, my lungs, and my blood vessels with a rich, lavender aroma that I now recognized as the smell that had filled the the closets of my parents' house as a child, the smell of a home I never had, the smell of my mother.

A full minute passed with the confusing combination of those sensual fingers titillating my skin and the ghost of my mother haunting my olfactory senses. I knew if I didn't break the silence soon, I was going to start weeping uncontrollably.

"So about the incident next door… You said you warned them."

The humming stopped, as well as the jet of warm breath, and I shuddered at its absence. With her her eyes still closed, she made a long-suffering face. "I said I *tried* to warn them. Calm your mind. Relax your aura." She moved her hands lower and I held my breath. I desperately wanted her to touch me. Every molecule in my body seemed to pull toward her hands, as if her skin was a magnet and I was a pile of metal shavings. "I love Mountainview, Samuel. It is a pure community, and I want to keep it that way. Can you feel that? The energy moving from my center to yours? Inhale through the nose, exhale through the mouth. There, that's better. Allow the universe to flow through you. You're doing very well. I have nothing against that place, of course. In fact, I have an incredible amount of empathy for those young women. They are caught in a vicious cycle of exploitation and shame they cannot extricate themselves from. We should certainly help them climb out of the patriarchal abyss they have fallen into, but that does not mean we need to join them in the darkness. Don't you agree?"

"Yes…" I would have said almost anything in that moment to gain her approval.

"Of course, you do. You are a good soul, Samuel. I knew it from the beginning. When we first met and I read that horrendous story you wrote, I was upset, but then I realized it was not your fault. It was your naiveté that was the cause. You are pure, like the air, like the mountains. But you must understand that the world does not share your purity. There is negative energy in the universe, Samuel. There is corruption and pollution. In the past, Mountainview has been isolated from these unpleasant realities, but it will not remain so forever. We cannot save the whole world, but we can protect our small part of it. We just need to focus our positive energy and drive out the negative. You will feel a warm circle in the middle of your abdomen followed by a tingling sensation in your fingertips and a sense of well-being."

Maybe it was the sound of her voice, maybe it was the drugs, maybe it was the partial erection, but my stomach was suddenly filled with a hot glow that expanded to my fingertips. Everything was going to be alright.

"I knew this would happen. Not this exactly, but something like this. I tried to warn them, but they would not heed me. When you allow a negative force into your center, it can take over your entire qi. You cannot invite criminals into your life and not expect crime."

"Crime?" I said. My voice sounded hollow and distant. I was so relaxed that I couldn't move. "The police said she fell and hit her head."

Liliane stepped away from the table, and my body went cold. "This is what I am talking about," she said. "You cannot afford to be this naïve, Samuel. These are drug dealers running a strip club. Do you really think a dead employee in the alley is just a coincidence?"

I opened my eyes and sat up. Liliane was washing her hands in the sink, her back rigid and disapproving. Steam rose from the sink.

"Did you see anything?" I asked. My head was starting to clear again. I felt great.

"They were always in that alley. Day and night. Talking and fighting and smoking cigarettes. The law specifically says you have to be fifty feet away from businesses and residential buildings to smoke those disgusting things. I told the police about that, and do you know what they did? Nothing. Warnings. Who knows what else they were doing behind there? I know it, Samuel. I know these types of people. They cannot follow the rules. There is something broken inside of them. They ruin everything around them. They are drawn to negative energy. We have to stop them. You have to help me stop them. I need you, Samuel. Mountainview needs you."

She turned around, and her hands were bright red, the skin boiled by the hot water. What she said did actually make sense. The Larkmans had a long history of defying the law, and they did sell drugs. Of course, marijuana was legal in Colorado now, but who knew what else they were selling. And then there was the needle I'd just found in the alley. Liliane didn't even know about that, so it wasn't like she was putting these thoughts in my head. Victoria would want more evidence, of course, but we were on the right track, I just knew it.

I hopped down off the table, my body as light as a feather, and grabbed my hat.

"Don't worry, ma'am," I said. "I'm on the case."

Chapter 10: The Red Shoes

MY CONVERSATION WITH LILIANE LEFT ME SURPRISINGLY INVIGORATED, and I was ready to get out of the alley and proceed to the next step in the investigation. I walked to the pink door with leading-man confidence and beat on it with the meat of my fist. Nothing. I tried again.

Maybe I should call the front desk, I thought. I reached into my pocket for my cell phone before remembering it was dead. Damn. I became aware of the cold seeping through the cheap lining of the trench coat and turning my bones to brittle icicles. I needed shelter soon or I would die. Okay, I probably wouldn't die, but frostbite was an actual possibility. It was too early for businesses on Pearl Street to open, and my apartment was at least a twenty-minute walk. My hands were stiff and red. I shoved them deep in my coat pockets and kicked the bottom of the door. "Let me in," I whimpered. My throat contracted, and my eyes began to burn with the expectation of tears. I blinked rapidly and tried to will the sensation away, but it was no use. Snot gathered at the tip of my nose and instantly began to form a yellow icicle. I wiped it away. I was tired and hung over, and feeling like a hunted animal on the edge of a cliff.

Frustrated, I reached out, grabbed the doorknob, and gave it a yank. *Why did everything bad happen to me!* To my surprise, the doorknob turned easily and the door flew open, almost knocking me on the ground with the force of its release. I stumbled backward several steps, regained my footing, and returned to peek inside. There was a gust of warm floral-scented air and the distant thrum of hip-hop music from below. I looked around quickly to see if anyone was watching, and then I wiped away the tears and walked through the Pink Door's pink door.

Like most of the bars and clubs in Mountainview, the Pink Door was underground. In an effort to protect the legendary view of the mountains that was the town's namesake, the powers that be had passed stringent building ordinances that restricted the height of all public and private structures to three stories. Therefore, in order to seek out new real estate, enthusiastic entrepreneurs were forced to dig beneath the surface, so to speak.

The stairs were steep, dark, and covered with a thin layer of frayed maroon carpet that needed to be vacuumed. There was still some of that slick grease on the sole of my shoe, and I clutched the bannister tightly as I descended. The music grew louder and I recognized the smooth, lazy voice of Snoop Dogg dropping it like it was hot. A strip club classic if ever there was one.

At the bottom of the stairs, there was more maroon carpeting leading to a black curtain, and on the other side of the curtain was the infamous Pink

Door, a mid-sized underground strip club with a polished oak bar, a deejay booth hidden away in the corner, and a rectangular wood floor in the center with two silver poles sticking out of it. The dance floor was surrounded on all sides by long cafeteria-like tables, where, during business hours, men sat wide-eyed and mouths agape, sucking down cheap drinks and pausing periodically to slip crumpled dollar bills under the elastic G-strings of the beautiful women who pretended to seduce them. The ceiling was too low for an elevated stage, and on at least two occasions, I'd seen dancers attempt to perform complicated upside-down maneuvers on the poles and accidentally knock off chunks of plaster with their high heels. Instead of neon lights and mirrors on the walls, there were photographs of staff members wearing silly hats, framed pictures of celebrities, movie posters, and a taxidermied moose head with giant sunglasses covering its glassy eyes. Behind the bar was a large picture of Elvis looking impossibly cool on the set of *Kissin' Cousins* next to a sign that said, "Tipping Ain't Just a City in China."

Currently, the dance floor was occupied by an enormous white man named Curly, who usually stood at the entrance to the club, straw cowboy hat on dimpled head, handlebar mustache cocked in a suspicious sneer, arms crossed in a Mussolini pose. It was rumored that he had served several tours in Iraq and knew a dozen ways to kill a man without breaking a sweat. It was also rumored that after arriving home from his military service, he put his unique skill set to good use for the Russian mob, which had cornered much of the legalized marijuana market in Canada before expanding into the United States. These experiences would be useful to, say, a family of criminals who were trying to expand their operations. I had never heard more than two words come out of Curly's mouth, and his face was always set in an expression halfway between boredom and anger. At the moment, however, he was gyrating in the middle of the floor with his shirt off, his enormous belly undulating like a hairy Jell-O mold with every lascivious thrust, his purple-nippled man-breasts flopping shamelessly back and forth to the beat of the music. There were five women sitting at one of the nearby tables, screaming encouragement and periodically tossing crumpled dollar bills onto the floor, which Curly would then catwalk over to, bend down in dramatic fashion, and pluck off the ground with his teeth. He was surprisingly limber for a man of his girth. The women were dressed in normal winter clothing: sweaters, jeans, comfortable shoes that did not force them to wobble around on their tiptoes like newborn foals. On the other side of the room, in the VIP lounge, there were two women sitting on a stained faux-leather couch locked in an eternal embrace, perhaps crying. Everyone was clearly drunk.

Behind the bar stood a stunning strawberry blonde named Rae, whom I'd had a hopeless crush on for several years. She was halfway through a PhD in sociology at MU, paying for graduate school with the tips she made at the Pink

Door, and, I always assumed, doing a bit of research for her degree along the way. She was a fan of cinéma-vérité (nobody's perfect), but if you got a few shots of tequila in her, she would admit that her favorite movie was *Cinderfella* with Jerry Lewis.

Currently, Rae's attention was focused on two women across from her, one of them wearing a yellow jumpsuit with a red racing stripe down the side, the other a familiar sequined ball gown. V. was talking loudly, her raspy voice periodically rising above the bone-rattling baseline of the song, while her hands painted pictures of drama and hilarity under the blue glow of a Coors Light sign. The younger women leaned toward V. with wide eyes and eager smiles, clearly hanging on her every word. It was a cozy scene, and for a moment I considered not interrupting it. No one had noticed me yet. The main office was in the back of the house, behind a large one-way mirror, and I could easily slip in there without drawing attention to myself. Mouth was probably inside having an early morning cup of coffee or whiskey or both, and I could interview her and then sneak back out the way I came. No one would be the wiser.

And I was about to do just that when I spotted the half-empty bottle of brown liquid sitting on the bar next to Rae. It was difficult to tell from this distance, but the label looked top shelf. My mouth began to water and I felt a tingling in my extremities. Before I knew what had happened, I was sliding onto a wooden stool and pouring two fingers of Johnny Walker Black into a short cube-shaped glass that may or may not have been clean. I tipped the glass to my lips and felt the smoky bite of the liquor burn its way down my esophagus and ignite the comforting, familiar fire in my belly. Half the glass was gone before I could stop myself. When I finished, all three women were staring at me with a combination of concern and annoyance.

"Well, look what the cat puked up," said V. "I was wondering what you got up to last night."

Rae picked up a white rag and began to polish the bar, a tic that signaled her irritation. "Yeah, Sam, what brings you here in the daylight? We don't have a breakfast buffet, you know."

I was about to make a clever retort, but V. got there first. She put her elbows on the bar and leaned toward Rae. "You wouldn't believe what happened last night," she said. Sometime during the course of the evening, the elaborate scaffolding of pins, spray, and barrettes that held up her cathedral-like hairdo had come undone, and the winding towers and gothic spires now fell in ruins past her shoulders. In the dim light, her white hair appeared blonde and she looked almost girlish.

"Is that right?" said Rae, purposefully not looking at me. She'd gotten a haircut since the last time I saw her, short and lopsided, a cross between 1920s flapper and 1980s punk, and she brushed the bangs out of her eyes as she refilled V.'s drink. "Tell me more."

"Mama found him in an alley crying like a baby. Oh, you never saw such a scene. He was going on and on about some girl who cheated on him with his best friend in college. How she broke his heart and stole his movie. It was pathetic. Finally, I told him I'd take him to a titty bar if he shut the hell up. And then guess what he did."

"That's not what happened," I protested. But they ignored me.

"What did he do?"

V. took a long drink for dramatic effect. "He left me there."

"No."

"Yes! Can you believe that? A defenseless old woman out at night on the dangerous streets of…where the hell are we?"

"Mountain—"

"Doesn't matter. Who knows what nefarious end I could have met."

"Nefarious end?" I said. "Really?"

"That is appalling behavior," said Rae. She shook her head and clucked her tongue. "Unfortunately, it's not exactly surprising. It's like my mother used to say, 'Never trust a man you meet in an alley during a film festival.' "

"Wise woman," V. said. "So how do you know ol' Sammy-boy here? Were you two hot and heavy for a while? Let me guess, you were hot and he was heavy."

"Oooookay," I said. "We don't have to go into that, do we?"

Rae arched a challenging eyebrow, but before she could say anything the woman in the yellow jumpsuit took pity on me and extended her hand. "We haven't met. My name is Kate."

Kate had soft, dry palms and nails the color of bubblegum.

"Sam Drift, reporter for the *Mountainview Chronicle*. And I wasn't crying, by the way. She's making that up."

"He's not a reporter," said Rae. "He writes movie reviews. He's a blogger."

"That's not…completely true," I said.

"I like your coat, Sam Drift Reporter for the *Mountainview Chronicle*," said Kate. She reminded me of a young Carol Burnett—long, thin features, wide eyes, large teeth constantly breaking free from her crimson mouth. "My dad used to watch *Columbo* reruns on Saturdays. His weird eye creeped me out. Columbo's, that is. My dad had normal eyes."

"What? Peter Falk?" I sputtered. "I'm not… I mean, if anything, I'm Humphrey… Never mind."

V. threw her head back and let loose an insulting cackle. "You serious, kid? You think you look like Bogart in that rag?"

"I think he looks handsome," said Kate diplomatically. "Like Cary Grant in *His Girl Friday*."

I smiled. "Madam, you're a cock-eyed liar, and you know it."

Kate didn't miss a bit. "Oh, Walter, you're wonderful in a loathsome sort of way."

"Cary Grant was overrated," said Rae. "Too tan."

These were fighting words, and I started to protest but Kate interrupted. "Wait, I know who you are."

I sat up straight and gave Rae a smug glance.

"You're the guy that wrote the blog about Rebecca."

"Who?"

"Rebecca Kint," said Rae. She glared at my blank face. "My friend and coworker who passed away two nights ago."

"Oh, the dead dancer."

"Rebecca Kint."

"He knows who she is," Kate continued. "He's writing a story on her for the paper, right?"

I swirled the contents of my glass for effect and took a satisfied sip. "That's true."

Rae and V. exchanged a dubious look. "You're writing an article, and you don't know the girl's name?" said V.

"That's why I'm here. To do, you know, research and interviews and stuff."

"I think you're supposed to know the person's name before you conduct the interviews, Woodward."

"Yeah, well, I have my own methods."

The music transitioned from Snoop to Beyonce's "Drunk in Love" and we all turned for a moment to watch Curly expertly twerk.

"How did you know about Governor Buttface?" asked Kate.

"Who?"

Kate turned to Rae. "You know that older guy I was seeing for a while? The one with the chin that looks like a butt?"

"The silver fox with the wad of cash. Yeah, I remember."

"Turns out he's some hot-shot politician from Denver. He was getting his kicks in Mountainview so no one would recognize him. And, get this, he's *married*."

"Everyone knew he was married. That was not a secret. Mouth told you he was married. I told you he was married. Literally every single person who works here told you he was a married man."

Kate waved her off. "Yeah, well, *he* didn't tell me he was married. Lying asshole. Anyhow, Sam here called him out in his blog. Didn't you?"

"I have no idea what you're talking about," I said.

"Sure you did. You said there was some cover-up involving a politician at the Pink Door, and he's the only politician who was here that night. That's what you should write a story about. I'll go on the record right now. That guy's a lying bastard."

"I don't know anything about that," I said. "I'm supposed to interview Mouth."

Rae looked at me skeptically. "Does she know you're coming? No one told me about it."

"Of course she knows. You think I'd just show up here unannounced at this hour? I'm supposed to talk to her about…you know…"

"Rebecca," Kate said.

"I knew that."

"Maybe you should write her name down."

"That's a good idea." I set my glass on the bar and leaned in conspiratorially. "You guys have any idea what happened to her?"

Kate and Rae looked at me like I was crazy. V. shook her head.

"She slipped and hit her head," said Kate. "Haven't you talked to the police? You seriously need to do your research, man."

I nodded vigorously. "Right, right. That's the story the police are trying to sell us. But just between you and me, was there any, you know, foul play?"

Kate wrinkled her nose. "Foul play? You mean like with the senator? I think he's just a liar."

"Sure, with the senator, or maybe with, you know, the mob."

Kate laughed. "Are you serious?" She turned to Rae. "Is he serious?"

"I honestly have no idea," said Rae. She gave me a warning look and then motioned with her head for me to follow. "Come with me. Let's go ask Mouth if she wants to talk, and then you gotta go. Understand?"

I followed Rae to the end of the bar, where she grabbed me by the shoulder and pulled me toward the dance floor. Curly was now completely naked, his blue jeans hanging over the side of a nearby chair like the discarded skin of some large, denim reptile. The music had transitioned once again, and now we were listening to the dulcet tones of Sarah McLachlan singing "I Will Remember You." Curly's eyes were closed, and his large, naked body was swaying gently back and forth to the rhythm as he sang along with Sarah, his bone-white buttocks trembling with emotion, the purple mushroom head of his penis barely visible through a thick bush of dark pubic hair. On his right arm, there was a poorly done tattoo of an eagle perched on top of a globe, and down his right side, starting just under the ribs and ending at his pelvic bone, there was a long, white scar that squirmed and writhed like a giant earthworm. The women who had been throwing money earlier were now weeping and holding one another.

I was completely absorbed in this strangely touching scene until Rae dug her nails into my flesh and hissed, "What do you think you're doing?"

"Ow," I cried. "What?"

"You can't just show up unannounced the day after an employee dies and start asking idiotic questions like that?"

"Why? What's going on? Does Mouth have something to hide?"

"Something to hide? What the hell? No, she's not hiding anything. It's just a really difficult time for everyone. Rebecca worked here for two years. Everybody loved her." She waved her hand around the room, her eyes filled with tears. "On top of that, it's never good when a dancer gets hurt, especially in a town like this where everyone's looking for an excuse to close us down. And then you come in asking questions about *foul play*? I mean, come on. Get it together, Sam." She grabbed my face and took a closer look. "And you're high, too. I can't believe this. What are you on?"

"It's just a little Vicodin," I mumbled. "I was hung over. It's no big deal."

"Look," said Rae. "I like you. I've always liked you. I mean, you're a pain in the ass, but you're sweet in your own way and you make me laugh. So I'm going to say this for your own good. I can tell you're going through something right now, but honestly, I don't care. Just get your shit together, okay? Because Mouth is in no mood to deal with your bullshit today. She likes you, too, but she has a lot on her plate. Get in, ask your questions, get out. Understand?"

I nodded. I knew Rae had my best interests at heart, but her speech just sort of fluttered by me like a paper bag in the wind. Why was everyone getting so upset? I was on to something, and they were clearly trying to get rid of me. I needed to keep pushing.

Rae led me to the back office, a small room behind the VIP lounge decorated with 1950s pinup posters and framed prints of paintings I didn't recognize. I had been there only once, when I wrote the first article about the Pink Door. Nothing had changed. The place was immaculate, a fact that had shocked me then and was still surprising. True, I had never been inside the office of any other strip club owner, but I had seen dozens in movies and none of them were this clean. They usually featured piles of loose cash, lines of cocaine ready to be consumed, and a thin greasy-haired man behind the desk wearing a jacket that either featured sequins or leather fringe under the arms. This place was neat, the desk was polished oak, there were no drugs in sight, and the owner was wearing a gray herringbone business suit with a white blouse underneath.

"Sam!" Mouth exclaimed as we entered the room. "Come in, come in. How's my favorite movie reviewer?"

She motioned for me to sit in an empty chair in front of her desk. Mouth was a stout fireplug of a woman who had spent her entire life being underestimated because of her size and gender. Her age was impossible to determine. Somewhere between thirty and fifty. The only piece of personal information she refused to share the last time I interviewed her was her birthday. She had shiny raven-black hair, olive skin, hatchet-blade cheekbones, and the long hooked nose of a bird of prey. The Larkmans claimed to be one-tenth Arapahoe, but no one knew if this was true or just something they said to make the wealthy white liberals of Mountainview nervous. Either way it worked.

"I'm fine," I said. "Could use a drink though."

Rae gave me a sideways look and said, "He already had one on the house, boss."

Mouth opened a drawer in her desk and pulled out a bottle of top-shelf bourbon. All ten of her fingers were covered in rings, each one larger and gaudier than the next, and they clinked against the bottle as she opened it. "This is more than a one-drink kind of day," she said. She poured an inch of brown liquid in two coffee mugs and handed me one. "To Rebecca." We saluted and sipped.

"He says he's here to do an interview," said Rae.

Mouth looked at me curiously over the top of her cup. "An interview? No one talked to me about it."

"Don't know much about it myself," I said. "Victoria called me into her office yesterday and told me to do a story on the dead stripper. I guess she figured I still had some friends over here."

Mouth continued to smile but her eyes went flat. "Exotic dancer. Her name is Rebecca Kint," she said.

"Right," I said, gulping more bourbon and shuddering uncontrollably as it went down. "Rebecca. I knew that."

"Kint. K-I-N-T."

"Got it."

"Why don't you write it down to make sure."

"Oh, right."

Panicked, I reached inside my raincoat and began rummaging around. There were half a dozen pockets inside that thing, and it took a while to search all of them. I didn't plan on finding anything; I just wanted to put on a show so it looked like I knew what I was doing. However, to my own amazement, in the third pocket my fingertips came in contact with something long and hard, and I pulled out the pen I'd stolen from Victoria's office yesterday. I held it up like a torch.

Mouth nodded, unimpressed. "What're you going to write on? Your hand?"

I reached back into the magic coat, and lo and behold, out came a little notepad. This time I acted nonchalant, as though I did this every day. I wrote *Rebecca Kint* in the notepad. It felt great to write those two little words, like a real reporter.

I cleared my throat. "So what can you tell me about this... about Rebecca Kint?"

Mouth's eyes softened and she settled back in her chair. "She was from Kansas. Small town. I can't remember the name. You'll have to ask her family about that. Came here to see the mountains. They don't have mountains in

Kansas I guess. She couldn't ski, but she liked to go sledding. She lived with a roommate over at Garden Village. Kate Miller. She works here too."

"He just met her," Rae said.

"I did?" I asked. Rae gave me a look. "Oh, right. Kate. Yes, I met her."

Mouth nodded and continued. "Kate's a good kid. You should talk to her, get some idea of Rebecca's home life. I do know that Rebecca recently got her GED and was planning to go to community college. Wanted to be a veterinary technician, take care of sick animals. She was kind of ditzy, but I think she could've done it." Mouth leaned forward and pointed a warning finger at the center of my forehead. "Don't print that part about her being ditzy."

I continued to write down what she was saying, but none of it was very useful. It was obvious I was going to have to brace Mouth if I wanted real answers. I shifted in my chair and crossed my legs in what I hoped was an authoritative manner.

"Okay, that's fine," I said. "How about something more…interesting?"

"Sam," Rae warned.

Mouth cocked her head. "Like what?"

"Like how did she die?"

Mouth sucked at her teeth. "Haven't you talked to the police yet?"

"That's a good idea," snapped Rae, glaring at me. "Why don't you go talk to them, and then come back when you're more informed."

I stayed my course. "The police said she slipped on some ice and hit her head. Can you, um, confirm that?"

"Ice?" said Mouth. "No, no, she didn't slip on the damn ice. When was the last time you saw snow on the street, much less ice?"

I sat up in my seat and readied my pen. Now we were getting somewhere.

"She slipped on grease. *Grease*, not *ice*. Or some kind of slick chemical at least."

I slumped back in my chair and scribbled the word *grease* in the notebook.

"I see," I mumbled. "Like mechanical grease?"

"No, like oil."

"Oil?"

"From that spa next door. They use it to massage rich ladies' hoochies over there or something. They call it Ayurvedic therapy. It involves some kind of solution from India that's supposed to make you look ten years younger. These old ladies are bathing in that shit. Why aren't you interviewing *them*?"

"Who?" I asked.

"Liliane Easton," growled Mouth. "I've told that snobby skeleton a million times not to dump that shit in the alley. They're supposed to pay the city to recycle it properly. Layton County Environmental Ordinance 39-H, section five, paragraph three."

I just stared at her, not quite following the sudden turn the conversation had taken, the alcohol and pills making her words a little mushy around the edges.

"Do you have any idea what's going on in the city you live in?" she said. "Jumpin Jesus on a kangaroo, you work for the goddamn newspaper. Don't you ever read it?"

"Of course I do!"

I didn't.

"Then you should know. Your editor wrote a front-page story about local environmental regulations two months ago. What's her name? Wood. Victoria Wood. Now that's a journalist. I filed four EP-7 reports with the county clerk's office in the last six months. An inspector stopped by for a few minutes, took some notes, and then nothing. I haven't heard jack rabbit squat about it since then."

She opened a filing cabinet behind her and pulled out a manila file an inch thick. She slapped it on the desk. "Those are copies of the reports. Everything filled out all nice and legal like. I even had our lawyer take a look before we turned them in. The city is required to examine the property within three months and serve the establishment with an official compliance request within five. They should've served them three weeks ago."

"But you're sure she slipped?" I said.

Mouth screwed up her face like she'd just bitten into a lemon. "Of course I'm sure. What else could have happened?"

I tugged on the brim of my hat and gave her a hard look. "Maybe she was asking questions she shouldn't have been asking. Maybe someone pushed her or hit her on the back of the head. Maybe there's more to the story."

Mouth nodded and placed her hands in her lap. "And why would someone want to hurt Rebecca?"

"Right," I said. "Exactly. That's the big question. Maybe because of, you know, the drugs."

"The drugs?"

Mouth looked down and began fidgeting with her hands under the desk. It was obvious that the pressure from the interrogation was too much. She was going to break any second.

"That's right. Maybe drugs were involved. It wouldn't be the first time. Nice kid like that moves from a small town in Kansas to the big city, takes up with a bad element. No offense. Happens every day. It's fun at first—good times, fast men—but then the money runs out. She needs to feed the monkey, so she looks around for ways to make extra cash. Soon she's in over her head. I'm not accusing you, Mouth. Maybe it's someone in your family. Things have been moving so fast lately. If we work together, maybe we can get to the bottom of this."

When Mouth looked up, she had an unusual expression on her face. Not guilt, exactly, but something just as intense. "Get out," she said.

"Huh?"

"Get out of my office."

She brought her hands back up and laid her rings on the top of the desk. One particular ring—a large silver band topped with a turquoise rock the size of a dung beetle—broke free from the pile and rolled drunkenly into the middle of the wood surface. We both watched it wobble around until it finally found a settled position.

"You mean leave?" I said. "Like now? But I'm not done yet."

Suddenly, she shot out of her chair and flew at me. She was around the desk and on top of me before I had time to react. She knocked my hat off, grabbed my hair, and wrenched my head up until I was looking into her furious brown face. I could smell her Chanel and her apple-scented shampoo. Rae quietly closed the office door.

"Listen here, you little shit," Mouth hissed. "I care about these girls. This is a weird, fucked-up business and we attract a lot of weird, fucked-up people, and I'm one of them. It's not a healthy place for a young woman to be, I realize that, but I do the best I can for them. I don't care that you're stupid. That's not your fault. I don't expect you to care about these girls as much as I do. But I do expect you to do your damn job."

"That's what I'm trying to do," I cried.

She pulled my hair harder. "What's her name?"

"Why?"

"I read that little blog of yours last night. You called her a stripper three times. No name, just a stripper. She has a name. She was a person. Say her name."

"It's, um, Rrrrrrachel?"

Mouth cocked her tiny ring-less fist back and punched me in the eye. It wasn't a vicious punch. Just a jab, really. I could tell by the way she threw it she knew how to hit someone hard, and she was purposefully holding back. That didn't make the pain any less real though.

"Rebecca!" I cried. "Rebecca Kint, Rebecca Kint, Rebecca Kint."

Mouth let go of my hair and smiled. "Say it again."

"Rebecca Kint."

She walked back to the other side of the desk, drained the rest of her whiskey in one swallow, and began putting her rings back on.

"Get the hell out of my club," she said. "And don't you ever call her a stripper again. She was a good girl, and she deserves better. You get your facts straight, or next time I won't be so gentle."

Chapter 11: The Kid

OUTSIDE THE CLUB THERE WAS A BLACK SUV IDLING in the alley with the word "POLICE" stenciled on the side in white capitals underneath the smaller yellow "Mountainview." I made what I thought was a nonchalant right turn and headed in the opposite direction, the cool breeze coming off the mountains a welcome relief to my rapidly swelling eye.

I had what could be described as an uneasy relationship with the local authorities. I'd never actually been arrested as such, but over the years there had been a certain number of incidents—mostly involving public intoxication, and urination, and, on one occasion, nudity—which had caused me to be detained temporarily against my will in the Mountainview Police Department's detoxification center, a windowless white room with an uncomfortable cot and a surprisingly clean toilet that I filled over and over again with the contents of my stomach. Furthermore, although I had written only one real news story for the paper, that story had painted the Mountainview PD in a less than ideal light, causing resentments and hurt feelings in the department, or so I assumed. In light of that (and the fact that I currently had several bottles of prescription medication on my person that did not belong to me), I thought it would be better to avoid interaction with the authorities if at all possible. I briefly entertained the thought of making a break for it. Just taking off at a full sprint down the alley, sliding over the hoods of parked cars, upending trash cans in my wake to deter my pursuers. They'd call for backup, but by then it would be too late. I'd steal a horse and head into the mountains where no one would find me, grow a Jeremiah Johnson beard, survive on rainwater and grubs. What was a grub exactly? Some kind of insect larva. That didn't sound appetizing. Maybe I could learn to fish.

I was dressed in deerskin, hip deep in a river with a sharpened stick raised over my head as I tracked the progress of an approaching trout, when my revelries were interrupted by the vinyl-like crackle of car tires on pavement. The SUV soon pulled up beside me, and the driver's-side window descended with a mechanical purr, releasing a blast of heated air along with the poetic lamentations of Townes Van Zandt singing about waitin' around to die.

"What are you doing here, Mr. Drift?" asked the man behind the wheel.

If I was making a movie about a murder in a small mountain town that was being investigated by a brilliant, intrepid reporter, I would absolutely cast Henry Moss as the handsome, black sheriff with a complicated past and a cool disposition. He was a thin, neat man with a mocha complexion and the type of sleepy blue eyes that caused people to stare at him longer than was comfortable in normal social interactions. The eyes were his mother's—a Danish beauty who taught history at the local high school for nearly three decades—and the disposition was his father's. The Moss family had deep roots in Mountainview dating back to the early 1900s, when Henry's great grandfather opened up the fourth black-owned business in town. It was a small grocery store called Value Foods across from the university that had been passed down through the family for almost a hundred years. It had survived fires, floods, vandalism, and a variety of attempts to shut it down by racist government officials, which local historical record keepers tried desperately to gloss over. Then Whole Foods came to town in the late nineties just as Henry's father was renegotiating a ten-year lease. The drop in business combined with the rising cost of rent drove Value Foods out of business in less than five years. Henry's father had a stroke ten months later, and his broken-hearted mother moved back to Copenhagen to be with her family, where she passed away soon after. Henry had enlisted in the army directly out of college, and he was in Iraq fixing broken tanks when he heard the news. He came home to an empty house and a pile of debt. His experience in the military and his degree in sociology qualified him for a job in the Mountainview PD, where he demonstrated a cool head and an uncanny ability to avoid controversy. He was unfailingly polite, referring to everyone, no matter their age or station, as *mister* and *miss*, but also efficient and direct with his intentions. He kept his personal opinions to himself and stayed out of local politics. In fact, he had done so well in Mountainview, there were rumors of an administrative appointment to the Denver Police Department, where a more diverse demographic made a black man who knew how to handle white people an attractive asset. On this subject, as usual, Henry had no comment.

"Good morning, Henry," I said, too brightly, making sure I kept a safe distance from the SUV and faced east, so he couldn't smell the whiskey on my breath or see my black eye. "Crazy weather we're having, huh?"

Like most mountain communities, Mountainview citizens were obsessed with the weather, and it was usually a good opportunity to change the subject.

"Stop trying to change the subject," Henry said. He reached through the car window and put his finger on my chin, applying gentle pressure until I turned my head and looked at him directly. "Why are you stumbling out of the Pink Door at ten in the morning with a black eye?"

I tenderly massaged my cheekbone. "Mouth hit me," I whimpered.

I hadn't meant to rat her out so quickly, but you never know how you're going to react in the heat of interrogation.

Henry lowered his head and looked at me over the top of his glasses. "Do you think it's such a good idea to mess around with the Larkmans, Mr. Drift?"

"I wasn't messing around with her," I said. "She was messing around with me."

"And you didn't do anything to provoke her?"

"I was just asking her questions about the dead…about the young woman in her employment who recently died."

Henry let go of my chin and reached for a metal thermos shaped like a small torpedo that was sitting in the passenger's seat. He removed the lid and filled its contents with steaming brown coffee. "And why were you asking questions about Rebecca Kint?" He blew and sipped.

"I'm writing a story for the paper."

"Right," he grunted.

"No, really."

"Don't you write those asinine movie reviews?"

"They're not asinine," I said weakly. There was something about Henry Moss that always made me want to earn his approval, despite (or perhaps because of) the fact that over and over again he'd made it quite clear I wasn't going to get it. During those visits to the detoxification center, it was Henry who stayed up with me all night, berating me for my life choices, listening to my various sob stories, making sure I didn't fall asleep and choke on my own vomit. He'd attended Mountainview High School at the same time as my mother, and although he was several years her junior, he remembered her as a pretty, kind-hearted theater nerd who had once danced with him at homecoming. Since Henry had also lost his parents unexpectedly, I suppose he felt responsible for me in a way, as he was always pulling me out of trouble and giving me gentle, taciturn advice. They say orphans spend the rest of their lives searching for families to replace the ones they lost, and while no one wants their existence reduced to a cliche, it seemed to be true for Henry and I.

He snorted. "You think getting high and ranting about Frank Capra makes you some kind of genius? Trust me, they're asinine."

"Well, this one isn't a movie review," I said.

He squinted at the Flatirons in the distance and took another swig of coffee. "And Victoria assigned this story to *you*?"

"Sure. Why wouldn't she?"

"Reyna and Michael were busy, huh?"

"Well, yeah. But that had nothing to do with it. Gerald asked for me specifically. In fact, he wants to make me the new editor." I stopped there, realizing with the usual drinker's remorse that I'd said something I shouldn't have only after I heard it coming out of my own mouth.

"Victoria's quitting the paper?"

Victoria and Henry had been a hot item when I first started writing for the *Chronicle*, and their breakup was the subject of much gossip at the bar after hours. Most believed it had something to do with an investigative piece Victoria wrote several years ago about a California real estate mogul that was secretly funding efforts to usurp political power in Mountainview. It was all very cloak and dagger, and I didn't actually read the article myself but everyone was talking about it. The gist was that the mogul in question was attempting to stack the town council with California transplants so they could alter certain aspects of the town charter that interfered with business opportunities, such as zoning laws and liquor licenses. It turned out nothing the mogul and his cronies were doing was technically illegal, but Victoria's article drew unwanted attention to their efforts and temporarily squashed their plans. After that, she wrote an op-ed piece challenging local politicians and community leaders to speak out against outsiders trying to influence Mountainview's politics and economy. Many did just that, but Henry remained silent. His reasoning was that, as police chief, his job was to catch criminals, and since no crime had been committed, it was none of his business how wealthy assholes in California conducted their affairs. They stopped seeing each other shortly after. Henry would neither confirm nor deny the cause of the breakup, and Victoria refused to acknowledge Henry's existence, unless there was a newspaper story involved.

"She turned in her letter of resignation last week," I said. "She's leaving us."

Henry rubbed his chin and ignored my dramatic proclamation. "And Gerald wants to make you the new editor? *You*?"

"Why not me?"

He held up a small fist and began listing the reasons, raising a finger with each one. "You drink too much. You have no experience running a newspaper. Your colleagues are more qualified than you. You don't have a degree in journalism. In fact, you don't have a degree at all because you dropped—"

"Okay, okay, I get it," I said. "Let's just stop there. You're running out of fingers."

"I have another hand."

I adjusted my hat and stood up straighter. "I'm the most popular writer at the paper," I said. "There was a graph with…with circulation numbers. That's why Gerald wanted me on this story in the first place. The readers like me."

He shook his head and blew a blast of incredulous air out of his nose. "God, you really are dense. It's a newspaper, Mr. Drift. If people like you, you're not doing your job."

"That's why I'm working this case."

"Case?"

"I mean story."

Henry sighed and screwed the lid back on the thermos. "Okay, fine. Have it your way. What have you uncovered so far, Columbo?"

I looked down at my trench coat. "Why do people keep...? Never mind." I glanced sideways down the alley and lowered my voice. "I think there might be more to this than they're telling us."

"Who's 'they'?"

"Well, Mouth, for starters."

He pointed to the right side of my face. "Because of that?"

"Yes!" I said. "That's what I'm talking about. Why would Mouth hit me unless I was on to something?"

"I don't know. Maybe you were being an annoying asshole, so she popped you one."

I nodded vigorously. "Maybe. Or maybe she has something to hide."

"Like what?"

"Like this," I said, pulling the used syringe out of my pocket and presenting it to him, careful to hold the tip between my thumb and index finger so as not to destroy any fingerprints.

"Whoa," said Henry, recoiling slightly. "What the hell is that?"

"I found it in the storm drain behind the dumpster. It's a heroin needle."

"Heroin?" He leaned in for a better look.

"Well, okay, I don't know for certain. Crack or speed or meth. I mean, you guys will have to test it down at the lab. I'm sure there's, like, residue inside it and stuff, right? And there's probably blood on it somewhere, as well. The needle part broke off, but I'm sure you can still find something. Particles or molecules. How many blood molecules do you need to make a positive identification?"

"Let me see that," said Henry, taking it from me in a motion so fast that I almost didn't see it.

"No, but..."

It was too late. The syringe was in his hand before I could protest, the fingerprints being rubbed out right before my eyes. Maybe Liliane was right about the local police. Here I was providing the highest-ranking officer in the Mountainview PD with evidence in a murder investigation, and he was fumbling with it like a freshman frat boy with a bra strap.

Henry examined the plastic tube for a few seconds, turning it around like a piece of meat on a rotisserie.

"It's not heroin," he finally said.

"No? Is it crank? Smack?"

"Nope." He turned the needle on its side and held it out so I could see the small, white prescription tag. "It's insulin. Belongs to one Charles Bledsoe, whoever that is. Probably a customer at the Pink Door had a diabetic episode, and he came out to the alley for some privacy. You're not supposed to dispose of used needles in public, but I don't think I'll arrest him for it."

I squinted at the words on the syringe. "Maybe he's a witness. You should bring him in for questioning."

"A witness to what exactly?"

"Rebecca Kint's murder."

"What are you talking about? The woman slipped on the ice and hit her head."

"On the grease," I corrected.

"What?"

"She slipped on some grease in the alley. Or chemicals for old ladies. I don't know. It smells like sunscreen. Mouth said she filed complaints with the city, but nothing happened. Wasn't that in the police report? Of course, that's probably just a smoke screen. Liliane said there's a lot of shady things happening at the Pink Door."

"Liliane?"

"Easton. The owner of Nirvana & You."

"Yeah, I know who she is. Her lawyer files complaints with our department about once a week." Henry finished his coffee and put the lid back on the thermos. "Did she see what happened?"

"Well, no, but her business is right next door and she sees…things. She was giving me a reiki massage and we were talking about…"

"A what?"

"A reiki massage. There's energy in the, um…in the hands, and then she focuses it into, you know, the auras in your chest for maximum positive… stuff. It's supposed to align your qi."

Henry turned to face the mountains again, this time glaring at Pike's Peak as though it was a suspect that had tried to pull something over on him. He gripped the steering wheel, his knuckles stretching and his tendons tightening. It was an unnecessarily long pause.

"Get in the car," he said.

"Why?" I asked, suddenly paranoid. "Where are we going? Am I under arrest? I don't have to go with you if I'm not under arrest. Do you have a warrant?"

"Mr. Drift?"

"Yeah?"

"Shut up."

"Okay."

"Miss Wood has been looking for you all morning. Something about a blog post you made last night. They've been trying to call you, but your phone is dead. I'm going to drive you to the office so they stop bothering us."

I let out a relieved sigh. "Oh, yeah. Ha ha. Ran out of battery last night, and I haven't had time to recharge it. Victoria probably just wants an update on my progress." I trotted around to the other side of the SUV and climbed inside, where it smelled like cigarette smoke, bleach, and the faint acidic hint of vomit, like every police car I'd ever been in. "So you talked to Victoria?"

"No," said Henry, putting the car in gear and pulling out of the alley. Van Zandt sang about the tragic relationship between Poncho and Lefty. "The bald one with the tattoos."

"Chloe."

"Yeah, that's her. She called the station looking for you. She's a talker, that one."

Henry took a left on Elm and immediately got stuck behind a small battalion of middle-age male bikers, all wearing neon spandex and aerodynamic helmets, their belly flab undulating which each thrust of their hairy-sausage thighs. Instead of riding single file down the bike lane, they were spread out across the road in a misshapen V-formation like a flock of balding geese flying south in search of warmer climates and unregulated Viagra. Henry honked at them and for his efforts received several peevish looks and one middle finger, which quickly wilted when the owner saw the police insignia. The bikers moved over and allowed us to pass.

"You were at the MIFF opening last night," said Henry, his eyes focused on the road.

It wasn't phrased as a question, but he clearly expected a response. "Yeah, it was great. Bigger than last year. It's really taking off."

"Did you meet the keynote speaker?"

I shifted nervously in my seat. "The keynote what?"

Henry gave me an annoyed sideways glance. "The special guest. The actress who was in all those old horror movies. You know what I'm talking about."

"Oh, *right*," I said. "I came late so I really didn't get to see much of the beginning. And there were so many people there. You know how it is. All those actors and directors, and everyone wants to buy you a beer. Liliane was there, too. Seemed like everyone in town showed up."

The business district faded away and soon we were driving past the university, where students were streaming in and out of large stone buildings, looking like so many attractive ants carrying backpacks instead of leaves. As usual, I was hit with a tiny dose of college nostalgia, and I felt the weight of Maggie's letter in my pocket.

"She's missing," said Henry.

"Who? Liliane?"

"The actress woman from Hollywood. She wandered off last night and no one has been able to find her."

"I thought you had to be gone for, like, forty-eight hours before you can file a missing-persons report."

"You watch too much TV," he said. "Her granddaughter was in my office all morning screaming about suing the city. Says she's going to raise a stink on the internet if we don't find her. My guess is the old lady got invited to a party and stayed out all night. What do you think?"

"How would I know?" I said quickly. "I mean, I didn't see…or talk to anyone. I left early because I had to work on this story. So how would I know?"

We passed a construction site where large, yellow machines scooped dirt out of the ground and men in hardhats pounded nails into the wooden skeleton of a future condominium. The northwest corner of the would-be condo had once been the location of Value Foods.

"I didn't say you knew anything," Henry said. He stared at the condo with a blank expression, possibly contemplating the wealthy young app inventor who would soon be sleeping in an organic bed on the spot where the Moss family had once tried to make a life for themselves. "I just know you go to a lot of those parties, so I was going to ask you to keep your eye out for her. As a favor."

"Oh…"

V. hadn't specifically instructed me not to tell anyone where she was, but it was clear she did not want to be found yet and I was fairly certain I knew what her reaction would be if I showed up at the Pink Door with the police in tow. There was a scene in *Bride of Mars* where V.'s character, Queen T'andaaria, discovers she's been tricked by the American astronauts that have landed on her planet, and she pulls back the human skin covering her face to reveal a slimy alien lizard creature beneath, and then she spits blood-acid into the face of the chief science officer, melting him into a gory puddle.

"I'll keep an eye out," I said. "Probably won't see anything, but I'll do what I can."

I tried to think of something else to say, but the air was suddenly heavy. The countenance on Henry's face did not change, but there was a ripple along his jaw that seemed to indicate he was grinding his teeth, attempting to masticate history into a digestible form. I remembered my own attempts to eat the past, and I left him alone.

We soon pulled into the *Chronicle* parking lot, and Henry parked in the space furthest from the building. He reached for the thermos and poured himself another lid of coffee.

"You want to come in and say hello?" I asked.

Henry shook his head. "Probably not a good idea."

I reached for the door handle, but it was locked from the driver's side.

Henry sipped the coffee leisurely while I waited. He seemed to be working something out in his head, a slow mental grind that he wasn't quite ready to articulate.

"Here's the thing," he said. "You're a good kid. Dreamy, kind of stupid, but a good kid, nonetheless. I don't know what is going on here, but it stinks. You shouldn't be assigned to this story."

I started to protest but he cut me off.

"You're a lousy journalist, Mr. Drift, and I think somewhere in that odd brain of yours you realize this. I don't know what you're going through right now, but it must be something big. You're erratic, you reek of alcohol, and your pupils are dilated. I don't know what you're on, and I don't want to know. Just promise me that you'll slow down and stay grounded in reality. No more drugs, no more liquor, and stay off the internet."

"Okay," I lied.

"I know you're lying," said Henry. He gave me a resigned look and shook his head. "I assume you'll want those EP-7 reports then."

I furrowed my brow. "What...um?"

"The paperwork regarding that spa's health-code violations."

"No, I don't really think it's relevant."

Henry closed his eyes and pinched the bridge of his nose. "Mr. Drift, I can't officially obtain departmental paperwork for a journalist unless you request it. This paperwork is directly connected to the article you're working on. Trust me, your editor will want to see these reports. Just tell me to get them for you."

"Okay."

"Okay what?"

"Okay, get me the..."

"EP-7 reports."

"Yeah, those. Please can you get me the EP-7 reports?"

"Yes, Mr. Drift. I will have those for you first thing tomorrow." The lock on the door clicked open. "And just think about what I'm telling you. Slow down. Talk to Victoria. Tell her what you're going through and share your information with her. She's an excellent editor. She will get you through this in one piece."

Chapter 12: Citizen Kane

WHEN I WALKED THROUGH THE FRONT DOOR OF THE *MOUNTAINVIEW CHRONICLE*, Chloe greeted me with wide eyes and an index finger across her lovely throat. I couldn't tell if she was saying I was going to die or that I should kill someone, and before I could clarify the meaning of her macabre miming, Victoria grabbed my shoulder.

"What happened to your face?" she asked, placing a gentle hand on the cheek just under the eye where Mouth had punched me. Her skin was soft and cool, and I was disappointed when she pulled her hand away.

"It's nothing," I said brightly. "Just a little misunderstanding."

"Are you sure? Do you want some ice?"

I desperately wanted a glass of ice drowned underneath four fingers of whiskey, but I shook my head.

"Alright then." The concerned expression melted away, and her features hardened. She pointed toward the stairs. "We're in Gerald's office, Sam."

"I'm glad you're here," I said, trying not to make direct eye contact. "My phone died last night, so I didn't get your calls. Do you guys have an extra charger around here? Henry found me this morning and drove me in. He says hello by the way. You two should really patch things up. Anyhow, no need for the meeting. Rest assured I have been diligently following your instructions. I started pounding the pavement as soon as I woke up this morning. I already interviewed—"

"That's fine, Sam," she said, turning my shoulders toward the stairs. "Why don't you step inside the office and we'll talk about it?"

I didn't like the way she kept repeating my name, as though she was a cop in a police drama about to break the news that my husband had been killed in the line of duty.

We ascended the stairs.

The building that housed the *Mountainview Chronicle* was divided into three floors. Editorial and layout were crammed into the first floor, advertising and distribution were on the second, and the penthouse suite was all Gerald. It wasn't as extravagant as it sounds. For some reason, possibly due to flooding concerns, the water heater and fuse boxes had been placed on the top floor along with a sizable storage room, which took up a quarter of the space. On top of that, in order to comply with local building codes, the ceiling was about six inches lower than the other floors and tilted ever so slightly to the east for drainage purposes, giving the place a cramped off-kilter feel, like the captain's cabin on a second-hand yacht or the attic of a suburban condo built on the edge of a swamp. Still, Gerald had done everything in his power to give the impression that this was the office of an eccentric high-powered CEO. There were Brahma carvings, Shiva tapestries, and Vishnu altars. The door to the storage room was hidden by a four-paneled black lacquer screen depicting a trio of white cranes standing in front of a waterfall. A framed original pressing of *Are You Experienced* by Jimi Hendrix hung on the wall next to an ancient yellowed poster advertising a Grateful Dead concert in San Francisco. The rich hardwood floor was polished to a glassy shine and covered with expensive Middle Eastern rugs. In the far corner, beside a brass statue of Ganesh sitting in the lotus position, there was an antique bookcase filled with leather copies of the *Tao Te Ching, Bhagavad Gita,* and *The Art of War* making nice with *Atlas Shrugged* and *The Power of Positive Thinking.*

I started to step inside the office, but Gerald held up a traffic-cop hand. "Namaste," he said and pointed at my feet.

"Oh, yeah. Namaste to you, too," I said, doing an awkward half-bow for no particular reason. "Sorry about that. Namaste."

I took off my shoes and tossed them in a wicker basket near the door that already contained three pairs.

"Nice socks," said Victoria.

I looked down at the mismatched stockings covering my feet and scrunched my toes.

"Laundry day," I mumbled.

Gerald was sitting behind his enormous oak desk, back erect, hands flat on the surface in front of him, his face a mask of inscrutable serenity. At fifty-two, he was a good-looking man and he knew it, with a thick pile of wavy brown hair brushed with silver at the edges, a wiry yoga-toned frame, and a tan so deep and rich he practically glowed in the dark. Altogether, he looked like gerbil-era Richard Gere. Except six inches shorter.

Above the desk hung a large gold-framed oil painting that was completely out of place with the rest of the Eastern-bohemian decor. It featured a distinguished elderly couple dressed in formal wear, the man silver of hair and square of jaw, the woman a sharp-featured, bird-like creature with a perfectly coiffed gray nest on top of her head and a look of eternal disappointment on her face. This would be Martin and Emily Dawson, Gerald's California in-laws and the newspaper's financial backers. According to River, when Gerald first borrowed the three hundred thousand dollars necessary to start the paper, one of the conditions Emily Dawson insisted on was that he hang the portrait above his desk until the loan was paid in full. They had not approved of the marriage, and this was the punishment for taking away their daughter. I always assumed this was the reason Mrs. Dawson's thin lips were pursed into an almost rectal pucker and why her cold gray eyes seemed to glare downward from the painting, as if assessing the worth of her son-in-law below and finding him wanting.

Gerald was one of those guys who always saw something bigger on the horizon. Maybe it was his California blood. They said, "Go West, young man" but what if you started out on the edge of the Pacific Ocean? Where did you go to make your dreams come true? Gerald came to Mountainview in 1978 to be a big fish in a small pond, and now that the pond was getting bigger, he saw himself shrinking again, transforming from a shark back into a guppy, and he was desperate not to be eaten. He tried to play the easy-going West Coast business guru, but he was too passive-aggressive for the role, and whenever something went wrong, his petty, vindictive nature won out. Gerald wanted more. More of what? Money? Power? Serenity? A sense of oneness with the universe? It didn't matter. He just wanted it. The newspaper wasn't his only source of income. He was always investing in stocks and buying real estate, but despite these various financial ventures, he could never quite pay off the debt to his wife's parents, and so they hung there, year after year, staring down at him in judgment.

Without smiling or blinking, Gerald nodded toward a trio of low-slung wicker chairs in front of his desk, one of which was already occupied by Reyna, who grunted at our arrival but otherwise remained silent. I didn't know the etiquette regarding Buddhists and hats, so I took mine off just in case. (I realized too late that more than half my wardrobe belonged to River, and there was a chance Gerald would identify his daughter's clothes and jump to the obvious conclusion that I'd spent the night with her and fire me and yell at me and possibly punch me in the face. But his eyes stared directly at the hat without a flicker of recognition.) I positioned myself in front of one of the tiny chairs and squatted as far down as I could, then sort of leaned back and prayed that I was lined up correctly. There was a moment of vertigo and I swung my arms out to break my fall, but at the last possible second my ass found purchase, and I landed with a graceless plop. I cringed—the old tailbone was really taking a beating today. Gerald smiled. Like the tapestries and statues, the chairs were from India, and Gerald claimed they were more ergonomic than "Western" chairs, which did not explain why he never sat in them.

In theory, they positioned the body in a more natural state of rest, but in practice, they were virtually impossible to get in and out of, and they made you feel like a child in the principal's office waiting to receive punishment. This was most certainly the real purpose of the chairs. At five-foot four-inches tall, Gerald was always devising small ways to tower over people, both physically and emotionally, especially those in his employment. Forcing everyone to take their shoes off was one. The chairs were another.

Gerald pressed his palms together in front of his nose and went around the room giving each of us a full ten seconds of intense eye contact followed by a little bow. Reyna and I awkwardly returned the gesture. Victoria gave him a thumbs-up. When he was finished, he inhaled deeply through his nose and then dramatically expelled the breath through his mouth. Finally, he was ready to speak.

"I'll be right back," said Victoria. And without waiting for permission, she turned on her heels and walked out the door.

Gerald's face remained unmoved, except for his jaw muscle, which rippled several times as he clenched his teeth.

Victoria was the only one who was allowed to defy Gerald's office rules, a privilege she had earned by guiding the newspaper through decades of scandal, financial hardship, and infighting. Also, as she told me more than once, she'd survived an emotionally abusive father and a physically abusive husband, so she was immune to Gerald's little mind games. She had no problem with removing her shoes but refused to fold her substantial six-foot frame into the tiny furniture, no matter its Eastern origins, and despite several screaming battles overheard by the entire staff, Gerald had not persuaded her otherwise. "I am fifty-five goddamn years old," she said the last time I heard them discuss the matter. "I have earned the right to wear comfortable shoes, eat whatever the hell I want, and sit on a real goddamn chair, and there is nothing in the world that is going to make me squat on your doll furniture. Your chakras will just have to deal with it."

With Victoria gone, the air was heavy with Gerald's disapproval.

"Hi, Reyna," I said, attempting to lighten the mood. "How's the writing going? I liked your last article on…um…politics."

Reyna scowled in my direction but said nothing. She was sitting on the very edge of a chair identical to mine, feet flat on the floor, as though she might have to leap into action at a moment's notice. In her right hand she held a pen, and on her lap there was that spiral-bound notebook opened to a fresh page. It was true that Reyna and I had never been close, but she had never snubbed me before and I wondered what I had done to deserve her cold shoulder.

Victoria finally returned carrying her black office chair on her shoulder like some sort of mechanical corpse. She set it down directly in front of Gerald and sank into it with a satisfied sigh.

"Go ahead," she said.

When we were all seated, Gerald stood up. He now towered over everyone except Victoria, who was just under chin level. His feet were bare and professionally manicured. He wore a pair of loose white pants with a drawstring around the waist and the type of ninety-dollar designer t-shirt that rich people put on when they want to appear casual.

"I would like to start this meeting with a quote from the Buddha," he said. " 'Just as a solid rock is not shaken by the storm, even so the wise are not affected by praise or blame.' " He paused to let this sink in. "What do these words mean to us? There has been a lot of blame cast in the past twenty-four hours."

Reyna pointed a long finger at me. "That's because he—"

"*Tranquility!*" Gerald snapped. Reyna and I jumped. Victoria rolled her eyes. "Tranquility is the river that smooths the rough stone. In order to become smooth like the stone, we must learn to become one with the river. I invite everyone here to meditate on these words."

He closed his eyes and brought his prayer-hands to the middle of his chest. We sat in silence for several minutes, Gerald in a deep trance, Reyna and Victoria both giving me the evil eye.

Originally from the upper-middle-class suburbs of Santa Cruz, Gerald's spiritual beliefs were a seemingly contradictory mishmash of Buddhism, self-help jingoism, and unregulated capitalism with frequent references to Bob Marley and Tony Robbins. Normally he wasn't quite so annoying about it, but when the Moores took their yearly pilgrimage to India, Gerald always came back with a fresh set of quotes from his guru, a man named Samar, along with a dozen new business ideas that would make him rich both financially and spiritually. But mostly financially.

Finally, Gerald opened his eyes and smiled. "Isn't that better?" he said. "Our minds are clear, our hearts are open. We are all part of the river. Now we can discuss the issue in a civilized manner."

"You need to stop posting internal shit on your blog," Reyna said.

I leaned backward to get away from her accusation and almost fell over. "My blog?" I said. "Is that what this is about?"

My mind reeled as I tried to remember what I had written yesterday. The whole night was a blur of alcohol and sex, and nothing cohesive came to mind. Something about the stripper story and Victoria's retirement. If only they would let me plug my phone in.

"Yes," said Victoria. "That's what this is about. Come on, Sam. We spoke about this. You need to act professionally when you represent the newspaper."

"It was just a joke," I replied, trying to catch up to the conversation. I turned to Victoria. "I didn't actually use your name. No one could possibly know I was talking about you."

Victoria wrinkled her brow.

"Oh, shit," said Reyna. She looked at Victoria. "It's worse than we thought. He doesn't even know what he did."

I bristled. It was one thing to be called an asshole and another to be accused of idiocy. "You're angry because I said Victoria's quitting." My eyes volleyed from Victoria to Reyna. "Right?"

Reyna threw up her hands.

"Be mindful, ladies," said Gerald. "Remember the river. Don't pollute the waters with your negative energy."

Victoria glared at me. "I am pissed off about that, yes, but that's not what this meeting is about. I got a call this morning from the *Denver Post*. Guess what they wanted to talk about."

I shrugged. "How should I know?"

"Tranquility, tranquility," cooed Gerald. He put his hands out, palms down, and fluttered his fingers, which I assumed was supposed to simulate the flow of a river.

Victoria ignored him. "He asked me whether or not a certain blogger who writes movie reviews for my newspaper is claiming that a Colorado politician murdered an exotic dancer and then used his influence to cover up the crime." I laughed. No one else did.

"Are you serious?" I said. "I was joking. I make jokes on my blog all the time. No one takes them seriously."

"The difference is this time you were making jokes about a real story that you are really working on for a real newspaper," said Victoria.

"And you're going to screw up my article," Reyna said. When she saw the blank look on my face, she sighed and continued. "About Joe Fullerton." Another blank look. "Seriously? You don't know who the governor of Colorado is?"

A dim light bulb went on in my head and I recalled a political commercial featuring a smiling man with a chin dimple saying that he approved the message. I nodded, happy for even the smallest ray of light. "Oh, you mean *Joseph* Fullerton. Right. Yes. Good guy. What's going on with him?"

Reyna balled her hands into fists, and I automatically flinched. "He's been accused of at least three different sex scandals in the past two years," she said. "But he always weasels out somehow. I finally found a concrete lead, and I'm working the story. Then you come along dropping accusations about dead strippers, which diminishes our credibility and makes it look like we have some sort of vendetta against the governor."

"But I didn't say anything about Fullerton."

"You didn't mention him by name," said Victoria. "But you said the dancer might have been killed by a prominent politician that was in town. Who else could it be?"

"The governor was in Mountainview this week?" I asked.

Reyna groaned. "You can't possibly be this stupid. He was cutting the ribbon on the new science building at the university. It was in all the newspapers. It was in *our* newspaper."

"There's no need for name-calling," said Gerald. "Let's be proactive, not reactive."

"But it was just a joke," I said. I was directing my comments to Gerald now, as he appeared to be the only one on my side. "I wasn't talking about the governor. I wasn't talking about anyone. I was just making a joke. I'll call the *Denver Post* and explain the whole thing. It's really not a big deal."

Victoria shook her head and pointed her finger at me. "You won't call anyone. I spent the entire morning on the phone with their editor, assuring him that you are an idiot and there is absolutely no story here whatsoever. They're not going to print anything this time, but rest assured they're reading your blog. So you need to keep your mouth shut."

I nodded so vigorously that my wicker chair began to rock. "Yes. Totally. I can do that. I completely understand. I mean, really, aye-aye, captain. I've got it."

Victoria started to say something else, but Gerald clapped his hands together twice, bringing the focus back to him.

"Blessings," he said. "I think this has been a productive conversation. You have expressed yourselves fully. Sam understands your concerns and has promised to correct his actions. We have all learned and grown. Now it is time for reflection. That is enough for today."

"No, it's not," Reyna said.

Gerald's smile tightened. "Yes, it really is."

Reyna cringed but stood her ground. "No, it's really not." She looked at me with pity. "I'm sorry, Sam. I really am. It's not personal. You're a nice guy and a good writer, but you are a terrible reporter. This is not how a responsible journalist behaves." She turned to Victoria. "You should pull him off the story. Give it to one of our other freelancers. John just finished up that series on the education bill. He should be available."

"No!" I cried. I hadn't wanted the story in the first place, but the thought of losing it now made me frantic. "You can't... That's not... I already went to the Pink Door and interviewed Mouth...I mean, Monica Larkman. The stripper's name was Rebecca Kint. She liked sledding. Look, I took notes like you told me to." I dove into my coat pockets, and as I was desperately rummaging around, the syringe fell out and landed on the floor. Victoria's eyes widened. "You see, that's...that's evidence. There are drugs involved...maybe. I don't know for sure yet. That's why I need more time." I pocketed the syringe and went back to the coat until I found the notebook. I ripped it out and waved it above my head like a flag. "I think there's been some foul play over at the Pink Door. I don't have all the pieces yet, but I've got a hunch. Front-page news. I'm about to break the case wide open."

"You see there," said Gerald, spreading his arms wide. "He's already started. There's no need to take him off the story now. He's sorry. Aren't you, Sam?"

"Yes," I said. "I'm very very sorry. It won't happen again. I won't make any more blog posts while I'm working on this. I promise."

"There you go," said Gerald. "The kid stays on the story. Let's move on."

Victoria shook her head. "It's my fault," she said, her voice pinched. "I shouldn't have assigned you this story in the first place, Sam. You just don't have the tools for hard news yet. We'll give it to someone else, and you can write about the film festival."

"But I can do it," I insisted. "I really can. Just give me one more chance."

Victoria's eyes glistened and she gave me an empathetic smile, but her resolve did not waiver. "I'm sorry. You crossed the line."

Gerald stepped between Reyna and Victoria, and gave each of them a hard look. "You are not listening to me," he said. His face was still placid, but the serene smile was now gone. He pointed at Reyna. "I need you to receive my words with an open spirit."

Reyna kept shaking her head. "But this is wrong—"

Gerald cut her off. "Who owns this newspaper?"

Victoria leaned forward in her chair. "Gerald, everyone is fully aware—"

"I didn't ask you," Gerald hissed. He turned to Reyna and leaned down until his face was several inches from hers. "I need you to receive my words with an open spirit. Who owns this newspaper?."

Reyna looked Gerald in the eyes and said calmly, "You own this newspaper, Gerald."

Gerald smiled and stood back up. "Okay then. I'm glad we cleared that up."

"But you don't own journalistic ethics," she continued quickly, her voice rising. "You don't own media integrity. We do things a certain way for a reason—"

"Shut up!" Gerald said. "Shut up! Shut up! Do you understand, young lady? You persist on being disrespectful and insubordinate. I have tried being mindful and you did not listen, so now I am going to be blunt. If you interrupt me again, you are fired. Is that clear enough for you, missy? I will say what I want to say and you will shut up, or you will pack your desk."

Reyna held her tongue and looked at Victoria, who was leaning so far forward in her chair that she looked like a jaguar ready to pounce. She continued to stare at Gerald, but she gave Reyna a subtle shake of the head.

When Gerald was certain Reyna wasn't going to speak again, he continued. "Sam is going to continue working on this story," he said. "That is not a request. It is not up for debate. He is going to follow up this lead on the Pink Door, and you two are going to stay out of his hair. He will report directly to me. I will be responsible for his progress and for the content of the story. You will have nothing to do with it. He will file the story on Tuesday, and we will run it on Wednesday. This will happen, and there is nothing you can do about it. Do you understand?"

This time the staring contest was between Gerald and Victoria, and I honestly had no idea who would back down first. It was clear that if Victoria spoke up, she would be fired, but Victoria was already quitting, and besides that, I had never seen her back down from anyone or anything, much less a diminutive publisher dressed like a skateboarding monk. Slowly she stood up, which placed Gerald at chin level and forced him to raise his gaze. Victoria opened her mouth and Gerald clenched his fists.

And that's when the office door flew open and River burst into the room, a loud yapping noise emanating from her Armani purse.

"Gerald!" she squealed. "Namaste!"

She was a complete mess. Her hair was wet, her eyeliner was smeared, and she was covered from head to toe with red streaks that I knew to be paint but everyone else logically construed as blood. I had never been so happy to see anyone in my life.

"Good God," exclaimed Victoria as she turned toward the young woman, the mother and newspaper editor in her both ready for action. "What happened? Are you injured?"

River looked down at herself and forced a laugh from her mouth that did not reach her eyes. "My goodness, no," she said. "I didn't even *realize* I was such a mess. You know how artists can be. Always in our own little worlds. It's just *paint*, sweetie."

Victoria sank back into her chair, still not convinced that the scene did not require emergency assistance.

River placed her purse on the floor next to me and managed to kick me in the thigh with the toe of her shoe in the process. While I writhed in pain and massaged the muscle, Rothko growled at me. His head was clean, but the rest of his body was smeared with a scabby layer of dry paint. He snapped at my hand, and I carefully scooted away.

"Well, this is a pleasant surprise," Gerald said, after the initial shock of River's wild entrance had subsided. "Namaste, my dear."

They exchanged bows and then Gerald kissed his daughter on the lips for several disturbing seconds. Everyone else in the room averted their eyes.

River and Gerald had one of those modern father/daughter relationships that involved kissing on the mouth and calling each other by their first names. This was supposed to demonstrate how enlightened and untraditional they were, but to most people it was just weird.

"Did I *interrupt* something?" River said innocently. "Your faces are all so serious." She looked pointedly at me, and I mouthed the words "I'm sorry," which she ignored. "I hope *Sammy* isn't in some kind of trouble."

My earlier happiness regarding River's unexpected appearance faded, and I attempted to melt through the floor. River and I had always maintained an unspoken pact to keep our sexual trysts a secret from her father for obvious reasons, but I knew that if she ever got mad enough, she'd throw me under the bus. After all, I had more to lose than she did.

"Not at all," said Gerald. "Why would you say that?"

River shrugged. "He has such a guilty look on his face. If I didn't know better,

I'd have thought he'd been caught *red*-handed doing something just awful."

Gerald's face grew stern. "Now, darling, Sam has already been through an ordeal this morning. Let's not throw gasoline on the fire."

"Oh, I bet this morning has been trying for poor Sammy," River continued. "He probably woke up on the wrong side of *someone's* bed."

I could feel Victoria glaring at me now from one side and Rothko from the other. Gerald was oblivious to the coded messages his daughter was sending, but it was obvious he was in no mood to be challenged by another woman this morning. The large vein on the right side of his forehead was starting to pulse, but River either didn't notice this warning sign or chose to ignore it.

"You don't know Sammy as well as you think," she continued. "He's got a *lot* of secrets. I'm not sure I would want someone like that working for me."

"And what would she know about working?" said Gerald. His words were directed at River, but he looked at me when he spoke, a commiserate smile on his moist lips.

"But Gerald," River said. "You don't understand—"

"Twenty-two years old and she's never had a job," Gerald continued, as if River hadn't spoken. "Do you know when I started working? Twelve. I started a lawn-mowing business in our neighborhood. It grew so fast that I had to hire help. This kid in my class, Jerry Norton. I paid him minimum wage, plus a bonus for any new business he signed up. But this girl has never earned a paycheck in her life. Never traded labor for monetary remuneration."

River stamped her foot. "I am an artist. You know I sell my paintings."

Scenes like this were the stuff of legend around the office. Gerald fawned over River most of the time, but he wasn't shy about humiliating her in public, especially in front of the staff. It afforded him the opportunity to yell at his employees vicariously through his only child, while simultaneously demonstrating that he did not play favorites with his temper. And it worked. After overhearing a screaming match between father and daughter, it was impossible not to think about the horrible things Gerald might say or do to someone who didn't share his DNA.

"It's my fault, I suppose," he continued. "I've spoiled her. You don't know what it's like to have children, Sam. You want them to have a better life than you, so you give them all the advantages. Dresses, shoes, cars, apartments, college educations. You believe you're helping them, but in the end, you can't give them the one thing they need most. Ambition, self-respect."

"But Gerald."

He glanced at Reyna and frowned. "This generation expects everything to be given to them. No offense, Sam. I know you're not much older than my River, but you're the exception to the rule. You work for a living. You have a job. Maybe I'm old fashioned, but it seems to me you shouldn't be allowed to complain about society until you start contributing to it. Samar says that if you want to drink, you must first fill your own cup one drop at a time. My daughter just expects her cup to overflow whenever she's thirsty. She's lived a privileged life. We can't expect her to understand what it's like to have responsibilities."

"It's not like *you* pulled yourself up by your bootstraps," said River, her chin quivering but defiant.

The room fell into dead silence. This was the first time any of us had heard River fight back, and we had no idea how Gerald would take it.

"Careful," he said, his voice frighteningly calm. "Don't say anything you will regret."

River swallowed hard and bit her lip, but there was a familiar look in her eye that I knew was not resignation.

"You didn't get the money to start this paper from mowing lawns." She pointed at the painting above the desk. "You *begged* Grandma for the money."

"You are out of line."

"And when she wouldn't give it to you, you made *Mom* ask her for it."

"I built this business with my two hands!" Gerald waved his arms around to demonstrate the scope of the empire he had created. "Everything you see here, *everything*, exists because of me."

River laughed. "What do you even *do* here? Victoria runs editorial, advertising makes money, circulation distributes the paper...and you just yell at everyone. You contribute *nothing*."

Aside from Victoria, I had never heard anyone challenge Gerald so directly, and I expected him to fly into a rage. Instead he calmly walked over to the Buddha statue on the other side of the room and lit an incense stick next to it. He leaned in and waved his hand in a circular direction, fanning the smoke into his face.

"I guess Samar was right," he said. "You really are an empty vessel desperate to be filled by any man who will have you. And when you don't get your way, your true nature comes out."

River's eyes widened and she let out a little whimper. "Those sessions were *private*. You promised, Gerald!"

At last, River's resolve broke, and her eyes filled with tears. She was too proud to let us see her cry, so she turned around and took several steps away from the group.

"Jesus, Gerald," said Victoria, standing up and putting an arm around River. "That is more than enough. She's a grown woman, not a child."

"When she starts acting like an adult, I'll treat her like one," said Gerald, coolly.

"Come with me, young lady," she said, taking River by the arm and leading her out of the room. "Let's get you cleaned up."

On the way out, River snatched up her purse, producing a startled yelp from Rothko as he was jerked up into the air. Reyna sighed and followed them out the door, and Victoria shot me one last poignant glare that said, despite Gerald's ultimatum, I was not off the hook yet.

When everyone else was gone, Gerald closed the door, his face once again a perfect mask of serenity and well-being.

"Alone at last," he said.

It was supposed to be a joke, but he came off sounding like Mr. Blonde in *Reservoir Dogs* before he cuts the ear off of the police officer in that empty warehouse. I tried to remember how to smile and failed.

"I should probably head out," I said, trying to push myself into a standing position. "I've taken up too much of your time already. Also, you know, got to get back to this story. So much to do. Interviews and…stuff."

"Sit down, Sam," he said.

Gerald strolled over to the wall mirror on the other side of the room and began to do stretches, pushing his hands toward the ceiling as though he was trying to lift an invisible box, bending down to the floor until his chest touched his knees. It was an impressive display. Not knowing what I should do, I sank back into the chair but turned my body so I was now awkwardly facing him. He made eye contact with me through the reflection in the mirror.

"Do you yoga, Sam?"

"Me? Not really, no. Although I do find myself in downward facing dog a lot."

"What do you do to relieve stress?"

I fidgeted with River's hat. "Oh, you know, the usual: watch movies, drink whiskey, pass out."

"That doesn't sound very holistic."

"No, I guess it doesn't."

He stood up straight, exhaled loudly, then bent his right knee at a ninety-degree angle and extended his left leg straight in the other direction. He stretched his right arm out like a spear in front of him and his left behind, palms down, both arms exactly parallel to the floor.

"This is called the warrior pose," he said. "It builds core power and strengthens my hamstrings, quadriceps, and buttocks."

I winced at the word *buttocks*.

"The warrior pose is a power stance," he continued. "You see how my legs are firmly planted and my chest is thrust forward. It indicates strength and virility. I am taking up as much space as I can here. I am making my presence known. Do you want to make your presence known, Sam?"

"Sure," I said. "I mean, I guess so."

"Victoria told you that she's quitting, didn't she?"

I nodded. "Yeah, but she's said that before."

"Oh, I believe she's serious this time." His front leg started to tremble slightly. "She gave me a letter of resignation, and when Victoria puts something in writing, she means it. She wants me to hire Reyna to replace her."

"Reyna is great. She would do a good job."

Gerald raised his right arm overhead and let his left hand slide down the left leg until his palm was resting on his calf.

"The reverse warrior pose opens the heart and stretches the back," he said. "This position demonstrates a connection to the universe and a willingness to receive knowledge. Reyna is a fine girl, but she doesn't have what I'm looking for in an editor."

"What are you looking for?"

Gerald brought his arms down to his sides and leaned forward. He straightened his right knee and lifted his left leg off the floor until his left leg and torso were aligned and his body formed a capital T. This pose stretched his loose pants at an unusual angle and I could see the outline of his circumcised penis perfectly beneath the fabric.

"Vision," he said.

"Is that the pose you're doing now?" I asked, trying not to stare at his crotch.

"No, no." His right leg wobbled and for one delightful moment it looked like he was going to fall. But he soon recovered his balance. "That's what I want from my editor. Vision. Reyna has no vision. She's all rules and regulations. She can't see beyond the archaic twentieth-century philosophies of print journalism. Her mind is not open."

"But I've never been an editor before," I said. "I've never even taken a journalism class."

"Exactly," said Gerald. "That's exactly what I want. Someone whose mind has not yet been influenced by the traditionalists. I want someone who is willing to reinvent everything we know about how media works in the digital age. I want a maverick."

He dropped his left leg down and stood up straight. His member disappeared from view and I let out an audible sigh of relief. He closed his eyes, pressed his palms together, inhaled deeply, and raised his hands to the ceiling. After holding that pose for several seconds, he exhaled with gusto, and returned his prayer hands to the center of his chest. He stood there for a while. I didn't know what I was supposed to do. It felt weird staring at him like that, but I thought it would be rude if he opened his eyes and I was turned the other way. My left butt cheek was going numb, so I nonchalantly leaned on my right elbow and tried to get the blood flowing through it again. Gerald was a big fan of long pauses and awkward silences. He liked to say that you could learn more about a person from their silence than from their conversation. I think what he learned mostly was that he could intimidate people without saying a word.

Finally, he opened his eyes and said, "I think this has been an extremely productive meeting."

"Um, yeah," I agreed, shaking my left leg. "It was fun."

"So you will continue the excellent work you have been doing regarding the poor woman who died at that club, and you will consider my offer."

"Offer?"

"Regarding the editor position."

"Oh, right. Sure." I scratched my head. "You're serious about that then?"

He crossed the room in quick strides and loomed over me. "Very serious, Sam. You are the future of this newspaper."

I shook my head and struggled to stand up. "Okay, I'll think about it."

After I was on my feet, there was an uncomfortable moment when the top of Gerald's head aligned with the top of my nose. Gerald cleared his throat and turned away from me. He walked to the bookcase near his desk. "Before you leave, I have a gift for you," he said. There was a polished wood box with a troop of elephants carved on the side, each one marching behind the other in single file. He opened the box, and withdrew a bulging Ziploc baggie. There was a solid ounce of prime Colorado pot inside and a few starter joints already rolled. My mouth began to water.

He smiled in the manner of an indulgent father and extended the bag toward me. I snatched it out of his hand before he could change his mind. "I read your blog, and I know you occasionally imbibe. I am a connoisseur myself, if you can believe that. The processed drugs created by Big Pharma will poison your mind, but this comes from the earth and can help one see beyond the façade of reality. Of course, you should wait until you're done writing this story before you partake."

"Of course," I said.

Chapter 13: Detour

BACK AT THE APARTMENT, I PLUGGED IN MY PHONE and then opened the bag of weed. It was good shit. Really good. Like cultivated-in-a-government-lab good. I put *Out of the Past* in the DVD player and watched Robert Mitchum's cleft chin compete with Kirk Douglas's cleft chin. It was a cleft-hanger. I sat down on the couch and reached for my pipe. It was a beautiful old Dunhill with a round, chestnut-brown bowl made of polished briar wood that fit perfectly in the palm of the hand and a long, curved neck that, in profile, gave the piece the appearance of a swan floating on the surface of a pond. I liked the feel of it in my hand, and in my most vain moments, believed it made me look like a young, stoned Lee Van Cleef.

I packed the pipe with Gerald's weed, lit up, and struck a contemplative pose in front of the mirror. Soon I was so stoned that I was hearing things. A baby crying. There were no children in The Trap, and it was kind of spooky to hear the distant wail, like the whine of a ghost in a nearby house. It sounded like it was coming from inside the walls.

Finally, I looked out the window and saw Audrey crouched on the dead tree branch, motionless, eyes closed, her striped gray-and-white lemur tail curled around her paws. She looked like a display in a taxidermy shop, and I felt my throat tighten with panic at the thought of her freezing to death out there during the night while waiting for me to come home.

I'd found Audrey in the alley behind The Trap several years ago when I was taking out the trash. She was a tough, proud street cat, and although she'd run wild from birth, she showed no fear when I bent down to scratch her greasy ears, instead arching her back and leaning into my hand as a quiet cricket-like purr emanated from her throat. I have no idea how she found my window, but there she was the next morning, waiting patiently for me to open it, after which she jumped gracefully onto the couch, sniffed around to make certain the accommodations were up to her standards, then promptly fell asleep on my lap while I watched *Cat People*. I'd never had a pet before and was wary about allowing a living creature to disrupt my tiny living space, but she wore me down. It was a slow training process, but eventually Audrey showed me where to put the food bowl, when to let her outside, how to sleep on my back so she could curl up in the crook of my left arm, and which ear to scratch first thing in the morning.

I was sleeping with a vet tech when this forced adoption took place, and she offered to give Audrey a free examination. She cleaned up a few scratches and administered the necessary shots, but aside from that, she said Audrey was in good health for a stray. There had been some trauma to the uterus in the past, possibly during a difficult pregnancy, and Audrey was no longer able to give birth. The tech posited that Audrey's mothering instincts were highly attuned, and when she realized she would never have a litter of helpless mewling kittens to care for, she sought me out as the next best thing. The tech and I were in the middle of a breakup at the time, but it was difficult to argue with this assertion, considering Audrey's tendency to bathe me with her tongue if I didn't shower regularly and her attempts to clean the apartment by carrying rotten food out the window in her mouth and dropping it on the heads of the fraternity boys below.

Over time, I grew accustomed to this interspecies mothering and tried, in my own way, to be a good son. I showered more frequently and cleaned up after myself. I gave her bottled water, which she preferred to tap, and I pulled back the blanket covering the window during the day so she could nap in the sunbeams without leaving her favorite spot on the couch. The only thing I couldn't seem to get right was when to arrive home. She expected me back every night at a reasonable time, and when I didn't show up, she would sit on the branch outside for hours like an angry gargoyle, staring at the window and twitching her tail. Once I came home after a three-day bender to find her there, dirty, gaunt, and bleeding from a wound she'd received in a fight with some other neighborhood animal, possibly the raccoon that lived in The Trap's dusty rafters. I rushed her to the vet tech, who said, with a definite tone of accusation, that the wound was infected and she was severely dehydrated. Since that time, my punctuality had not improved but the guilt I felt when I found her like this was a knife wound. It was alarming how quickly I'd become attached to her presence, the soft purr in the morning, the rubbing against my legs when I got the mean reds, bringing me back to the world. I just knew that one day I would come home and find her there, a frozen statue bearing eternal witness to my true nature.

"Audrey!" I cried as I jerked open the window.

Nothing. Not a flinch from her soft feline body. I moaned. I was a monster. A selfish, disgusting asshole who would die alone because I alienated and neglected everything I ever loved. I began to sob. Crying when you're alone and stoned is an incredibly cathartic experience. You can just let go completely, wail away without reservation or shame, the tears and snot running down your face.

I was sitting on the couch, my face buried in my hands, when Audrey pushed her head against the side of my arm and let out casual meow, as though asking what all the fuss was about.

"You're alive!" I cried and buried my face in her fur.

She was cold. The type of cold that went all the way to the bone. I closed the window and snuggled her into a blanket to warm her back up. She was somewhat annoyed by this, but allowed herself to be cradled on her back like an infant for a full minute, her peevish face poking out the top, before she started squirming and clawing at the blanket. Once free, she began to preen, cleaning the night's detritus from her fur.

"Why did you do that?" I said. "You could have frozen to death. Don't sit out there waiting for me. Next time go find shelter."

She looked at me like I was an idiot and began rubbing up against my coat.

"Oh, yeah," I said. I reached into my pocket and pulled out a handful of the stolen cat food. "I told you I'd remember. You have no faith in me."

Audrey jumped off the couch and trotted to her food bowl, where she began rubbing her head against the ceramic edge. I followed her and placed the food in the bowl. She looked up at me and began to howl.

"Okay, Jesus." I picked up a piece of the food and pretended to pop it in my mouth. "Mmmm," I said, rubbing my belly. "Delicious. I'm so full now. I couldn't eat another bite."

Satisfied, Audrey began to devour the food. For some reason, she refused to eat until I had taken a bite, perhaps some instinct left over from her time on the street when food was sometimes rancid or poisoned. Or perhaps she was being a mother still, making certain her baby was fed before she filled her belly.

I took another hit from the pipe and then made myself a cup of tea. I watched the movie to the end, the scenes fluttering by my stoned brain without any real recognition, and then I sat staring at the blank screen, enjoying the warm timeless fugue of a stoner coma, until I was rudely interrupted by a knock on the door. I held my breath and tried to ignore it, but after thirty seconds or so there was another knock, and then another.

"What do you want?" I yelled.

"I have an urgent message for you."

It was the Mayor, of course. Who else? At the sound of his voice, Audrey hissed and dove under the bed. She loathed the Mayor and always hid from him, which was for the best. I tried to coax her out the window, but she was having none of it.

"All right," I said. "Just a second."

I pushed Audrey's food bowl under the bed with the toe of my shoe, and then I opened the door. The Mayor was wearing an expensive silk kimono covered in nacho cheese stains and open at the front, of course, the better to display his expansive gut, and he clutched a white piece of paper in his right hand. We stood there staring at one another. He shifted from one foot to the other like a kid who needed to use the bathroom.

"Well, what is it?"

He looked up and down the empty hallway. "We should speak inside," he said. "I'm not sure it's safe out here."

"Oh, for Christ's sake."

I stepped aside so he could squeeze his bulk through the door.

"What do you want?" I said, positioning myself near the television, so the Mayor would be facing away from the bed should Audrey decide to peek out. "I'm busy."

I realized too late that I had left the bag of weed out in the open. I tried to block his view of it, but the Mayor was a world-class mooch, the type of man who had a sixth sense for free shit and weak character.

"What's that?" he asked. "I thought you said you didn't have any money."

I shook my head and picked up the baggie. "It was a gift. I didn't pay for it."

He held out his hand like a child demanding candy. "Gimme."

It wasn't worth having an argument that I was bound to lose, so I handed him the bag. He inhaled deeply and sighed.

"This is the good shit. Do you mind if I partake?"

"Sure," I said. "As long as it comes off my bill."

He cocked his head and gave me a hurt puppy-dog look. "I thought this was just a friendly smoke session between friends, man. Why bring money into it?"

"Oh, you mean like when a 'friend' asks to borrow *thirty-five cents* for the laundry, and his 'friend' puts it on his bill? That kind of friend?"

"I see. So it's going to be like that?"

"Yeah, it's going to be like that."

He gave a long-suffering sigh. "Fine, but I don't like this side of you, Sam. Very materialistic."

"Whatever. Roll the damn joint."

He produced a pack of rolling papers from somewhere on his person I didn't want to think about, sat down on the couch, and set to work. Clumsy and pachyderm-like in every other aspect of his life, the Mayor was a virtuoso when it came to rolling a joint. His fat sausage fingers suddenly became supple and graceful, and they danced over the coffee table like Baryshnikov pirouetting across the stage at Carnegie Hall. In less than two minutes, he was pinching a perfect fattie between his thumb and index finger, delicately suckling the end of it like a piglet at its mother's teat, and expelling great gasps of greenish-gray smoke. I watched in amazement as he finished the entire joint in five tokes and started to roll another.

"Okay," I said. "I think that's enough. What's this urgent message? I've got things to do."

Behind his back, I saw Audrey poke her nose out from under the bed and look up at the window. She was going to make a run for it soon, and I had ro clear a path for her and distract the Mayor or all hell was going to break loose.

"What are you looking at?" he replied, glancing over his shoulder.

"None of your business. Did I tell you about this cover story I'm working on for the paper. Very hush-hush."

"Is this about that stripper that died over at the Pink Door?"

My jaw dropped before I could stop it. "Her name was Rebecca Kint. And how did you hear about it?"

The Mayor shot me a smug look. "You forget I used to run this city. Nothing happens around here I don't know about it, man."

"You've been talking to that guy in two-oh-seven, right? What's his name? John or Jim or Jack." I waved my hand in front of my face and wrinkled my nose. "This stuff is really potent. I'm going to crack a window. Do you mind?"

The Mayor shrugged. "His name is Jake, and he's a reliable source."

I opened the window just far enough for Audrey to squeeze through and returned to my spot in front of the couch. Now all I had to do was keep him occupied long enough for Audrey to make her getaway. "Right. He still works for the sanitation department?"

The Mayor stroked his beard. "They tried to pick up the cans yesterday morning, and the alley was full of cops."

I shook my head. "This really is a small town sometimes. You probably heard about the murder before I did."

"Murder? I thought it was an accident."

I shrugged. "Maybe. Maybe not. I just had a meeting with the editor about it. And the publisher."

I knew I shouldn't be sharing this information, but there was no better way to divert the Mayor's attention than a juicy bit of gossip topped with a drizzle of conspiracy. Audrey's head appeared again and she saw the open window. I made eye contact with her and attempted to communicate the urgency of the situation telepathically.

The Mayor finished rolling the second joint and lit it with my lighter. "Let me guess. They tried to pull you off the story."

I turned my head quickly. "How did you know that?"

He gave me a patronizing smile. "This ain't my first rodeo, cowboy. That's how cover-ups work." He started listing items. "Number one, something happens that the powers that be don't want the public knowin' about. Number two, said powers attempt to cover up the event through various nefarious and illegal permutations. Number C, some honest citizen starts poking around where the powers don't want to be poked. And the last number is your number's up, man. This is just like what the Kennedys did to poor Marilyn."

"Monroe? I thought she overdosed."

Audrey was completely in the open now, eyes focused with hatred on the back of the Mayor's head while she crept silently toward the window.

The Mayor snorted. "Yeah, and the CIA didn't know about 9/11. If she ingested the pills, as the coroner claimed, why was her stomach empty, man? If she died alone, how did someone administer an enema hours before her demise? And where was the yellow residue from the Nembutal capsules, huh?"

I held my breath as Audrey crouched low to the carpet, twitched her tail several times, and then leapt onto the window sill, landing quiet as a ghost less than four feet from the Mayor's head. He seemed to notice something in his peripheral vision, but before he could look, I waved my arms in the air and raised my voice.

"But I just talked to the police chief today!" I said. "He confirmed the initial report! Rebecca Kint slipped and hit her head. Simple as that. I'm sorry but I don't see how there could be a conspiracy involved."

The Mayor hated Henry, and I knew the mere mention of his title would send him into a blind tirade. It worked like a charm.

"Moss? Are you kidding me?" he cried. "You're listening to the pigs now, man! Oh, wow! Oh, wow! Let me tell you a little story about your new best friend, Hitler Moss. Are you listening, man?"

"Yeah, I'm listening."

Instead of making her escape, Audrey now sat on the window sill staring at me in an oddly forlorn manner. I widened my eyes and jerked my head to the side, telling her to get a move on, but she just blinked and continued to look at me, as if attempting to pass along some macabre message that my idiotic human brain was not capable of deciphering. Her eyes were calm and spooky, and for some reason I got the feeling she was saying goodbye. I tried to tell her I loved her and she was being dramatic, but I didn't have the same ability to communicate with my eyes.

Finally, the Mayor heaved himself into a standing position, and that broke the trance. His massive bulk was in my line of sight, and by the time I could safely check the window again, Audrey was gone.

"Okay, okay. Where do I start? Oh, wow!" The Mayor and I had switched places. I was settling onto the couch and he was pacing up and down the length of my apartment, which was only about three steps. "About five years ago, man, I came across several hundred documents regarding the poll results from the fraudulent election that ended my political career. Remember that little doozie? Okay? Don't ask me where I got them from because I can't tell you. I *can* tell you that the information was never published by the so-called newspapers in this city. I *can* tell you that the documents in question contained disturbing evidence that I was being monitored both locally and nationally by various governmental organizations after I turned this city on its head by winning the mayoral race. I *can* tell you that said documents were retrieved through extra-legal means that I will not go into at this time. Any of this getting through, man? Oh, wow! Anyhow, less than two months after receiving these documents, guess who comes knocking on my door? That's right. Your best friend in the whole world, that's who. And he says he's arresting me for—get this—failure to pay child support. Now why do you suppose that happened?"

"Because you failed to pay child support?"

The Mayor stabbed the air with his finger. "Sure, okay, fine. Was there a paternity test? Yes. Did it come back positive? That's what *they* said. But I wasn't in the room when *they* processed that DNA. Were you? No, you were not. And neither was I, man. And neither was that bastard Moss, so he can just go right to hell for all I care. It's just awful convenient, that's what I think. It's awful convenient that he decides to arrest me for some trumped-up charge right *after* I receive concrete evidence of election tampering in this fair city. And then, after I get out of jail, and I get back to my room, where do you think those documents are? Gone. Just gone, man. I couldn't find them anywhere. The janitor *said* he came into my room while I was gone to take out the trash because people were complaining about the smell, but I don't have video footage of what he did in there. Awful convenient, man, that's what I think. That's what I think about your buddy Hitler Moss. He's a convenient son of a bitch, that's what I think."

"Alright, settle down," I said.

"I'll settle down when I'm dead." He took a long hit from the joint and shook his head. "You can't trust the police in this situation, that's my point. You can't trust anyone. Now tell me what happened. What's your little story about? What's the lowdown? The inside scoop? I can't help you unless I know the details."

I bit my lip and looked out the window. I'd always thought of the Mayor as a bit of crackpot, but it was true he had occupied the highest levels of government in Mountainview and dedicated his life to understanding the political machinations of the city, especially its dark underbelly. In a situation like this, you couldn't always rely on mainstream resources for honest information. That's the thing Victoria didn't understand. She was a good journalist, sure, but she followed the rules. Sometimes you had to break the rules to get things done, everyone knew that. What if Glenn Ford had followed the rules in *The Big Heat*? Then Lee Marvin would have gotten away with the murder of Jocelyn Brando and the crime syndicate would have remained in control of the city. Yeah, the Mayor was a little out there, but that didn't mean he was completely wrong. If the Larkmans were expanding their operation, it made sense they'd need someone on the inside to cover their tracks. And who better than an ambitious police chief? At the very least, I could bounce my theories off the Mayor and see where it went.

"Alright," I said, leaning back and motioning for the Mayor to take a seat. He ignored me, instead choosing to continue his pacing, the smoke from the joint puffing out of his mouth like an old-timey train. "I'm going to give you the dirt, but what I'm about to say doesn't leave this room."

He gave me an offended look. "Of course."

"I mean it. This is just between you and me. *Mono y mono*. This can't get back to my boss."

"Who you think you're talking to, man? Where were you during the Berkley riots? Where were you when Medgar Evers got shot? I'll tell you where I was. Fighting for your freedoms on the picket lines, that's where I was."

"Okay, Jesus. I'm just saying."

"That's what's wrong with your generation. You don't know how to keep secrets. All the social media and the twittering. Don't worry about me. You just give me the details, and let's go get these bastards."

So I told him everything. I told him about the conversation I had with Victoria and how Gerald wanted to make me the new editor of the newspaper. I told him about the amusing blog post I made later on that night at the MIFF. (I skipped the part about waking up in River's bed the next morning, as it did not seem relevant.) I told him about my visit to the Pink Door and the meeting with Mouth, during which she had committed an act of violence against my person. I told him about the needle I found behind the dumpster. I told him how Henry was waiting for me outside the club and the conversation we had in his car. I told him about the meeting in Gerald's office, how Victoria and Reyna ambushed me and Gerald came to my defense. While I spoke, we smoked two more joints, and the Mayor did not interrupt. He was quiet for the first time since I met him, only pausing once in a while to offer a wry chuckle or a knowing nod.

"So that's it," I said when I was done. "What do you think?"

"I think you're knee-deep in a pile of shit and you lost your paddle."

"It's that bad?"

He laughed. "Bad? You've got the whole system after you, man. The cops, the media, the government, the mob. Hell, throw the CIA in there, and you'll have your face up on a post office wall."

I put my head in my hands. "So it is bad. Do you think I should drop the story? I could tell them to give it to someone else. That's what they want."

He reached down and grabbed me by the shoulders. "Are you kidding? Did Woodward and Bernstein drop the story? Did Julian Assange say 'Aw shucks, let someone else handle this'? This is great. You have them right where you want them. They're on the run. You can't stop now. What you need to do is push harder."

"I don't know."

"Ah, Christ on a cracker. Look at you, man." He started talking in a high, whiny voice. "*Everything is so hard. The big bad police are after me, and I just want to sit on my butt all day and watch movies.* Your generation makes me sick."

"Fine," I said, pulling away from his fat fingers. "But I don't have any real evidence. All we know so far is that a woman died from a head wound. That's it."

"Evidence?" The Mayor scoffed. "Look at your eye. It's four different colors. I'd say that's evidence. Did or did not your editor try to pull you off the story? That's evidence. Why was a cop following you around? Seems to me you've got all kinds of evidence. You've got them on the ropes, Ali. They don't know what to think. Hot damn, man, I didn't know you had it in you. And you've got at least one friend on your side. This publisher fella... what's his name."

"Gerald."

"That's the one. It sounds like he's got your back. To hell with the rest of them. In fact, anything they tell you, just do the opposite and you'll probably be fine. You need to follow up on these leads, man. What's your next move? Where are you going next?"

"Oh, shit," I said. I looked at my phone. "I need to go."

"That's the spirit!"

"No, no." I pushed him toward the exit. "I mean I really need to go. I have an appointment."

When we got to the door, he planted his feet and placed his hands on both sides of the door frame. "You know, you still owe me sixteen-hundred and forty-seven dollars."

"What happened to the thirty-five cents?"

He ignored me. "It doesn't have to be money, per se. You have other items to trade."

"Damnit." I picked up the bag on the table, removed approximately half, and held the offering in front of me. The Mayor smiled and cupped his hands under mine.

"This makes us even on the drugs," I said.

"What?" The Mayor shook his head. "No way, man. I gave you an ounce. This is half at best."

"You gave me an ounce of ditch weed. This is grade-A shit, and you know it. Two-hundred off my tab or no deal."

The Mayor looked at my face and then looked down at the weed.

"Okay, deal."

I dropped the marijuana into his greedy palms, and he let out a gleeful squeal. He carefully placed the weed into a secret inside pocket on his kimono.

"I almost forgot," he said, pulling a white piece of paper from the same pocket. "Some woman came by today and knocked on your door. I told her you weren't home and she said to give you this."

"What woman?" I asked, pinching the damp piece of paper between my thumb and index finger.

He shrugged. "I don't know, man. Didn't give her name."

"What did she look like?"

"She looked…" The Mayor held his hands in front of his chest, palms up, as if holding an invisible puppy. "…womanly."

"That's it? She had big breasts. Nothing about hair color, eye color, height, age?"

He wrinkled his brow and stepped into the hallway. "Do I look like a police sketch artist to you?" he said as he made his way to the bathroom. "She looked like a woman. She gave me that note. You're welcome, by the way."

"Yeah, thanks," I said. "Your attention to detail is impressive."

I closed the door and opened the note. There was no name inside, just four words written in blocky capitals: I HAVE THE FILE.

Chapter 14: Casablanca

THE MOVIE WAS BEING SHOWN IN THE BASEMENT OF MORTON HALL, a crumbling gothic cathedral of a structure on the far east end of campus, hidden away from the rest of the college like a knocked-up daughter sent to live with distant relatives, past the new dome-shaped science building, past the hulking monolithic residence halls, past the music library and the freshman cafeteria and the tennis courts and the swampy trench the university tour guides insisted on calling a "duck pond" despite the fact that mosquitos and salamanders were the only creatures that could survive its fetid waters.

Almost ten years ago, as giggling, stoned sophomores, Eric and I had shot our first short film in that murky puddle, a seventeen-minute horror flick called *The Professor That Wouldn't Die*, which featured Eric as the zombified Professor Loveless, yours truly as his trusty lab assistant, Hugo, and more dry ice than three Ed Wood movies combined. We had not yet met Maggie, and our friendship was still pure, based on our mutual love of old movies, marijuana, and 2 a.m. conversations about our favorite William Castle productions over shitty cups of coffee in the 7/11 parking lot.

Before I met Eric, I was not doing well in college. The classes weren't the problem. I've never been accused of overachievement, but when it comes to academics, I have always been right of center on the bell curve, coasting safely downhill in C-plus/B-minus territory. No, it was the social scene I couldn't get a handle on. In high school, everyone knew me as the kid whose mother committed suicide, a designation that came with the type of mystique that automatically attracted some people and repelled others with no particular effort on my part, but in college I was no one. I tried out for different parts— Cool Nerd, Loveable Stoner, Sensitive Guy with Goatee Who Sits Alone in the Cafeteria Reading *Siddhartha*—but I didn't get any callbacks.

After spending two semesters in my dorm room living on Kraft Singles and watching every old movie in the film library's classics section, the loneliness evolved into serious depression. I lost ten pounds, which on my already-slim frame looked particularly unhealthy, and I attended classes sporadically. My roommate was a towel-snapping frat boy who, two weeks after orientation, moved his belongings into the Delta house, so I had the whole place to myself. I kept the curtains closed and the door locked. When the RA came by to ask how I was doing or invite me to events, I cracked the door and answered her chipper inquiries with terse dismissals. Eventually, she stopped coming by at all, and even though I hated her clumsy attempts to suss out the cause of my unhappiness, I missed her when she was gone. I stopped shaving and seldom showered. In order to stay stoned all day and complete my transformation into my father, I rigged up a system for smoking weed in the room that involved several fans, a bottle of Old Spice, and a plastic pipe that ran out the window. The room smelled terrible but not of marijuana. I felt like Vincent Price in *The Last Man on Earth*, a hopeless fool living alone in a manufactured American paradise, yearning for human contact and surrounded by monsters that hated and feared him. That's the state I was in when I met Eric.

It was Friday evening and I'd just changed into my pajamas in preparation for an all-night Peter Lorre marathon when I heard a soft, insistent tapping sound. At first I thought someone was knocking on my suitemate's door. He was a thick-necked goon with an easy-going Spencer Tracy charm that I envied, and people were always stopping by to invite him to parties or ask if he wanted to join their intramural Frisbee golf team. Almost a full minute passed before I heard the knock again, still quiet but somehow more determined, as though the person on the other side wanted me to know they would stand there all night if necessary. When I opened the door, I was greeted by a giant praying mantis with round coke-bottle glasses magnifying green-yellow eyes that never seemed to blink, a thick black flattop, and a galaxy of angry zits orbiting a pointy chin.

"Are you the one who checked out *Black Angel*?" asked the mantis. Like his body, his voice was thin and reminiscent of an insect, the unrelenting buzz of a locust formed into monosyllabic words.

"I just put it in," I answered.

He looked down at his shoes, shifted his weight from left foot to right several times, and cracked his engorged knuckles. In the months that followed, I would come to recognize this as the trademark dance Eric Cross performed when he was nervous but resolute in his purpose. "Mind if I join you?" he asked.

I shrugged consent but inwardly I was doing cartwheels at the thought of human company, any company, even this strange bug-like boy-man. Eric's arms and legs were skeletal sticks, and he had to sort of stoop down and fold his body to get through the doorway. Once inside, he immediately stretched his six-foot, four-inch frame out on the dung-colored carpet and did not move from that position until the movie was over. When it was finished, he awkwardly refolded his body into a standing position and started toward the door without saying goodbye or making eye contact.

"Wait!" I said a little too desperately.

Eric turned around, his eyes focused on his giant toboggan-shaped feet. I didn't have anything else to say; I just didn't want him to go. So I asked the lamest of all movie questions.

"How did you like it?"

Without pausing, he held up his left fist and began listing his critique points, raising a boney white finger for each one. "The script was a five, the directing was a four, and the cinematography was a six."

"What about Peter Lorre?" I asked.

He looked directly at me for the first time and grinned, displaying a set of teeth so crooked they were cartoonish. "Peter Lorre is *always* a ten."

From that point on we were inseparable. Eric was in the film program and I was a creative writing major, but we managed to plan our schedules so we could eat all our meals together and spend every minute of our free time watching movies. Eric lived off-campus in a rundown suburban ranch house with a small cabal of gloomy art and theater majors who paid rent by putting money in a jar labeled TIPS that sat on the dining table. The number of residents in the house changed from week to week and no one seemed to know whose name was on the lease, but somehow the bills always got paid.

By the end of the semester, I'd abandoned my lonely dorm room and started adding my own sweaty bills and pocket change to the tip jar. My new room was a cramped attic loft I shared with a dozen dusty storage boxes and a family of mice that danced a scratchy rodent tango inside the walls at all hours of the night. The floor was warped and the ceiling pitched to accommodate the upside down V of the roof, making the space disorienting and otherworldly, like an enchanted tree house. There was no insulation. In the summer I slept naked, and in the winter I wore two coats and a ski mask to bed. The one perk was the enormous dormer windows on the west side of the room that opened up to a rooftop perch that comfortably accommodated two lawn chairs and a wobbly end table, on which, like circus performers, we balanced an overflowing ashtray and a small tower of empty alcohol receptacles. Eric and I spent countless evenings on the roof of that house smoking weed and talking about movies while the sun lowered its fiery head to the bosom of the Rocky Mountains in the distance.

I was in that old house, haunting its attic like a stoned spector, when I received the news that my dad was dead. Since my grandparents were all gone and there were no siblings on either side of the family, I was the next of kin. The Denver Police Department called Mountainview PD, and Henry showed up at the door, dressed in officer blues, to inform me of the incident and take me to identify the body. On the drive back, I was practically comatose, and Henry kindly filled the silence for both of us. In a careful, professional voice, he told me that he knew my mother briefly in high school, and then, after I failed to respond, he spoke at length about the deaths of his own parents. When he dropped me off, he gave me his card and suggested I see a grief counselor, which I never did.

After that, I threw myself completely into writing and making movies with Eric. It had always been a passion, but now it became an obsession, an outlet for the grief I couldn't face and the creeping feeling of hysteria that haunted my waking hours. I began to drink and smoke heavily, which was barely noticed in the liberal arts culture where we circulated. I threw myself into the work.

Behind the house there was an old unused woodshed where Eric set up a small theater and editing room that smelled like mushrooms and gym socks, just large enough for five people, although Eric and I were usually its only occupants. We ran extension cords through the kitchen window of the main house to power the digital projector Eric had found in a dumpster behind Best Buy, as well as a fan or a space heater, depending on the season. The screen was a white bedsheet stretched tight and tacked to the wall. We boarded up the only window to block out the light, and from the basement of the house we commandeered a floral-printed camelback couch that had been ruined by cigarette smoke and cat piss. It was the finest movie-watching experience imaginable. The woodshed was a time machine that shut out the real world and took us back to the Golden Age of Hollywood in a way no crowded movie theater or living room television ever could. When we were in that smelly pitch-black shed, the modern world ceased to exist. We were no longer watching the movie, we were *in* the movie, *of* the movie—we were God's own voyeurs. We watched Cagney leer, Astaire dance, Monroe wink, and Garbo slouch. We were in cinema heaven.

Of course, we watched modern movies, as well, but I remember little of them. Don't get me wrong, I'm not discerning enough to be a snob. I like movies with explosions and car chases and romance—I just prefer them to have been made half a century ago. Seeing Brad Pitt and Angelina Jolie try to kill one another in *Mr. and Mrs. Smith* was downright boring after seeing Richard Burton and Elizabeth Taylor rip each other's guts out in *Who's Afraid of Virginia Wolf?* Eric said I was a romantic fool, but I didn't care. "It's not real," he would say. "Those painted backdrops, the vivid Technicolor. There's no realism. You're thinking of it as part of history, but that history never existed. It's nostalgia for a dream that was never ours in the first place." To which I would inevitably reply, "None of it is real. It's a bunch of people playing dress up in front of a camera. At least those old movies don't try to pretend they're real. They know they're creating a made-up world. When you think about it, that's more authentic than the so-called 'realism' in your precious indie movies." That usually shut him up for an hour or two.

The fights were almost as much fun as the movies. We sparred back and forth, testing one another's cinema knowledge, probing for weaknesses, making the type of grandiose statements only naïve would-be intellectuals can say without blushing at their own hubris. The arguments carried over into our creative projects. In those days, I wrote poorly but constantly, never pausing to consider how I might improve a piece, just finishing it and moving on to the next thing, like a shark, afraid that I'd die if I stopped moving. I had an old Olivetti typewriter in my room with such smooth key action that, when I was on a roll, sounded like a Civil War battlefield in full swing. I wrote short stories, poems, songs, plays—it didn't matter. Some were for class but most were just for my own amusement. My most rewarding projects were the scripts I wrote for Eric.

Eric had no imagination for original material, but he did possess a relentless analytic mind capable of taking someone else's half-formed story and shaving off the extraneous parts, sharpening the characters, defining the plot, until the end result was something sleek and fast instead of the lumbering cliché monsters that I generally churned out. I would hand him a fifty-page script on Monday and by Wednesday he'd have reduced it to seven pages of sharpened dialogue and action.

"But you took out the backstory," I would whine. "There's no description, no details. You gutted it."

"I know," Eric would answer coolly, his mantis eyes never wavering. "You didn't need any of that stuff. You were just showing off. This is the story. This is what we want to shoot. Now go back and write it again."

And I would, and of course, he would be right. I came to rely on Eric's brutal criticism more than the feedback from any classmate or professor. He never let me off the hook, never allowed me to cheat in my storytelling. Eric was sparse with praise, but when he gave it, it really meant something. When he raised an eyebrow and tapped the page with his finger (his usual response to a particularly well-written sentence), I'd know that I had impressed him, and my chest would tighten with pride. It was the only time I felt good about myself.

After the writing was done, it was Eric who did most of the work. I tagged along, carrying cameras, setting up lights, etc., but when it came down to the technicalities of filmmaking, I didn't have much patience. At first, I thought it would be exciting to shoot movies, but Eric found ways to suck all the fun out of it. If I wrote a big shoot-out scene in which twelve people get riddled with machine gun fire, Eric had to ruin it by spending five hours worrying about the consistency of the fake blood and choreographing the death scenes so that the actors fell at realistic angles. Sure, it looked great when it was finished, but did anyone in the audience actually care whether the villain's head flew back and to the left when he got his brains blown out? I didn't think so, but this was the type of minutia Eric wouldn't let go. Months later we would be sitting at the breakfast table eating cereal, and he would suddenly throw his spoon down in disgust, splashing milk and Froot Loops all over the place. "Damnit, I should have used a second camera on that car-chase scene in *To Have and to Kill*! Why did I let you talk me out of it? We have to reshoot." And then he would go back and reshoot the scene—even though the movie had already been shown and no one was ever going to see the new scene except the two of us.

It was early in our junior year that we met Maggie. I had just finished a script for a mobster movie in which the female lead, who was verbally and physically abused by the leader of the gang, ended up double-crossing everyone and taking Tarantino-like revenge on her abuser before splitting town with the money. After seven rewrites, Eric was finally satisfied with it, and we proceeded to casting. As usual, casting was exciting at first but quickly became dull as the usual parade of eager theater majors answered the call, reading from the script in an overly dramatic and loud fashion more suitable for the stage than the camera.

Maggie was a freshman majoring in literature, and she'd heard about the auditions from her suitemate who thought she would be perfect for the part. She'd never acted before, but she always wanted to try. After all, wasn't that what college was all about? Having new experiences? Becoming a different person?

I barely heard anything she said. As soon as she walked in the room, I stopped breathing. She looked exactly like my mother. Or, to be more precise, she looked exactly like the one photograph of my mother that I stole from my father's scrapbook when I left home. In the picture, my mother was in her early twenties, still single, standing in a field of wildflowers somewhere in Middle America, the setting sun casting a shadow on the right side of her face and lighting up the left side in an ethereal glow, the hem of her blue cotton dress lifted flirtatiously by the wind. Maggie was wearing a similar dress, and her hair was the same color of sun-streaked ochre, cascading over her shoulders at exactly the right angle.

I remember little of her actual audition, but she must have been impressive because Eric didn't argue when he saw her name at the top of my list. However, he was reluctant to put our first hour-long film in the hands of a novice English major who might suddenly decide she had to study for a midterm or attend some fraternity party on a whim instead of spending her weekends pretending to get shot by a man with an eye patch in an alley behind Conoco. In the end, we played it safe and cast Maggie in a minor role as the pampered, adolescent daughter of the mob boss. Although she only had three scenes and four lines, she was ecstatic to be in the movie at all, and when we finally premiered the film to an audience of twenty students (the usual film and theater majors, and a small, noisy gaggle of Maggie's friends who came to cheer her on) it was obvious to all that Maggie stole every scene she was in. Her makeup was ridiculous, her costume didn't fit, and her hair was all wrong for the part, but when the camera moved in for a close-up, your heart stopped for a split second. She had something, that "it factor," whatever the hell that meant. She had *it*, and in a place like Mountainview, *it* was a rare thing.

From that day forward, every script I wrote was for Maggie Chase, and when she left me, I stopped writing movies.

THE DOORS WERE CLOSED WHEN I ARRIVED AT THE THEATER, but after showing my press pass to an indignant volunteer with the creature from *Creature from the Black Lagoon* tattooed on her forearm and then browbeating her into submission, I was allowed to slip unnoticed into one of the empty seats in the back. The theater sat one-fifty and they'd managed to fill up the first five rows, an impressive turnout for one of these events considering the fact that there were currently two dozen other movies being shown by the MIFF at locations around town much more conveniently located and alcohol-friendly than this one. I recognized a few audience members several rows in front of me as students and professors from the past, no doubt here to kiss some Hollywood ass. It made me sick. I was surprised to see River there, near the front right, chatting loudly with an attractive Henry Fonda look-alike next to her. I scooted down in my seat, but I needn't have bothered. As usual, she was too engrossed in her own conversation to pay any attention to her surroundings. River often came to the MIFF parties, but I had never seen her at an actual movie. Her presence couldn't be a coincidence, but I didn't have time to dwell on it. I strained to spot Maggie and Eric, who surely had reserved seats in front, but there were too many strange heads in the way and I couldn't be sure which ones belonged to the traitors.

The film had not yet begun. The house lights were on and there was an elderly man standing in front of the audience wearing a tweed jacket and fire-engine red tennis shoes, the unruly cotton ball of curly white hair on his head bouncing excitedly as he spoke into a microphone. His name was Archibald Finch, and he was the most beloved professor in the film department. At the sight of his Burgess Meredith nose and Clark Gable ears, my heart did a nostalgic somersault.

"On the first day of class, I always ask my freshmen students the same question," Professor Finch said, his tiny head bobbing like a happy chicken, a physical tic he displayed during his lectures when he got excited. "'What do all great filmmakers have in common?' There is no right answer to the question, but it starts off a lively discussion about the art of filmmaking. Normally the students say things like 'talent,' 'vision,' or 'intellect.' All perfectly reasonable answers, if a bit dull. The pretentious ones might say 'gravitas.' The cynical ones, thinking they are clever, always say 'money.' When I asked Eric Cross this question, he said, 'They keep working when everyone else goes home.' That was when I knew Mr. Cross would make movies. I did not yet know what kind of movies he would make or how good they would be, but I knew he would have the perseverance and fortitude to bring his cinematic vision to life."

Professor Finch then went on to list all of the accomplishments Eric had achieved since leaving college, which was an impressive list, even though I couldn't help thinking it was a bit embellished. There were editing awards for advertisements, producer credits for internet shows no one had ever heard of, cinematography work for the California Tourism Commission, and blah-blah-blah. Afterward, he moved on to Maggie and listed every improv show and Shakespeare in the Park production she had ever appeared in. I was surprised and grudgingly impressed to learn that Maggie had been an informant in an episode of *CSI* and she had lines in an upcoming Richard Linklater movie. None of this changed the fact that she was a no good two-timing cheater, of course, but it was unexpected, nonetheless.

I still couldn't spot Maggie and Eric, but Professor Finch kept directing his comments toward the center of the front row, and I shifted my attention over there, boring a hole in the back of every nodding, self-satisfied head I could find with my venomous gaze. I imagined red beams shooting out of my eyes and those heads bursting one by one into flames. I imagined Professor Finch shrugging his shoulders nonplussed at the exploded brain matter and saying, "And now, let me direct your attention to the person who is *actually* responsible for this film... the brilliant, the incomparable Mr. Samuel Drift." Professor Finch would make a sweeping gesture to the back of the room, and a spotlight would appear on me. I would shake my head and attempt to ignore the acknowledgement, but the spontaneous burst of applause from the crowd would thwart my attempt at humility, and I would be forced to stand and take a bow.

Before I could even start my celebratory speech, however, the house lights dimmed and the movie began to play.

The opening scene was one of those moody, underwater, indie-film shots of a man diving to the bottom of a swimming pool and looking up at the undulating faces of the people on the surface, while the requisite folksy band played plinky-plunk acoustic guitar music in the background and a woman with a shy, warbling voice sang about being lonely in a crowded room. The waves on the surface bent the sunlight at odd angles, and the audience was made to wonder what exactly this man was doing underneath the water. Was this a recreational swim, or were there thoughts of suicide involved? It was all very symbolic.

And it was all very wrong.

This was exactly the type of thing Eric and I used to argue about. He was always trying to inject some sort of larger meaning into the script, as though the plot itself wasn't enough to keep audiences watching. He had an M. Night Shyamalan problem.

It took almost five minutes for the man to surface from the swimming pool—shocker, he didn't drown himself—and the movie finally got underway.

I had to admit, after the whole underwater fiasco, the plot moved pretty well. There's a young man working the overnight desk shift in a four-star hotel, and he has ambitions to one day become a high-class gentleman just like the people he's forced to grovel to for tips. One night, a wealthy businessman who is a regular guest of the hotel checks in with his young, attractive mistress. At two o'clock in the morning, the businessman calls down to the front desk in a panic. The desk clerk goes up to the room and finds the mistress on the bathroom floor with a pool of blood around her head. The businessman claims she slipped in the shower, and he begs the desk worker to help him cover up the accident. He's afraid his wife will discover his infidelity. He's willing to pay the clerk handsomely for his services. After some negotiating, the clerk finally complies, and they clean up the blood. The clerk disables several security cameras and uses a large rolling laundry cart to smuggle the body down to the parking garage in the basement. However, as he's putting the body in the trunk of his car, the girl's hand moves. She's still alive. The clerk doesn't know what to do. He locks her in his trunk, returns to the front desk, and nervously completes his shift. Afterward, he drives back to his crappy one-bedroom apartment, and lugs the girl to his bed, where he proceeds to clean her wounds and care for her. She's unconscious for several days, and during that time, the clerk falls madly in love with her. When she wakes up, the girl explains that what happened in the hotel wasn't an accident after all. There was an argument and the businessmen pushed her, which caused her to fall and hit her head. She thanks the clerk for saving her, and they have passionate (and slightly disturbing) sex. Afterward, the clerk and the mistress hatch a plan to blackmail the businessman.

Maggie played the mistress, of course. It was shocking to see her on the screen again after all those lost years, beautiful and charismatic and electrifying. Her natural mousy brown hair had been dyed a more cinematic chestnut, and she'd lost almost twenty pounds that she didn't need to lose, trading in her curvy girl-next-door figure for a more raw sexual appeal. Every time I saw her, a bolt of excitement and anger shot through my loins, on one occasion causing me to twitch so hard I accidentally kicked the seat in front of me, earning the annoyed half-turn side-eye from its scarved, mustachioed occupant. The scene in which she was found unconscious on the bathroom floor was particularly vexing, as she was wearing nothing but a thin cotton nightgown, the strap falling just so off her freckled right shoulder, exposing the slightest hint of rosy areola. I fished around my pocket until I found another Oxy and washed it down with whiskey from my flask.

The desk clerk was played by a pale, intense young man who'd built a typecast reputation as the "weird friend" in various cancelled sitcoms and indie movies over the past five years. He was stunningly handsome, but there was something slightly off about his features. It was hard to pin down—the blue Paul Newman eyes set too close together, the pouty Tony Curtis lips sneeringly off-center—but it had impeded his ability to land leading roles. Still, I could not fathom how Eric had managed to talk a recognizable actor into appearing in such a small movie. My heart filled with equal parts awe and jealousy.

It pained me to admit it, but it was a good movie. Really good, in fact. The plot was tight, the acting was strong, the cinematography was fantastic (there was a scene toward the end when the desk clerk and the mistress are standing in the hotel's mezzanine while the sun rises in the background that took my breath away). But aside from all that, there was a sense of desperate longing in the movie that came from no particular character or scene, it just seemed to emanate from the screen itself, an aura of haunted beauty that I recognized in the partnership between Eric and Maggie. They'd made something truly wonderful, and I hated them for it.

As the movie ended and the final credits rolled, the wounds were opened afresh when I saw the words "Written and Directed by Eric Cross" appear, followed, to my surprise, by "Story by Sam Drift and Eric Cross." It was impossible to describe how it felt to see my name on a movie screen like that. There was a flood of giddy excitement and vertigo, almost as if the layers of reality around me were being bent and readjusted to make room for the monumental shift in my perception of the world, followed quickly by intense anger as I realized the only reason Eric had included this pointless acknowledgment was as a bribe to prevent me from exposing the truth. Well, it wasn't going to work.

The house lights came on and the room erupted in enthusiastic, sincere applause that lasted a full minute. Afterward, Professor Finch returned to his position at the front of the room, gently wiping his eyes, standing alone in front of the audience in silence for a long beat before he gained the composure to speak.

"As my students know, I am seldom at a loss for words," he said. A consensual tittering trickled through the room. "I did not expect to be so moved by the film," Finch continued.

"It is of course the height of hubris to claim any part in its making, but I consider it a great honor that I once had this young man in my classroom, asking questions that would eventually, even in a minor way, influence the course of his art. It will take me days to process it all and I will need to watch it several more times, but in this movie, I saw aspects of some of the great directors—Kubrick, Hitchcock, Bergman, Welles—all of which Mr. Cross expressed interest in as a student." Here he turned to someone seated in the front row, and I recognized the back of Eric's head for the first time.

"Thank you for allowing us to take part in your vision, Mr. Cross. It was truly a pleasure. And Ms. Chase, your performance was divine." Professor Finch looked back to the audience and seemed a bit embarrassed. "But you don't want to hear the ramblings of an old hack like me. Let's get the auteurs up here to speak for themselves."

He motioned for Eric and Maggie to join him at a long table set up at the front of the room with several microphones sitting on it. When Eric stood up, I had a moment of nostalgic déjà vu, remembering those gawky long limbs unfolding at awkward angles. But I was surprised to see that some of the awkwardness was gone, along with the flattop haircut and acne. Eric now sported a gorgeous head of curly black hair that fell in gentle waves to his shoulders, and he'd traded in his clunky Coke-bottle glasses for a sleek pair of expensive frames. Dressed all in black from his designer skinny jeans to his fitted sport coat, he looked like the singer of some nerdy band with a cult following. However, just when I thought I'd imagined the goofy insect friend of my college years, he tripped over his own feet on his way to the front and performed a graceless tap dance to regain his balance. "Oops," he said when he finally found his way to the chair, his face flushed with embarrassment. Maggie displayed no such pratfall on her way to the front of the room. She'd always been graceful, but now she possessed a new confidence, something that could be seen in the playful swing of her hips and the almost dancer-like way she twirled into her chair, expertly crossing her legs and smoothing out her pants in one motion. Fortunately, she was not wearing a dress with chickens on it. I don't think my poor heart could have taken it.

Finch leaned in close to the microphone in front of him. "We will now have a question and answer period. There's no time limit here, but I would ask that you restrict yourself to just one or two questions per person. There is a microphone in the aisle on the right. If you would like to ask a question about the film, please line up and your questions will be answered in the order they are presented."

There was a short pause, and then half a dozen audience members stood and began the awkward crabwalk journey to the aisle, where a young woman with an official-looking lanyard stood protectively next to a microphone stand. Somehow the flock of cinema nerds all reached the microphone at the same time, and there was a brief moment of polite jostling before a clear winner emerged, bald of head and middle of age, a dandelion-yellow scarf wrapped jauntily about his pencil neck and a pair of enormous Charles Nelson Riley glasses magnifying eyes as flat and brown as tarnished pennies. His name was Wallace J. Mullholland III, but to his eternal annoyance, everyone called him Wally. He was a minor functionary in the university's film library, but he'd attended every student film on campus for the past three decades, doling out unsolicited criticism afterward as though the future of Mountainview's thriving cinema scene depended on his keen insights. In college, he had attended all of our movies, and after every one, he cornered Eric and I to discuss what he called "the inconsistencies in your artistic choices." Rumor had it that he had once been a film student at MU himself but had dropped out after a particularly scathing critique from a professor of one of his movies and landed in library sciences.

"Good evening," said Wally. "My name is Wallace J. Mullholland the third, and I write for an award-winning cinema publication."

Oh, yes. He also had a blog called *Waiting for Godard*, in which he wrote three-thousand-word rants about French experimentalism and the death of American cinema that no one read. The award he'd won was for a translation clarification in the subtitles of a short German film I'd never heard of. Apparently, the student director who made the film was grateful and convinced his university in Munich to bestow an award as a thank you.

"There are a few continuity issues that I would like to address in the film," he continued. "Is that alright with you? I assume you are open to criticism from colleagues."

Eric clenched his jaw and leaned down to speak into the microphone. "Sure, Wally," he said. "Go right ahead."

There was some immature snickering as Wally sputtered at the shortened version of his name, but he recovered quickly with a snappy scarf flip and began a long rambling series of accusations.

"Regarding aesthetic consistency, let me draw your attention to the first act, fourth scene, in which the protagonist drinks from a red coffee mug with the hotel's logo presumably on the side…"

As he was talking, I quietly got out of my seat and moved to the back of the line. No one paid any attention to me. When Wally was finally finished, he returned to his seat, and an excited young undergrad began asking a series of questions about lenses and camera angles that the entire audience enjoyed far too much. There were some actors with questions for Maggie about how to break into the film industry and then some more fan-boy drooling about scenes and locations. I watched Maggie and Eric closely through the interview hoping to detect a hint of guilt or an expression of apology regarding the script, but they exhibited absolutely no remorse, simply answering all the questions with excitement and even glee, as though they were having the time of their lives. I was also looking for any indication that they were still a couple, but could detect nothing on that front. They seemed friendly with one another but not demonstrative in any way, although it all could have been an act. After all, they had fooled me before on that account.

Before I knew it, the person in front of me had finished his question and I was suddenly next in line, all eyes turned toward me for the first time. For a second I froze. It wasn't too late. The table where Eric and Maggie sat was at least twenty yards away, and they had a light shining directly on them that made it hard for them to see who they were talking to. They were both squinting now, trying to see me better, wondering who this person was in a trench coat and fedora. I could turn around and just walk out, and no one would ever recognize me. Everyone would watch me go, people would chuckle, and there would be an awkward silence before the next person stepped up to the microphone, but that would be the end of it. That would be the end of it. And then I noticed River watching me, her mouth set in a smug grin, enjoying every moment of my discomfort.

I couldn't let that be the end of it.

"Do you have a question, sir?" asked Finch. He seemed both amused and concerned. "Please don't be shy. We're all friends here."

Finally, I took off my hat and stepped forward. I saw Maggie's eyes widen and Eric's mouth drop. They were definitely surprised, but I couldn't read the more complex looks on their faces. Was there guilt in those eyes? Did I see fear? In any case, there was no turning back now.

"I was wondering," I said. "How did you come up with the idea for this movie?"

I expected the question to boom like the voice of God, causing shock and fear to reverberate around the room, but it tumbled out at a normal amplified volume in my normal peevish voice. Eric had a strange smile on his face now. No, not a smile, a smirk. The asshole was laughing at me. I burned with the desire for vengeance. The look on Maggie's face was something different and more complicated. It wasn't fear, as I'd hoped, or guilt. Her brow was furrowed and her lips slightly parted, as though she were about to deliver a kiss to a long-lost lover. Suddenly I very much wanted to be that lover.

"As it says in the credits," said Eric evenly, "the story was created by me and my best friend, Sam Drift. We lived together in this weird old house in college, and we used to sit on the roof until three o'clock in the morning arguing about plot points and character development. Sam was a brilliant writer. He used to write all these weird, hilarious short films in college, and then we would make them together. Maggie was with us back then, too. It was great. But for some reason, I could never get him to write the script for *The Big Checkout*. We talked about it all the time, we even had the title figured out way back then, but he just wouldn't write any of it down. So one day I started taking notes. I wasn't secretive about it—I just brought a notepad with me and when we started talking about the movie, I wrote down ideas. I filled up that notepad in a week and started on another. After a month, I showed Sam the stack of notepads and tried to get him to start writing, but he just wouldn't do it. I told him if he wasn't going to do it, I would have to write the script without him. I don't think he believed me. I don't know, he was blocked or something I guess. And then Maggie and I moved to California, and we sort of lost touch with Sam after a while. I still had all those notepads, all those great conversations just sitting there. I'm not really a writer, but I started putting the scenes together from the notes. It took me almost three years to get a script out of it, but I finally made it happen. And that's where the story came from. But you already knew that, didn't you, Sam?"

There was a long moment of dead silence. I could feel the audience looking from Eric to me and back again, contemplating that last sentence. Had they heard correctly? What did it mean? I couldn't speak. I could feel River's eyes boring into me. I wanted to see if she was happy or sad for me, but I was afraid to look at her. There was no air in my lungs, and it felt like there was a cement brick sitting on my chest. Somewhere in the recesses of my brain, scenes from a long-forgotten movie began to play. There was no sound, just jumpy black-and-white figures moving across the screen that verified the story Eric had just told. But was it real? Did he tell me he was taking notes? Did he say that he was going to write the script without me? No, it couldn't be. It was my script, my story.

"So you stole that movie from me," I said.

A low murmur ran through the audience.

Professor Finch sat upright in his chair. "Now, now, let's not start throwing around accusations," he said. "I think he was clear—"

"Sam, we tried to contact you," said Eric. "We sent you dozens of emails and letters. You blocked me on Facebook. The letters came back unopened. We couldn't reach you. We didn't know what else to do."

I ignored him. "You stole my script and you stole my girl."

Eric laughed. "I did what?"

Maggie remained perfectly still.

"And you…" I couldn't let him have the last word, but I was all out of accusations. Suddenly, the mood of the room seemed to shift, and the eyes staring at me were filled with anger and pity. I saw at least four cell phones pointed at me. "You're a traitor!" I yelled. "And I'm going to… I'm going to sue you!"

With that, I turned on my heels and stormed out of the room.

Or I would have stormed out of the room if there had been a door available. Unfortunately, the closest exit was on the other side of the theater, which meant I stormed to the back of the room, spent several embarrassing seconds turning around in a circle like an idiot, then side-walked through the last row of seats until I reached the aisle on the other side, and *then* I stormed out of the room.

Chapter 15: North by Northwest

WHEN I GOT OUTSIDE THE BUILDING, I RAN. I have no idea why. I looked back to see if someone was chasing me, but there was no one. I kept running anyhow. It was what the scene required. I imagined the camera following me as I raced through campus, dodging around elderly professors and screaming "Get out of the way!" when I came upon a pack of slow-moving students. They jumped off the sidewalk to let me pass and looked behind me to see what I was running from. "No one is chasing you, dude," a male voice called out. Instead of stopping, I turned around with a look of panic on my face and ran even faster. I wanted to try that thing where the runner trips, falls to the ground, and then scrambles desperately to his feet, but I didn't know how to take a fall without injuring myself.

Finally, I rounded the side of the music building and placed my back flat against the wall like a spy hiding from the enemy. I peeked around the corner several times to see if I was being followed. My breath was ragged and my clothes were drenched in sweat. I saw several students running in my direction, and I ducked back behind the building to avoid detection. As they passed my hiding spot, one of them said, "I told you to set the alarm." The other one just huffed and puffed behind him. After they were gone and my breathing had returned to normal, I walked around the back side of the building just to be safe. Crosby Hall was a boring rectangular building that had served only one purpose as far as I was concerned when I was a student at MU. The back of the building was a dead-end alley next to a tall brick wall, making it one of the few public spots on campus where you could smoke weed without being detected. The alley was empty when I arrived, and I packed my pipe with marijuana while I watched the clouds accumulate in the sky above. They were large white clouds with engorged cloud muscles, the kind that looked like they had mass, as though you could put them on a scale and they would weigh hundreds of pounds. Most were marshmallow-white, but there was some darkness around the edges that perhaps alluded to a more sinister nature underneath. One looked remarkably like a puffy, overweight Orson Welles in *F is for Fake*.

I took out my phone and began to write.

I smell a rat, Mountainview! There's something rotten in our quiet, little city. In the past 48 hours, I've seen evidence of murder, drugs, political corruption, kidnapping, and intellectual property theft. It's happening right under our noses, and the local authorities have done nothing to stop it. I just came from a movie that sickened me to my core. Shocking that the MIFF would advocate plagiarism from their participants, but I guess you can't expect much from a corrupt institution like that. How does all this lead back to a young woman found dead in an alley? Stay tuned to find out. I won't stop until the culprits are behind bars and the rats have been trapped.

While the contents of the pipe turned to ash and the cannabis fairy tickled my cerebral cortex, I watched Orson tip his hat to a cloud shaped like Sophia Loren, and in response Sophia unhinged her jaw and swallowed big ole fat Orson whole, hat and all, like a cocktail olive, and kept floating by, a magical Sophia/Orson minotaur against an impossible blue sky. Where did Gerald get this weed? It was amazing.

The thought of Gerald caused the director in my head to throw up a few scenes from the past week, but it was a confusing montage and I couldn't quite make out what he was saying. My conscience and I had never been great at communication. I would get messages periodically from the nervous little fart, but I seldom knew what he was trying to say and he was easily distracted. It's difficult going through life with a conscience that has attention deficit disorder. This time it was something about Gerald and the job he had offered me, but he was short on details and soon turned its attention back to Sophia/Orson, which had transformed into a caterpillar that was now morphing into the form of an arrow pointing west. I followed the arrow out of the alley and through the campus, past my old dormitory and into the central courtyard, a large square guarded by enormous gothic structures on all sides and bordered by rows of giant elm trees, standing stark and leafless in the winter sun.

As I stood contemplating my past, slightly swaying from the force of an imaginary wind, Mouth crossed through my field of vision. At first, I thought I was imagining her. Perhaps she was a creation of the stoned director in my head, one of those clouds dropped down to Earth and walking around. I ducked behind a tree before I could think why. My right eye began to twitch and hum with fresh pain at the thought of her tiny, hard fist coming at it this morning. Could that have all happened just seven hours ago?

Mouth walked through the courtyard with quick purposeful strides. She wore a wonderful belted leather coat with a blood-red scarf wrapped around her throat. In her right hand, she carried a black briefcase, which she clutched—or so it seemed to me—protectively close to her body, as though the contents might be her undoing. What was Mouth doing on a college campus? Recruiting girls for the club? Meeting with one of her drug connections? Unlikely in the middle of the day, but not completely out of the question. After all, here she could blend into the crowd and pass through unnoticed and unmolested. No one would bother to stop and ask her questions. She walked past the fountain and started down the sidewalk that ran next to the Student Union. After a careful pause, I casually stepped away from my cover and began following her. I made sure to stay at least ten yards behind, but it wasn't as easy as I thought it would be. Mouth was small, and she kept weaving in and out of various groups of students, so I lost sight of her at least half a dozen times. If she made me and bolted, I figured I would probably be able to catch her, but I didn't know if she was carrying a weapon, so I decided I wouldn't give chase if it came to that. Mouth was smart. It wasn't like she was going to off me in the middle of a crowded campus, but the humming pain in my eye was a constant reminder of what she was capable of. Also, there was the rest of the Larkman family to consider. So far no one else had gotten involved, but who knows what would happen if I started exposing the inner workings of their empire. Better to play it safe and keep gathering information at this point.

There would be plenty of opportunities to face the music after I published the article—if Victoria allowed the article to reach publication, of course. I still didn't know where she stood in this whole caper. I always thought she was on my side, but now it seemed like maybe she was involved with the Larkmans. After all, why would she try to take me off the case just as I was starting to get somewhere? And wasn't it a little coincidental that she'd turned in her letter of resignation a week before the stripper was murdered behind the Pink Door? It was almost like she'd known it was coming and wanted to get out of town before the crime came to light. If she was on the Larkmans' payroll, it made sense. Who knows how much my investigation would uncover. If her name showed up on one of Mouth's ledgers, the story would be huge. *Newspaper Editor on Mob Payroll.* So what would a smart operator like Victoria Wood do? Maybe she'd cash in her retirement account and take a permanent vacation to Mexico, then make her way down to Argentina where the U.S. government couldn't touch her.

Mouth suddenly veered off the sidewalk and opened a side door into the Student Union. Thinking she might be on to me, I passed the building and then circled back around to a different entrance just to be safe. There were no classrooms in the building, just a small gift shop downstairs in which parents could purchase t-shirts and bumper stickers that announced the achievements of their offspring, and an advising center upstairs where students met with academic counselors to decide what classes to take in the upcoming semester. I caught a glimpse of Mouth's firm backside ascending the stairs, and waited a minute before I followed her.

The advising office was small and clean, much like the office of a foot doctor, and the young man at the front desk greeted me with clinical professionalism.

"Welcome to Academic Advising," he chirped. "How may I help you today?"

"Oh, yes, well, thank you, my good man." I was somewhat unprepared, I guess, although that did not justify why I was speaking like a confused British butler.

"I would like to…" And here I just couldn't figure out what to say next.

The poor kid was even more nervous than I was, and when I couldn't seem to find the words, he tried to find them for me.

"You're here to…sign up for classes?" he suggested. He had a constellation of zits on his shiny forehead that, when his eyebrows were furrowed, formed the Big Dipper.

This was a reasonable suggestion, considering this was the Academic Advising office.

"Yes," I said, eyeing the various smaller offices around the room, knowing that Mouth was in one of them. "I want to sign up for classes."

The eyebrows relaxed, and the Big Dipper flattened into Cassiopeia.

"Wonderful!" he declared. "We have many programs for nontraditional students here at Mountainview University. What type of degree are you interested in obtaining?"

The "nontraditional" thing sort of irked me. In university speak, nontraditional meant old, and although it was true that I was pushing thirty, it annoyed me that this little punk automatically assumed I wasn't a freshman.

"Actually, I used to go to school here, but I never finished my degree," I said.

"A returning student!" cried the assuming infant. "Welcome back, sir!"

Once again, that sir was not really necessary.

"Can I have your full name?" he asked.

Not wanting to leave just yet, I gave him my name and social security number. I nervously scanned the office doors while he typed in the information.

"It says here that you almost completed your degree. That's wonderful! We have a specific program for returning students who have completed more than seventy-five percent of their credits. We could sign you up for classes, and you would be done in one year."

"One year?" I asked. "But I was in my final semester when I dropped out."

The boy nodded. "Yes, that's true. However, you received incompletes in several classes that you would need to make up. Altogether, you are only twenty-six credits away from graduation, Mr. Drift. Isn't that exciting?"

I was about to tell the kid exactly how unexciting it was when Mouth appeared from an office on the other side of the room. I immediately dropped below the counter. The kid leaned over the side of the desk, the Big Dipper now glowing white against a flushed red sky.

"Mr. Drift?" he said. "Are you okay?"

"Sure," I hissed. "Just had to tie my shoe. Stop looking at me."

I waved my hand in the universal sign of Go Away, and slowly his head receded from view. To the left was the main exit, and to my right there was a bathroom with a blue sign indicating its gender neutrality. I began to crabwalk toward the bathroom, hoping I had enough time to slip through the door unnoticed before Mouth exited on the other side. I was just rounding the corner ready to make the leap through the bathroom door when my escape was blocked by a pair of short shapely legs attached to an alligator-green skirt and a matching pair of pumps.

"What the hell are you doing down there?" asked Mouth. She stood over me with her left hand set firmly on her hip and her right hand clutching the mysterious briefcase.

I looked up and smiled. "Lost my contact lens."

"I didn't know you wore contacts."

"I don't," I said, standing up. "Mystery solved. No, seriously, I was just thinking about going back to finish school." I turned toward my acne-faced partner in crime and gave him an imploring look. "Isn't that right?"

He smiled back with confused grace. "Yes. He only needs twenty-six credits to graduate."

"That's great," said Mouth with genuine enthusiasm. "I thought you were already an egghead. Good for you."

"What are you doing here?" I asked.

"Same thing," she said. "Well, not *exactly* the same thing. I'm starting my MBA in the fall."

"You have a bachelor's degree already?"

Mouth squinted, and I took a small defensive step backward. "Don't sound so surprised," she said. "Of course I have a BA. Who doesn't in this day and age? Art History." She wrinkled her nose. "I know, I know. What can I say? I was young and obsessed with Goya. It's not my fault."

"Goya?"

"You know, Francisco Jose de Goya y Lucientes, Spanish romantic painter of portraits and really creepy shit. Died deaf and possibly mad in 1828. God, if he were only alive today. Now I'm going back for a more practical degree."

She grabbed me by the elbow and pulled me over to the corner.

"I've been trying to talk to you."

My heart began to hammer. She opened her briefcase and reached inside. I brought my hands up to my face, closing my eyes against the inevitable gun blast.

"What the hell are you doing?" she said. "Look at this."

I peeked between my fingers and saw she was holding out a manila envelope for me.

"You left my office without taking it with you, idiot. I told you there were important papers in here. I came by your apartment yesterday to drop them off, but some fat guy with a beard told me you were out. I would have left this shit with him, but he didn't exactly seem like the reliable type. He kept staring at my tits and talking about JFK."

"Right," I said, gingerly taking the folder from her. "And what did you want me to do with this?"

Her eyes widened with menace and disgust. "Jesus Christ, don't you ever listen? Those are copies of the complaints we filed with the city against the spa?"

"What spa?"

She balled her tiny hand into a fist and I ducked behind the file.

"I swear to all things holy, if we weren't an educational facility right now, I'd make your eyes a matching set." She began speaking slowly with exaggerated emphasis, as if to a small child. "Nirvana. And. You. The spa next door to my club. Dumped chemicals in the alley. My girl slipped on the chemicals and hit her head. You are still working on this story, yes?" Her eyes suddenly lit up with hope, and she reached for the folder. "Or did it get reassigned?"

I pulled the folder back and squared my shoulders. "Of course it didn't get reassigned. Why does everyone keep asking that? It's my story. Mine. I'm all over it."

She gave me a dubious look and snapped her briefcase shut. "Fine. It's your story. You're all over it. Just get that file back to your editor and get the facts straight, or I'll be all over *you.*"

I opened the file, hoping there would be something interesting inside—damning photographs of political figures or a secret message that Mouth didn't want to deliver in public—but it was just like what she said, a bunch of paperwork. I closed the file, then folded it in half and jammed it into the breast pocket of my coat.

When I turned around, the guy at the Academic Advising desk was looking at me expectantly.

"Are you ready to sign up for those classes, Mr. Drift?"

"Sorry, kid," I said, tapping the pocket where I'd just stored Mouth's file. "I don't have time right now. I've got a murder to solve."

"Oh, my goodness. That's… Perhaps a Criminal Justice degree instead."

"I don't think so."

"Journalism then?"

"I already work for a newspaper. I might be an editor soon."

The kid's zits formed a concerned star map. "All the more reason to obtain a degree, sir."

I grunted. "I don't need… I'm doing fine, thank you. Leave me alone."

I turned to confront Mouth but she was gone. I ran after her.

"Well, alright then," he called after me. "We'll be here if you change your mind."

"Shut up," I yelled over my shoulder.

Mouth was already halfway down the stairs before I caught her. How did her little legs move so fast?

"Mouth," I said. "Wait up."

She paused and waited for me to catch up. She leaned against the rail and watched me until I came to a wheezing stop in front of her.

"Damn, how old are you?" she said. "You are in terrible shape."

"Uh…" I held up a finger, asking for a minute to catch my breath. She rolled her eyes. Finally, I asked her where V. was.

"Who?"

"The woman I brought with me to the club last night." Mouth's face remained blank. "Seventy-some years old, dressed in a sequined ball gown, started doing a striptease at about two in the morning..."

"Oh, right," said Mouth. "I like that old broad. She went home with Kate."

"Kate? Who's Kate?"

"Rebecca's roommate. Her...former roommate. She lives out there in Garden Village by the highway. Her address is in that file you barely looked at."

"Why would she go home with Kate?"

Mouth smiled. "Why do you think?"

I blinked several times. "I really don't know what you're talking about."

She shook her head. "You kids these days are too innocent for your own good. Go to the address, find out for yourself. In fact, you should go there tomorrow at 3 p.m. You got that?"

"Sure. Garden Village, three o'clock. Got it."

Mouth frowned and reached out her hand. "Give me your phone."

"Why?"

"Because I told you to and you're afraid of me."

"I'm not afraid of you."

She stepped toward me. I flinched and gave her my phone.

"What's your number?"

I told her.

She poked at the screen on her phone, and then she poked at the screen on my phone.

"There," she said, handing my phone back. "I sent you a text. Now you have my number and I have yours. I'm going to text you a reminder tomorrow, and if you're not there at three..."

"I said I'd be there."

"I know you did. You say a lot of things, Sam." She started down the stairs. "I like you, but you're not exactly reliable, you know. So I'm going to text you tomorrow, and I'm going to make sure you find that old lady, and I'm going to make sure you do your damn job, whether you want to or not."

She disappeared from view. I looked at my phone. Her text said, "Give the file to your editor."

"It's my story, Mouth!" I yelled down the stairs. "It's mine!"

Chapter 16: The Wizard of Oz

SINCE I'D SPENT MOST OF THE DAY ON NEWSPAPER BUSINESS, I decided to take the afternoon off to catch up on festival movies. I saw a subpar Korean horror film in the basement of the Student Union, a pretentious indie drama in the gymnasium of a nearby middle school, and an excellent documentary about homeless Argentinian circus performers at the library. I posted several insightful reviews and some text messages. There were three voicemails from Victoria requesting updates on the story, but I ignored those.

I was standing on the sidewalk trying to decide what movie to see next when I heard my name being called. I turned around and saw Maggie and Eric walking toward me across the quad. Eric was taking large strides with his enormous, spider-like legs, but he was still having trouble keeping up with Maggie, who was moving forward like a train engine. Her face was flushed, and as I watched, she called to me again. "Samuel Drift! Stay right there! Don't you dare move!"

At the sight of my two old friends walking toward me on the same campus where we met and fell in love, my heart broke open and I was transported back to the happiest period of my life, a time when I was surrounded by love and inspired by art. My mind began to play a montage of the greatest moments of our friendship: Eric and I running away from the campus police after shooting an action scene on the roof of the chemistry building; Maggie taking my hand for the first time in back of the Michener Theater during a midnight showing of *A Streetcar Named Desire*; the three of us getting drunk and falling asleep on the lawn in front of our house after a movie premiere. My eyes brimmed with tears, and I opened my arms to my friends—my heart filled with gratitude and longing—and I said, "I forgive you!"

That's when Maggie punched me in my one good eye.

THE BUTCHERED GOAT WAS A WINDOWLESS BRICK BAR located underneath Mountainview Manor, a historic hotel constructed as a private residence in the early 1900s by an eccentric millionaire named Augustus Livernash. This was back when they were pulling gold, coal, and uranium out of the Rockies by the ton, and the Livernash family owned half the mining equipment in the county. They built mansions all over the Front Range, in mining towns and logging communities, one gaudier than the last. Shortly after Augustus moved into his ugly mansion, there was a string of kidnappings in the area. Three children were abducted off the street during a five-month period. The police never found the abductor or the children, and rumors soon started that Augustus was keeping the kids locked up in a secret dungeon underneath his new house, although no one ever proved as much. Eventually, the Livernash fortune dried up and Augustus hung himself from one of the oak rafters in his expensive Victorian living room. The bank foreclosed on the property and sold it to a developer who tried to turn it into a swanky hotel. It never really took off, but the story and building became part of local lore and the bar in the basement where Augustus supposedly tortured innocent waifs was now a favorite watering hole for older locals and younger artistic types.

Perhaps predictably, the current owner was a horror movie buff; therefore, instead of football or hockey, the televisions were all playing *Night of the Living Dead* when we made our less-than-dramatic entrance. I felt very much like a Romero zombie in that moment. I hadn't been inside the Butchered Goat for six years, but it looked exactly the same: stone walls, dim lighting, Tammy Wynette moaning about standing by your man (see, Maggie, Tammy gets it!), a middle-age bartender with a push-up bra and an Elvira hairdo pouring drinks for a group of older men who started occupying those barstools back when she could pull off that outfit.

Like any good dungeon, the Butchered Goat was filled with dusty passageways and secret alcoves. If you took a left at the gnarled oak bar, elbowed your way through a group of surly young men who were perpetually shooting pool on a lopsided billiards table, and another left at an ancient jukebox that played, strangely enough, only classic country and hardcore punk, you would find yourself in a dead-end hallway with a single booth at the end shaped like a crescent moon. Above the booth hung a framed black-and-white photo of Bela Lugosi dressed as Dracula. This was where Maggie, Eric, and I spent the better part of our final years together, drinking alcohol, celebrating movie premiers, discussing story plots, telling jokes, arguing about cinematic minutia, and becoming best friends. For all I knew, this was also where Eric and Maggie fell in love and made plans to stab me in the back.

After Maggie punched me in the eye outside the Student Union, there had been a bit of yelling (mostly Maggie), a bit of crying (all me), and then an exasperated campus security officer told us to vacate the premises. Without even discussing the matter, we began walking to the Butchered Goat, and now we were here, in our old booth, drinking our old drinks—Fat Tire for Eric, Moscow Mule for Maggie, and two Old Fashions for me. I took an ice cube out of one of my glasses, sucked the precious alcohol off it, and then pressed it to my newly injured eye, earning a micro-grin from Eric and a macro-eye roll from Maggie.

After the dramatic exchange at the Student Union, we were all a little sheepish, and we sat drinking in silence for several minutes, no one able to figure out where to start the conversation. My emotions were rollercoastering between anger, excitement, and fear. I had thought about Maggie and Eric every single day for the last six years. They occupied my dreams and fantasies. I argued with them, drank with them, confided in them, and screamed at them. In fact, I was just realizing that I had known the real Maggie and Eric for less than three years, and I had been living with the fantasy versions of them in my mind for more than twice as long. Now both worlds were colliding, and my head was reeling from the mental whiplash.

Finally, Eric, ever the diplomat, looked up at the television, where a horde of black-and-white zombies were stumbling toward an old farmhouse, and said, "Remember the days when zombies didn't run? What has happened to this country?"

"Here-here!" I said, raising my glass. "And when did vampires start to glitter?"

"And werewolves are not teenage heartthrobs."

"This nation has gone to Hell in a handbasket."

"Can I get a harumph?"

"Harumph!"

Maggie shook her head, but I saw a shadow of a smile flicker in the corner of her mouth. For a moment, I thought she might join in the banter, and we could jump back into our old relationship and completely forget about everything that had happened between us. But then a dark cloud passed over her face.

"It took us four years to make that movie," Maggie said quietly. I started to respond but she held up her hand. "Four years of location paperwork and producer meetings. Four years of weekends and holidays. Four years of credit card debt. I had to borrow money from my parents. Eric gets calls from collection agencies every day. We killed ourselves making that movie. And you weren't there for any of it, Sam."

"Yeah, well, who's fault is that?" I mumbled.

"Yours. It is your fault. We invited you to come with us to Hollywood. Eric practically begged you. You refused to leave Mountainview, and you wouldn't tell us why."

"That wasn't..." I looked over at Eric with astonished eyes, expecting him to return my perplexed expression and denounce Maggie's preposterous claim, but he was staring down at his drink in silence. "I don't remember it like that."

"Well, that's how it happened," said Maggie. "And you never wrote a script. You talked about it for months, but you wouldn't write anything. Eric took a screenwriting class in L.A. and rewrote that script for three goddamn years before he was finally satisfied with it. You have no idea how hard he worked."

She reached over and squeezed Eric's hand.

"It was my idea," I said. It was all I had.

"That's why we gave you credit for the story, you little shit," Maggie said. "Nobody wanted us to do that. The producers wanted Eric to have that written-

and-directed Tarantino thing, but he refused. We had to fight to put your name on it."

"Oh, a story credit," I sulked. "Big fucking deal."

"It is a big deal," said Eric, finally getting angry. "And you know it. Don't pretend like seeing your name on that screen wasn't a big deal. I know exactly how much that means to you, and that's why I made them put it up there."

In all the scenes I had constructed over the years in preparation for this moment, none had gone like this. It was not fair. I was the one who had been wronged. I was the one who was supposed to accuse and then be redeemed. I was the spurned hero.

I drained the rest of my drink in three long swallows and slammed the empty glass on the table, causing Eric to flinch and Maggie to lean back. "You left me," I said with all the conviction I could muster. "You broke my heart, and you left me here. We were a team. I was in love with you, Maggie. Love. Do you remember love? That promise of dedication and passion we once pledged to each other. I remember it. I remember it every day."

That was better. The leading-man dialogue was coming back to me now. I was going to make a scene. Maggie tried to interrupt, but I was too quick for her.

"And, Eric, you were my best friend. The brother I never had. The one person in this world I trusted beyond all others. How could you do that? How could you steal my girl and my movie? What kind of a man does that? Does the bond of brotherhood mean nothing to you? You should be ashamed."

Maggie and Eric sat frozen before me, mouths open, twin looks of shock and horror on their faces, feeling the full weight of their betrayal perhaps for the first time. They seemed to be waiting for me to break the silence, but I wanted them to suffer as long as possible.

Finally, after what seemed an eternity, they turned to one another and began laughing hysterically. I felt my face burn.

"That's right," I said. "It's all a big joke to you. Betray your friend, crush his heart, and then laugh about it." I stood up to leave.

"What the hell are you talking about?" said Eric. "We were never together. We just both wanted to make movies, and California is a scary place, so we moved there together to support one another. Once again, you were supposed to come with us."

"But you broke up with me," I said to Maggie. "You left me."

She nodded vigorously. "Damn right, I did. You were a terrible boyfriend, Sam. I mean, you were great in the beginning. You kept leaving notes on my door and you called me all the time. My roommate thought you were a stalker. And then finally I decided to give you a chance, and as soon as it became official, you started getting moody and distant. You did that guy thing where you stopped talking to me and acted like it was my fault. I said I wanted to meet your parents. You remember that? You didn't speak to me for like a week. So, yeah, I broke up with you. Can you blame me?"

The movie screen in my mind began to go haywire with a series of jump cuts, splices, and dolly zooms. My memory shuttered, went soft focus, and then there was a disturbing fisheye angle that made me want to puke. Or maybe it was the drugs. It was difficult to tell.

Eric's smile faded, and he leaned in to look at me closely for the first time. "Sam, don't you remember?" he asked. "What's happened to you? Are you okay?"

It had been a long time since anyone had asked me that, and the sincerity in his voice caused an acidic lump to form in my throat. Suddenly, I couldn't breathe.

"I'm sorry," I whispered. "I didn't mean to ruin your movie. I was just…"

Maggie sighed and put her hand on my arm, causing a bolt of energy to shoot through my body. "You didn't ruin the movie." She gave me a motherly look. "I mean, what you said was stupid and it really pissed me off, but somehow it worked out. In fact, you might have done us a favor."

"What are you talking about?" I sniffled.

"We met your little girlfriend," said Maggie, tapping a maroon fingernail on the edge of her glass, the corner of her mouth twitching with either amusement or jealousy.

An invisible ice-cold hand grabbed my testicles and squeezed. "Who?"

"Lake," Eric said. He gave me a not-so-subtle thumbs-up.

"River," Maggie corrected him. "River Moore."

"She's not…"

"I like her," Maggie said. "She's a little…not what I expected."

"What did you expect?"

She shrugged. "You know, someone with a sense of humor. Or a driver's license."

"She's got a… She's a junior in college."

"I'm kidding. Seriously, she seems nice. Smart, sort of bossy, but, well, kind of impressive."

"Oh?"

"She offered to promote the movie," Eric said. He bared his teeth and pulled back his head, as though he was preparing to be slapped in the face.

I let out a hollow laugh. "She's not an agent. She's just fucking with you guys to get back at me."

"Get back at you for what?"

"Nothing. She has this dog… It's nothing. She's not an agent. She's just an art student that's pissed off at me. She can't do anything for your movie."

Maggie picked up a coaster featuring Elsa Lanchester dressed as Frankenstein's bride. "She already got us two more viewings, and we have a meeting with a producer next week. She says she can get us into Sundance."

I put my head in my hands and groaned. It was true that Gerald owned an art gallery in Denver, and River often organized events for the various painters, sculptors, and videographers who showed their work in its minimalistic white rooms. On top of that, she coordinated several upscale fundraisers every year that raised tens of thousands of dollars for various local charities and nonprofits. She had a special gift for connecting people and controlling social exchanges with such a deft hand that everyone involved thought it was their idea to give River what she wanted. She certainly had the connections to pull strings at the MIFF if she wanted, but why would she?

"We don't have any other options," said Eric. "It's not like we have agents and producers knocking down our door. We literally have nothing to lose."

"Fine," I said. "But don't come crying to me when she finds some other charity case and dumps you. Mark my words, River Moore does not care about your movie."

"It's your movie, too," said Eric.

Maggie made a sound in the back of her throat that was halfway between a hiccup and a growl.

"It's true," Eric insisted. "You're part of this. We have two more festivals, and whatever else River can get us. You should come with us and do the panels." He looked from me to Maggie and back again. "Wouldn't that be great? The three of us together again?"

This was the last thing I expected him to say, and there was a part of me deep down that hated him for it. I was sure he was just rubbing my nose in their success.

"Wouldn't that be a little weird?" I said, cocking my eyebrow in a knowing way. "I don't want to be a third wheel."

"Oh, for fucksake," said Maggie. She threw the coaster like a Frisbee and hit me right between the eyes. "For the last time, Eric and I are not together, you idiot. Get it through your head."

"I need a drink," I said.

"I think we all need many more drinks. This is going to be a long night." She stood up. "I'll get the first round, but you tightwads are next in line."

When she walked to the bar, I looked at Eric and saw him crack his knuckles like the old days, and I couldn't stop smiling.

Chapter 17: The Bad Seed

THAT NIGHT I DREAMT OF SCAR-FACED GANGSTERS in pin-striped suits driving enormous black Duesenbergs up and down the Chicago streets of my subconscious. I was one of them, a snitch, a rat, a hunted man on the run from the law and a merciless, jowly crime boss. There was a dame, of course. Isn't there always a dame? She was blonde and sharp-tongued, with a clever glint in her eye and a pearl-handled pistol tucked under a garter belt on her creamy left thigh. The gangsters chased us all over the city, over dark streets and through empty warehouse districts, until we took a wrong turn down a dead-end alley and they cornered us against a wall, our bodies casting elongated shadows on the stark brick surface in the background. The jig was up. I turned to the dame for one last kiss, and realized too late she was my mother. "Forgive me, Sammy," she said, as she clutched me to her bosom. I wanted to pull away, but my dream-world body was in cahoots with my Freudian brain. Instead of escaping, I leaned in close and said, "Please don't leave me."

We locked lips as the bullets began to fly.

I awoke with a confusing erection and the sound of gunfire outside my door. Audrey had been curled up on my chest, and when I jumped up, eyes dopey with sleep and mouth agape, she clawed a three-inch crop furrow into the tender meat of my left pectoral as she scrambled for her usual hiding place under the bed. My brain was still foggy with the false memory of the nightmare, and when I saw the blood oozing from my chest, I drew the obvious conclusion: I'd been shot. I put my hand on the wound and watched in amazement as red teardrops dripped from my fingertips. "The horror," I said. "The horror." Shots rang out again, and as the gash in my chest began to sting with urgent, undreamlike pain, I swam back to reality and realized that someone was knocking on my door. Well, not knocking, exactly. Banging. Pounding. Accompanied by muffled shouts. The blood pulsing in my head was so loud that it took me a few seconds to make out what the pounder on the other side of the door was saying, and even then I couldn't believe it.

"Sam Drift! This is the police! We know you're in there! Open the door!"

I pulled back the blanket that had cocooned me through the cold night and swung my feet around to meet the floor. My body stopped moving when I was sitting upright, but the room did not. It yawned and spun with frightening force, and I had to shut my eyes to keep the universe from flying apart. In any other circumstance, I would have declared the rest of the day a bust and tried to sleep off the poison that was canoeing through my bloodstream, but the noise coming from the front door made that option impossible. The police? It couldn't be. I rewound the projector in my head and tried to locate recent scenes that might have caused members of local law enforcement to come knocking on my door at nine o'clock in the morning. Unfortunately, there were several to choose from.

"Okay," I said. "I'm coming, I'm coming."

I meant to yell these words with self-assurance, but my throat wasn't up to the task and they came out a croaked whimper. With a truly Herculean effort that no one would ever appreciate, I managed to rock back and forth several times, using the momentum of the third thrust to push myself into a standing position. Unfortunately, my legs were not yet operational and I slammed into the back of the couch before I could catch myself, bounced off, and staggered backward into the closet door. The doorknob hit my beleaguered tailbone at just the right angle, sending a painful zing up my spine and finally waking the slumbering alcoholic director inside my skull. "Aaaaand *action!*" he said.

I rubbed my butt as I walked to my peeling sea-foam door and, without ceremony, swung it open.

At first, the explosion of light was too much for my poor dilated pupils to bear. I ducked my head and closed my eyes, as if trying to dodge the illuminated particles bombarding my retinas. Finally, after much squinting and blinking, I was able to make out two blurry human-like shapes in police uniforms and one that was not. The blurry human-like shape that was not wearing a uniform pointed a long finger at me and screamed, "That's him! That's the man who kidnapped my grandmother!"

"Huh?" I said.

The sound of her voice was like a fire alarm inside my skull, and I took several steps backward to escape its shrill vibrations.

She started after me, raising her hand as though she was going to take my head off with one swift karate chop, an act of which she seemed entirely capable, but at the last moment the female officer grudgingly stepped between us and said, "Let us handle this, ma'am."

I cringed and retreated further into the darkness of my hovel.

"I see you did not heed my advice," said the other officer.

There was a familiar timbre to his calm, paternal voice, and I rubbed my eyes until the source came into focus.

"Hi, Henry," I said. "How are you?"

"I'm fine," he said, looking me over with an air of disappointment that had become all too familiar in the past couple of days. "Are you injured?"

At first, I thought he was talking about my eyes—the right one was now badly swollen and the left was hot to the touch—but then I saw he was gesturing with concern at my chest.

I looked down and saw the blood still flowing freely from Audrey's scratch, dribbling down my ribcage in rivulets that had enough steam to make it over my hairy little hummock of white abdominal fat and then into the knobby hollow of my belly button. There was a large patch of sticky gore smeared across my torso. My hands were covered in blood, as well, and I realized it was probably all over my face and in my hair.

"What did you do to her?" screeched the fire alarm. "You sick bastard."

My eyes had finally adjusted to natural light, and when I turned to look at the woman, I discovered, without much surprise, it was V.'s sexy granddaughter, Nina. She was dressed less extravagantly than she had been the last time I saw her—a pair of painted-on jeans, leather boots with some sort of brown fur fringing the top, and the type of flimsy, body-hugging jacket worn by those who have never lived through a real winter—but I noticed that she took the time to do her makeup and hair before rushing out in search of her lost grandmother.

She narrowed her eyes at me and said, "He killed her in there. Now he has to clean up those stains before he leaves."

It was a strange phrase, said in a dramatic flourish that sounded hollow, as though it had been practiced too many times in front of a bathroom mirror, and after searching my memory banks for a second, I remembered its origin.

"Hitchcock," I said.

"What was that?" asked Henry.

I looked at Nina and smiled. "Stella in *Rear Window*, right?"

Nina's face turned scarlet with either anger or shame, or both. "Where's my grandma?" she sputtered.

"Is that your blood?" asked Henry.

"Yes," I said. "It's just a scratch. Literally. I was sleeping with Audrey…"

"Who?" he asked, glancing around the room, slightly startled at the prospect that he had missed the presence of another human in this tiny space.

"Audrey Hepburn. My cat. I mean, I wasn't sleeping *with* her. No bestiality or anything like that, haha. Just, you know, good, old-fashioned pet-owner spooning."

"Hey, Mr. Drift," said Henry.

"Yeah?"

"Stop making jokes."

"Yes, sir."

"We have some questions about this young lady's grandmother. Do you know her?"

"Not intimately."

Henry gave me a look.

"Sorry, sir. I just met her the other night at the MIFF opening. She wanted to leave the Blue Dick…I mean, um, the theater, so I took her to the Pink Door. The last time I saw her she was there."

I didn't mention V. was still there the next morning, chatting with a much younger stripper that she apparently went home with later. It didn't seem like pertinent information at the moment.

"You took a seventy-eight-year-old woman to a strip club?" said Henry.

"That's where she wanted to go," I said. "I advised her to go back to her hotel room on several occasions, but she wouldn't listen to me."

"Liar!" screamed Nina. "You are such a liar. She's here somewhere, I just know it. Check the closet."

"She was fine last time I saw her," I said. "I'm sure we can track her down. She's not here."

"Then what's that doing here?" Nina said, pointing to the corner of the room by the television, where I noticed for the first time there was a giant glass lifetime-achievement award sitting on the floor.

"Oh, yeah," I said, unable to hide a smirk. "She gave that to me the night we met in exchange for a shot of Petron."

"That is such bullshit," said Nina. She turned to Henry. "I hope you're not buying any of this. I insist that you search this room immediately. If this man is not arrested this instant, I will call CNN and FOX and…" Here she stumbled, unable to recall anymore three-letter news stations but not willing to quit at two, which was sort of anticlimactic under the circumstances. "…And I have more than eight thousand followers on Twitter!" she finally exclaimed triumphantly.

Henry's back stiffened and his jaw set in a manner that indicated he had been dealing with this situation for several hours.

"Excuse me," he said in an overly controlled tone, "I allowed you to accompany us here as a courtesy. I asked you to remain silent during these proceedings, which I can now see you are not capable of doing. Therefore, I am going to ask that you wait in the car while I speak with Mr. Drift alone."

Nina didn't quite know how to react to this reproach. First, she stuck out her plump bottom lip in a manner common among certain attractive women trying to convince a certain type of man to change their mind, but the realization that this technique would not work on Henry must have clicked in fairly quickly because her jaw dropped seamlessly into an indignant scoff designed to save face and send a warning.

"I cannot believe the way I have been treated," she said. "I don't know how you do things here in the sticks, but where I come from, we like to arrest criminals when they commit crimes. You will be hearing from my lawyer."

Henry accepted this news with cool indifference. "You may tell him or her to call my office. Officer Norton will escort you to the car and give you my contact information."

Nina's jaw dropped further at this, but before she could discuss more legal proceedings, Officer Norton—a solid no-nonsense woman with zero makeup and a face so blank you could project a double feature on it—took her firmly by the elbow and guided her toward the stairs.

Before they were out of the building, Henry leaned out the door and asked Officer Norton to bring him the first aid kit from the car.

When they were gone, he sighed and closed the door.

"Sit down," he said, motioning toward the couch.

I sank into the cushion with relief. Henry stayed standing, feet shoulder-length apart, ropey arms crossed over his Kevlar chest, as he surveyed my room. I followed his eyes as they took in the single, unmade bed, the piles of unwashed laundry pushed against the walls, the Marx Brothers blanket covering the window, the movie posters covering the walls, the bookcases filled with DVDs, and, finally, the phalanx of empty liquor bottles and drug paraphernalia covering all surfaces. Somehow, through all this, his eyes landed on the photograph of my mother sitting on the dresser, the glass cracked from some long-forgotten accident.

"I have a picture of my dad at home in his high school football uniform," he said picking up my mom's picture. "It's one of those old, corny photos they used to take back in the Fifties. You know, with the player posed like they're about to throw a pass downfield. My father was a quarterback. All-state. Would have gone to college on a scholarship if my mother hadn't gotten pregnant."

"How old were you when he died?" I asked.

"I was nineteen. Gulf War. Dad didn't want me to join the military. Said it was a fool's war. I told him to go to hell and signed up anyway."

There was a light knock on the door. Officer Norton entered, handed Henry the first aid kit, and then left. Henry sat down beside me on the couch and put the kit on the coffee table. He removed a bottle of hydrogen peroxide and a large package of cotton balls.

"Was that the last thing you said to your dad?" I asked

"What?"

"You told him to go to hell. Was that the last thing you said to him?"

He soaked one of the cotton balls in peroxide and applied it to my wound. I winced.

"No, we made up. I called him a week later crying about how I didn't think I could make it through basic training, and he talked me through it. We were on good terms when he died."

Audrey came out from under the bed and slowly approached Henry, tail up and vibrating, nose extended forward, body tensed to flee the moment danger presented itself.

"Who's this?" said Henry.

"That's Audrey," I said. "Don't take it personally if she hates you. She hates everyone."

Before I could stop him, Henry leaned down and put his hand near the ground, close enough to receive a finger-severing swipe. To my amazement, Audrey took a whiff of his hand and then pushed her face into his palm, closing her eyes and emitting a long satisfied purr as his fingers quickly found the sweet spot behind her ear.

"Good girl," he cooed, as she rubbed figure eights around his legs. He turned his attention back to me. "What about your mother?"

I shrugged and swallowed a lump the size of a monkey fist in my throat. "What about her?"

"It sounds like you didn't get much time with her. Have you ever tried looking her up at the high school? They keep pretty good records over there. Grades, senior photos, old yearbooks. It's not much but it's something"

I looked away and blinked back the hot tears building up behind my eyes. "She didn't want to get to know me. Why should I try to know her?"

Henry nodded. He finished cleaning the blood off my chest in silence and pressed a large cotton bandage over the wound with adhesive around the edges to keep it in place. By this time, the scratch had almost bled itself dry. I put on my shirt and tried to compose myself. Audrey jumped onto the couch and made her way to the top of the bookshelf, where she could survey the room from the highest possible point and strike down her enemies if necessary.

"So enough chitchat," Henry said, standing up again and returning to professional mode. "Let's talk about this missing woman. Where is she?"

"I honestly don't know," I said. "Like I said before, she was at the Pink Door last time I saw her."

"Doing what?"

"Just, you know, having a good time."

"Fine," said Henry. "Let's go all the way back. Tell me everything that happened after I saw you yesterday."

The truth was I couldn't remember much about the previous night, aside from seeing *The Big Checkout* and meeting with Maggie and Eric at the Butchered Goat. I didn't know how I got home, for instance, or why there was a lifetime achievement award in the corner of my apartment that belonged to an elderly scream queen. I assumed someone had called me a cab, and I hoped Mouth had seen to V.'s safe return to her hotel room, but the fact that her granddaughter was accusing me of murder did not bode well for the latter. I told all of this to Henry in an abbreviated and sanitized form, making our evening seem like a jaunty romp and his presence in my room a misunderstanding, but I was certain he didn't buy it—primarily because he looked at me after my little speech with his sharp, lupine eyes and said, "I don't buy it, Mr. Drift."

I tried to explain myself again, and he waved me off. "Here's the thing. There's a furious woman down there who has every right to be furious. I have spoken with her for almost two hours, and I don't think she cares for any living thing on this planet, including her own grandmother, but she loves attention and if we don't resolve this issue quickly, she is going to turn this whole thing into a media circus and you, my friend, are going to be the clown at the center. Do you understand?

I don't think you know where this woman is right now, but you know the people over at the Pink Door better than I do. I'm going to ask them some questions, but Ms. Larkman and I aren't exactly on good terms right now. So I want you to help me figure this out. Do you think you can do that?"

"Of course," I said, with the confidence of someone who wasn't entirely paying attention. The hangover was killing me, and I wanted desperately for Henry to leave so I could smoke a joint.

Henry shook his head and exhaled sharply through his nose to indicate that my overconfidence was not a good sign. Audrey flopped onto her back and reached her paw toward Henry. He smiled and reached out to scratch her chin.

"And one more thing," he said, packing up the first aid kit. "I want you to give something to your editor."

He reached into his back pocket and produced a sealed white envelope with the words VICTORIA WOOD written on the front.

"Don't open it, don't write about it on your blog, just give it to Ms. Wood. You think you can handle that?"

"Of course," I said again, this time a little miffed. "Why are you giving this to me?"

"I'm not giving to you. I'm giving it to your editor."

"Right. But why?"

He sighed. "These are the papers you requested yesterday. You asked for information regarding Rebecca Kint. I am simply delivering that information to you. I can't get involved in the political squabbles in this town. Things pass through my office, but it's not my place to intervene. If the law hasn't been broken, I just keep my mouth shut. Do you understand?"

"No."

"Good," he said. "Let's keep it that way. I have that statement for you, as well."

"What statement?"

"Yesterday you asked for a statement from my office concerning the death of Ms. Kint."

"Oh, right," I said, looking up at him expectantly.

He shook his head. "Don't you want to get a pen and write it down?"

"Right. Yes, yes, a pen."

I looked around the room until I spotted my trusty trench coat crumpled on the floor like an old drunk that had fallen asleep in a strange position. I hopped over the back of the couch and retrieved it. My sudden movement surprised Audrey, and she jumped up into a crouched position, ready for action, emitting a concerned meow. I found my notebook and pen on the first try this time and tried to take a serious journalistic pose, despite the fact that I was still in my underwear.

"Ready," I said.

"I want you to write this down word for word," said Henry. "The Mountainview Police Department is continuing to investigate the cause of Rebecca Kint's death. At this time, we do not believe the incident was premeditated in any way. However, the case remains open. Our condolences go out to the Kint family."

"Wait, slow down," I said, scribbling frantically. I finished writing and reread the statement. "But this doesn't say anything. You think the whole thing was an accident? What about the drugs? What about the Larkmans?"

"That's our statement," said Henry. He gave Audrey one last fond rub and headed for the door. "I am not prepared to take follow-up questions at this time. Just get that envelope to your editor, and give her that statement. And Mr. Drift?"

"Yes."

"Don't open the envelope."

"Sure," I said. "Scout's honor."

Henry nodded and closed the door gently on his way out.

I let out a sigh of relief and quickly crossed the room to bolt the door. I retrieved the trench coat, found the baggie of marijuana, fished out my pipe, and fired it up. Immediately, a sense of confidence and well-being spread through my body, and I knew everything was going to turn out alright. I took several more hits from the pipe, feeling a warm cloud envelope my head. I put *Rear Window* into the DVD player and watched Jimmy Stewart mumble and stutter his way into my heart. My brain hummed dreamily with the siren song of tetrahydrocannabinol and the beautiful, horrific Hitchcockian universe, where painted backdrops made reality look drab and every piece of action and dialogue contained insight to a larger revelation.

Audrey jumped off the bed and forced herself onto my lap, circling three times and then finally settling into place with a long-suffering sigh. I picked up the envelope Henry had given me and opened it.

The contents of the envelope were disappointing. I had hoped for some kind of coded note or hidden clue that would lead me in the direction of Rebecca Kint's killer, but it was just a Xerox copy of some paperwork, dull and official, from a local governmental office, marked at the top with a stamp that said APPROVED and signed at the bottom in an indecipherable squiggle. I turned the pages upside down and held them up to the light, looking for a message concealed by Henry or perhaps a mole in his department who might be secretly attempting to communicate with the outside world, but there was nothing. The top of the forms read *6913-F: Health Inspection Extension Request,* and I wondered if perhaps 6913-F was some sort of cryptological puzzle that contained information. I took another toke on the pipe and tried substituting each number with a letter from the alphabet. I came up with either FIAC-F or FIM-F. This did not seem helpful at first, but then I got the idea to reverse those first three letters. There wasn't anything familiar about CIAF-F but MIF-F was a different story. Mountainview International Film Festival. Was it possible the MIFF was somehow involved in Rebecca Kint's death? It made sense. If you wanted to get away with murder, make it look like an accident and do it during one of the largest events in town so the police are preoccupied with security and media control. Furthermore, there were people here from all over the world this week. There were documentary filmmakers from Norway and French cinema nerds and representatives from the BBC. If you wanted to hire a professional hitman from the other side of the globe, they would easily blend into the international crowd during the event. No one would think twice about some guy named Sven wandering the streets at night with a large camera bag filled with semi-automatic weapons slung over his shoulder. It was so simple and obvious it was almost brilliant.

I stuffed the papers back into the envelope and pushed Audrey off my lap. I got dressed while I finished off the rest of the pipe. Audrey was not happy about me interrupting her nap, and she was now rubbing her face against the windowsill and making a pathetic, warbling noise. I opened the window and watched her jump onto the branch.

"Wait," I said. She turned around to give me a snotty look. "I'll be home early tonight, and I'll bring you more food."

She turned around, stared directly at me, and let out a long, strange wail that sounded exactly like, "LIAR!"

I shook my stoned head. "I promise."

She sniffed and turned her back on me. The morning light was soft and yellow and it shimmered on Audrey's white fur, surrounding her body with a downy aura, as though she were an angelic being that had crossed the heavens on a sunbeam. My heart lurched at the sight of her and I tried to grab her for one last comforting stroke of her soft head, but she slipped through my fingers and disappeared from sight. Outside, the air was still and the sky was draped with thin clouds that hung down like a mourner's shroud. There was an unnatural silence, like the entire world was holding its breath, waiting to see what would happen next.

I closed the window and sat down on the couch to smoke another bowl. While I broke up the weed and packed the pipe, I watched Jimmy Stewart and Grace Kelly snipe at one another about their stalled relationship and Stewart's increasing obsession with his neighbors' windows. Hitchcock was a genius. Narcissistic and possibly a sadist, but a genius, nonetheless.

The prescription bottles of Xanax, Valium, and Oxy were still in the coat, although I was surprised to discover two of the bottles were half-empty, and I was down to two Vicodin. Knowing I needed to ration my supplies if they were going to last the rest of the week, I took only one Xanax and, after considering the state of my hangover, emptied the Vicodin.

I opened my laptop and was surprised to find a dozen new emails with subject lines like: *is this really u?*, *THATS MESSED UP*, and *Nice Trench Coat,*

Columbo!!! Every message contained a link to a video that showed me standing in front of a small crowd at a movie theater, wild-eyed and angry, accusing Eric and Maggie of plagiarism. "And you…" I screamed, jabbing the air with my index finger. "You're a traitor! And I'm going to…I'm going to sue you!" I cringed at the sound of my own voice and watched in horror as the video tracked my long, embarrassing exit from the theater, while Nancy Sinatra sang "These Boots Are Made for Walkin'" in the background. It had to be River.

I logged onto my website and began to type:

The problem with modern society is that the human race is too interconnected. People find out things about each other instantly, and they tell things to other people instantly, and those people share their opinions about those things instantly. It's probably causing some kind of worldwide existential crisis, but that's not what I'm concerned about. I'm concerned that it's ruining movies.

Take Hitchcock, for instance. The plot of pretty much every Hitchcock movie would fall apart if you introduced smartphones into the equation. Strangers on a Train. *Five minutes on Google and you're not a stranger anymore.* Pycho. *"Hey, police, I'm being attacked by a psycho, send help!"* The Birds. *"Hey, police, I'm being attacked by birds, send help!"* Rear Window. *"Here's a video of my neighbor doing weird stuff. Do you think he murdered his wife?"*

That's why there's no suspense in suspense movies anymore. No thrill in the thriller. Everything happens so fast in the Internet Age that nothing can creep up on you. We're drowning in a flash flood of kitten memes and superhero movies that feed our eyes but not our souls. "Hey, police, I'm being attacked by an informational overload that's killing our cultural metanarrative, send help!"

p.s. If anyone has seen an attractive septuagenarian wandering the streets of Mountainview cursing like an ice road trucker and wearing a sequined ball gown with enough cleavage to choke a baby hippo, please call the Mountainview P.D. and ask for Henry Moss.

I took another hit off my pipe. I was worried about V., but I couldn't go looking for her just yet. I rummaged around in my trench coat until I found the crumpled envelope. There was a mystery afoot, and I was going to solve it.

Chapter 18: Breakfast at Tiffany's

THE LAST DAY OF THE MIFF WAS A MAD DASH to the third act. Lovers who hooked up during the opening credits threw drinks in each other's faces at closing ceremonies. Directors who kissed up to network executives following private screenings loudly denounced mainstream television in public bars. Awards were handed out, drinks were consumed, and celebrity guests of honor who had been missing for several days were (hopefully) found by the police before their fame-mongering granddaughters started accusing innocent journalists of kidnapping on the internet.

I'd seen a measly eight movies thus far and consumed less than thirty free drinks, an all-time low for me. The Pink Door story was really throwing off my game. I knew Victoria wanted me to wrap it up, but there was no way in the world I was going to miss the Gossip Brunch. I pulled on my clothes from yesterday and restocked my marijuana supply. The fedora was upside down on the floor in the corner. The pheasant feather had been chewed down to a nub and there was a neat little pile of cat puke in the middle of the crown. I scraped out the vomit and headed for the door.

The Gossip Brunch was not on the MIFF schedule. It was not in fact an official festival event. In order to attend, you simply had to know when and where the gathering took place. How did you find out such a thing? You just did. It was like that secret menu for In-N-Out or knowing that Sean Connery wore a toupee when he was James Bond. When did you learn that information? Who told you? No one can remember, but the knowledge exists nonetheless.

The time for the brunch was always around noon, but the location varied from year to year. Inevitably, the event was held at the house of a festival committee member or private donor. In other words, someone extravagantly wealthy who wanted to be recognized as extravagantly wealthy while simultaneously appearing to be charitable. As fate would have it, this year the event was to be hosted by Liliane Easton.

The Easton estate was located several miles west of Mountainview, literally inside of Long's Peak. There was a large cave opening at the base of the mountain that had once been the home of bears, cougars, coyotes, and various vermin. When the Eastons decided to build a mansion there, it was occupied by several thousand rare bats that had to be removed humanely and relocated to a similar cavity on the other side of the mountain, where experts said they would almost surely die off within two generations. Construction took almost five years, and when the guano settled, the former opening was filled with an enormous edifice featuring several stories of reinforced glass walls stacked on top of each other like stairs and held up by oak pillars that, when examined closely, contained totem-like carvings of images from American Indian, Hindu, and ancient Babylonian cultures. The estate was featured in the glossy pages of a half dozen architectural and interior design magazines, which called it, "Breathtaking," "Inspiring," and "A harmonious blend of Jungian symbolism and Frank Lloyd Wright's suburban bohemianism." Locals called it, "the bat's cave."

I took an Uber to the house and knocked on the hand-carved ivory front door. An elderly Hispanic woman let me in and then disappeared without a word. I was left in a large, empty room with twenty-foot-tall tiled mosaic ceilings, white marble floors covered with Persian rugs, Navaho blankets hanging on cedar walls, and a chandelier made of what appeared to be bamboo. There was an enormous red stone fireplace on the north wall with half a cord of wood stacked up next to it in a precise rectangle. The wood and the fireplace were almost certainly for show, as it did not seem possible that this underground domain could have a working chimney. The centerpiece of the room was a polished obsidian sculpture of an Apache brave standing proud and defiant on a large pedestal with his arms folded over his muscled chest. It was at least six feet tall. The poor bastard was completely nude except for a single feather in his long hair and a turquoise arrowhead necklace. His penis was enormous, and, oddly, circumcised, and his smooth buttocks were clenched perfection. I circled him once, and, unable to resist, reached out and tapped the mushroom head of his giant member with my index finger. "Lucky bastard," I mumbled.

From the bowels of the house, I heard the distant clatter of expensive glassware followed by the gurgle of forced laughter. There was a strange echoing effect that made it difficult to tell what direction the noise was coming from, so I took a chance on an arched hallway that appeared to lead toward the back of the underground estate. I passed through a drawing room filled with uncomfortable sofas, a library filled with Easton Presses that had never been opened, and the requisite meditation room filled with nothing. The ethno-porn décor continued throughout the house. There were more naked warriors, paintings of unclothed African tribes, and a collection of fertility goddesses large enough to impregnate every woman on the Front Range. I tried every door along the way, but they were all locked. I was hoping to find a secret wet bar stocked with dusty bottles of rare wine or a case of bourbon stolen from the Kremlin, but no such luck.

Finally, after circling back several times, I turned down the correct hall and found myself in a large, open room populated with tipsy people trying to impress one another. In the far corner, there was a baby grand being played by an elderly woman in a dapper little tuxedo, the light tinkling music just barely rising over the muffled din of the guests, "Heaven Knows I'm Miserable Now" by The Smiths. The far wall was completely made of glass, and there were floodlights on the other side, so viewers could see deep into the recesses of the cave. There were giant stalactites hanging from the cave ceiling and minerals of every color glittering on the damp walls. It really was a breathtaking sight.

The crowd was a who's who of Mountainview's moneyed and artistic community, peppered with a few foreign directors, MIFF regulars, and party crashers to keep things honest. Every member of the MIFF board of directors was here, drinking and spilling secrets, which was why they called it the Gossip Brunch. Officially, the festival ended tomorrow evening with the award ceremony, but unofficially, the winners were revealed long before the sealed envelopes were opened. Everyone who was anyone knew this, and that's why everyone who was anyone was here.

I tiptoed around the side of the room until I found the wet bar, which was being manned by an attractive young man who looked like he'd just stepped out of sepia photograph from the 1920s, plaid pants, red suspenders, a long mustache waxed into the shape of a question mark on each end. I ordered an Old Fashioned, drank it in six thirsty swallows, and then ordered two more. Mustache McHipster gave me a dirty look but didn't argue.

I grabbed my drinks and looked around for a friendly face. The room was divided into three camps. The money was gathered near the cave window, holding fragile glasses with long stems and mumbling in well-mannered conspiratorial tones about stock tips or blood diamonds or whatever rich people talked about at parties. Liliane was among them, of course, dressed like a bohemian cowboy in a brown, flat-brimmed hat, knee-high boots with fringe dangling off the sides, and cream camel-hair shawl with various animals printed across it. She was leaning down to speak with a short man wearing what appeared to be very expensive pajamas. Even from the back, I could tell who it was and quickly turned away before either could recognize me. It wasn't unusual for Gerald to be at an event like this. In fact, he reveled in these types of gatherings, where he could rub elbows with his financial betters, swap community gossip, entertain suggestions on what stories to run in the paper, and generally hold forth on what he perceived to be Mountainview's future. It was a mutual ego-stroking affair. The wealthy citizens of Mountainview were allowed to believe that they were powerful enough to influence the local media, and Gerald was allowed to believe he was important enough to be influenced.

On the other side of the room, behind the piano, there was a contingent of bored media representatives wondering why they were drinking wine inside of a cave. And, finally, the talent was huddled near the appetizers, drinking too much and laughing noisily. Normally I would join their group, if for no other reason than to blend my impending drunkenness with theirs, but then I spotted Maggie at the epicenter of it all, telling stories and basking in the glow of their attention. River was next to her, smiling and whispering encouragement, like

Fay Wray trying to calm down Kong before he breaks out of his cage and trashes the city. They looked so comfortable together, even though they'd known one another for less than twenty-four hours, and I felt a wave of hot jealousy rise in my chest. How had this happened? Three days ago I was a simple movie reviewer with a broken heart and a minor drinking problem. Now the former love of my life was suddenly in business with my current paramour, promoting a movie directed by my former best friend based on ideas we came up with in college, where he did not apparently have sex with the aforementioned love of my life, and was currently slouching miserably against the wall under a framed painting of Sitting Bull (miraculously clothed). Looking at him now, picking nervously at his beer label, I realized this was the only person in the room I actually wanted to talk to, so I headed in that direction, moving slowly so as not to attract attention to my presence.

Eric raised his microbrew when he saw me approach. "You're late."

I showed him my two glasses. "That's why I'm catching up. What did I miss? The bloodletting? The virgin sacrifice?"

"You know perfectly well there are no virgins here."

We clinked receptacles and spent an awkward minute drinking, smiling, and trying to find a way to slip back into our casual friendship. Finally, I couldn't stand it any longer.

"What's happening over there?" I asked, nodding toward the growing crowd gathered around Maggie and River.

"She's always been better at the networking thing," said Eric. "I get all... you know."

"Frankenstein when he sees fire?"

He grinned. "Fuck you. And it's Frankenstein's monster, you ignorant asshole. Frankenstein was the scientist."

"Not in the movies. Seriously, why are those vultures hanging around Maggie? I mean, I know she's charming and all, but that's quite the crop of heavy hitters."

Eric cracked his knuckles and looked away.

"What?"

"It looks like we...um... well, maybe *The Big Check-Out* possibly could have won the Audience Choice Award."

"Oh," I said. "Congratulations."

"It's no big deal."

The Audience Choice Award was a big deal, especially for a small film like *The Big Check-Out*. It wasn't an Oscar or anything like that, of course, but it could create a buzz, even at a minor festival. Several years ago, a pair of sisters from Ireland won the Audience Choice Award with a clever little family comedy, and the movie eventually found a home on Netflix. They went on to make a mediocre horror flick with Nicole Kidman, and they were currently in talks regarding a Marvel movie involving one of those lesser side characters no one cares about. The Audience Choice Award was a big deal.

"The thing is," Eric stammered. "I don't think you meant to, but it looks like maybe you helped us out. That video of you that River posted is getting a lot of buzz." His knuckle-cracking became more earnest now. "I was skeptical about her at first, but she really came through. The movie got another showing last night and two more today. Our website is blowing up, and I'm getting phone calls from people I've never heard of asking me what my next project is."

I finished off one of my glasses and started on the other. On the one hand, I was happy for them, and on the other hand, I wanted them to die in a large fire and then spit on their charred remains.

"That's…great I guess. I mean, seriously, that's really good. Good for you. Very positive and good."

Eric finally managed to remove the beer label, looked around for a trashcan to put it in, and then stuffed it in his pocket.

"Yeah, I can feel the love. The problem is I don't have any ideas. I mean, nothing concrete. I've been working on this thing for almost five years. Now they want me to come up with something new on the fly."

"Yeah, that's rough. I feel for you."

He leaned over and lowered his voice. "Have you been working on anything lately?"

"Seriously?"

"Come on, man, this is what we always wanted. The three of us making movies together. Come back with us."

I made a face. "California? I told you I've got this newspaper job."

"You don't want to be a journalist. I know you. You love movies. You live movies. This is an opportunity of a lifetime. We could be a team again. Me, you, Maggie. Just like in the old days."

"Right, just like the old days."

"Will you shut up. We already talked about that. Maggie didn't cheat on you. I didn't steal your girlfriend. That's a fantasy, Sam. This is real."

There was a stir of motion in my peripheral vision, and I looked up to see Maggie and her entourage staring at us. There was a large, panicked smile on her face, and she was waving her arm in circles, motioning for Eric to join them.

"Oh, shit," said Eric, standing up and buttoning his blazer. "I've got to go. Think about California, okay? Maggie will be pissed off at first, but she'll get over it. Especially if you write her a good part. Our plane leaves at two o'clock tomorrow."

He handed me his empty beer bottle and headed toward the group on wobbly legs, looking like a newborn deer walking toward a pack of wolves. I took another drink and contemplated his offer. California? La-La-Land?

Impossible. It was another world. Besides, I had obligations here.

As if reading my thoughts, Liliane suddenly appeared at my right elbow and dug her talons into the soft meat of my bicep.

"Samuel!" she said. "We were just talking about you? Weren't we, Gerald?"

"Namaste," Gerald agreed.

He took my left arm, and together they marched me down the hall and through a door that resembled the lid of a royal coffin. When we entered the room, Gerald immediately recoiled and the words "Dear God!" came tumbling out of my mouth before I could catch them. The entire space was covered in swastikas. There were black swastikas and red swastikas and purple swastikas and rainbow swastikas. There were swastikas embroidered on large tapestries hanging on the walls and swastikas hand-painted on ceramic pots inside of glass cases. There were swastikas carved into the foreheads of wooden statues and swastikas sewed onto elaborate quilts.

"Anyone want a drink?" asked Liliane, ignoring our awe-struck faces.

"I do," I said.

She walked across the room and stood in front of a large globe made of dark, rich wood polished to a high shine. Every country on the beautiful orb was carved from a mineral taken from the soil of that nation, transforming the world into a colorful, glittering mosaic. Liliane reached underneath the planet, flipped some switch near Antarctica, and the Earth split open at the equator, revealing an impressive wet bar inside its core.

"You'll have to fix them yourselves," she said. "I'm not a bartender."

I rushed to the globe and cracked open a bottle of whiskey that was so expensive it didn't even have a brand name. I poured four fingers into a fancy tumbler and drained half in a relieved gasp.

Gerald stood in the same spot, gazing in horror at the swastikas. "Um...Liliane?"

"Yes?"

"My grandfather was half Jewish."

Liliane rolled her eyes and shot a jet of derisive air through her nose. "Why does everyone say that?"

"It is a lot of swastikas for one room," I said.

"The swastika—or *sauwastika*, as they say in India—is a Hindu symbol of spirituality and divinity. In Sanskrit, the word *swastika* means 'conducive to well-being.' For centuries it has represented peace and enlightenment to millions of people. This room is a shrine to all things holy. I don't understand why everyone focuses on the Nazi stuff."

"What about that?" Gerald said, pointing to a giant, tattered Nazi flag inside a glass-covered frame on the wall behind Liliane's head.

Liliane turned around and raised her right arm toward the flag, a gesture that was supposed to be presentational but looked disturbingly like a Heil Hitler salute.

"That's exactly what I'm talking about. This was one of only four flags recovered from Joseph Goebbels' Berlin home. It used to hang on the wall behind his desk, and now it is here in my house. Every morning I come to this room, sit on the floor in the lotus position, and meditate in front of this flag. Don't you see? I am cleaning it. This is our history, our karmic essence, and I am realigning the chakras of human existence here. I am removing the negative energy. I am reclaiming the swastika."

"Oh," said Gerald. "I get it. That's...beautiful."

"Wouldn't it be better just to burn it?" I asked.

Liliane frowned at me. "Do you have any idea how much it's worth?" She reached out to the wet bar with her creamy right hand, grabbed Russia by the quartz, and slammed the globe shut. "But we didn't come here to talk about swastikas, did we? I want an update on your progress, Samuel. Have you uncovered the true cause of that poor girl's death?"

"Well, it's sort of...complicated," I said. "I do believe there was foul play involved, but I haven't been able to prove anything so far. There was this needle, you see, but it turned out to be diabetes, and then I spoke to the chief of police and the Mayor said—"

"You talked to the mayor?" Gerald asked.

"No, not that mayor, the one in my apartment building. I mean, he used to be...but he isn't anymore. Never mind. It's not important. The thing is I just need more time. I'm sure Mouth is up to something. She gave me all these papers to go through."

"What kind of papers?" Liliane snapped.

"I don't know. I didn't really look at them. Just, you know, government papers or something. I think she was trying to throw me off the scent. When I asked her about the drugs, she punched me in the eye, and I think—"

"Wait, she assaulted you?"

Liliane gave Gerald a poignant look, and leaned in to get a better look at my face. He grabbed my jaw and pulled my face one way and then the other, causing pain to shoot through my cheek bones. I took another drink of whiskey.

"Did Monica Larkman do this to you while you were representing the newspaper?" he asked.

"Well, one of them was actually my ex-girlfriend. I went to see a movie she was in, and afterward there was kind of a scene. No, not a scene really. I was just asking questions like everyone else, but then she got mad—"

"Sam, shut up. This is important. Did Monica Larkman attempt to suppress your First Amendment rights?"

I scratched my head. "Which one is the first?"

"Freedom of Speech."

"Oh, no, not really. I just kept getting Rebecca Kint's name wrong."

"Who?"

"The young woman who died."

"Oh, yes. Sad. But this Larkman woman assaulted you while you were performing your journalistic duties, yes?"

"Right. Like I said, she punched me because…"

"It doesn't matter why."

Gerald looked at Liliane and nodded. "This is it," he said. "This is what we need."

"Need for what?"

"Shush."

Liliane closed her eyes and inhaled deeply, bringing her hands together in prayer at the center of her chest, and exhaling with a satisfied smile. She put her arms around me again, and I leaned into her warm, toned body and allowed myself to be enveloped in her intoxicating aroma. Gerald gave me a weird look but I ignored him.

"You have done an outstanding job, Samuel," she whispered. "You are my hero."

"But I didn't—"

She released me and stepped away, and I felt her cold absence. "My hero," she repeated, and then she turned and walked out of the room.

Gerald watched her go and then turned to me, his voice dropping several octaves as he transformed back into the alpha male.

"Sit down," he said, pointing to a chair in the corner with a swastika doily draped over the back. I complied, and Gerald stood in front of me, leaning over me in a paternal manner. "You are going to write this story from your point of view. Put in everything you saw in the alley and in the strip club. Talk about your interview with Ms. Larkman and—this is very important, Sam—describe how she assaulted you. Discuss your theories on how the unfortunate incident took place. Write it just like one of your entertaining and erudite movie reviews."

"Victoria will never let me do that," I protested. "You know how she is about sources and facts and stuff."

"Don't worry about Victoria. You're going to write this on your blog. You will mention the fact that you were working as a reporter for the *Mountainview Chronicle* at the time these events took place, and you will say that Victoria threatened to take you off the story. I was there. I'll back you up."

"Right. But you know that's not how it happened. Victoria just wants to get the story right."

"You know what Victoria wants? She wants me to hire that insolent little girl to edit the paper instead of you. Did you know that? She explicitly told me you should not be the next editor of the *Mountainview Chronicle*. She said you were inexperienced and unreliable. But I disagree with her, Sam. You bet I do. You know what I see when I look at you?"

"What?"

"The future of journalism. The future of my newspaper. The future of Mountainview."

He held out his hand, and I took it.

"This is the beginning of a beautiful friendship," I said.

"What?"

"Nothing. So I got the job?"

He patted me on the shoulder and walked to the door. "The job is yours, son. As soon as you write that blog, you will be the new editor of the *Mountainview Chronicle*. You should feel incredibly proud of yourself."

"Thank you."

He closed the door on his way out, and I found myself sitting alone in a room full of swastikas. I finished the rest of my drink and then went to the globe. I spent several minutes trying to find the switch on the bottom before finally giving up and prying the thing open with my fingers. I filled up my glass and took a drink. I was an editor. I was a college dropout who fought his way up from the bottom and was now in charge of a newspaper. It was the classic underdog story, but somehow victory seemed hollow. Maybe it was the decor. I felt bad for Victoria, of course, but it really was her own fault for not believing in me. And she was quitting, so it wasn't that big of a deal. Reyna would be mad at me, but Reyna was always kind of mad about everything anyhow. If Gerald tried to fire her, I would put my foot down and fight for her job, and then she would be grateful. Everything would be alright.

I was forgetting something. The director in my head was running through a series of images from the past forty-eight hours, trying to tell me something important, but the poor little man had completely lost track of the plot. I took another drink.

My phone buzzed. It was Mouth. *I swear to God if you're late for this thing I will break every bone in your scrawny body. COME. HERE. NOW.*

Chapter 19: Invasion of the Body Snatchers

GARDEN VILLAGE WAS A TRAILER PARK located on the far east end of town, in between a storage-rental facility and a cemetery. As far as trailer parks go, it was nice. There were thirty trailers lined up in four neat rows with about five yards of dirt between them. The flimsy rectangular structures were painted various bright colors (canary yellow, stop-sign red, carnation pink), and about half had rusty cars parked next to them. There were a few barbeque grills behind the trailers and plastic children's toys were strewn about, but aside from that, the property was well maintained. There was even a small playground at the back next to a community garden.

Despite its small size and generally tidy nature, Garden Village had a strained relationship with the rest of the Mountainview community. Over the years, no less than five attempts had been made to close the place down based on allegations of cleanliness, noise, crime, and drug trafficking, but so far none had come to fruition. The owners were a stubborn old hippie couple who'd made a modest fortune in the '70s by creating line of all-natural beauty products using beeswax as the primary ingredient. Their first home in Colorado had been a small trailer in Garden Village, and they bought the property for sentimental reasons, vowing to make it a safe space for poor young couples in Mountainview no matter how high the rent prices got in the rest of the city. Because of this, of course, Garden Village attracted an eclectic group of outcasts and misfits that would have been forced to leave the city if not for this financial oasis. Over the years, it had housed transients, grad students, folk musicians, street buskers, war veterans, drug dealers, and apparently strippers. I had not been to this side of town in years, and I was not excited to be back.

I took out two Xanax and a Valium and washed them down with a drink from my flask. When I got off the bus, I found a hiding spot behind an enormous pine tree and packed my pipe. The puffy theatrical clouds of yesterday had gathered together and turned dark, forming an ominous gray wall across the sky that pressed down on the atmosphere, forcing its weight upon the town, smothering the city like a damp blanket trying to suffocate every last one of us.

Maybe it was the sky, maybe it was the drugs, maybe it was this strange place I didn't want to be, but something inside me had broken loose, some essential gear or belt that kept the mental mechanisms running on time, and now there was an unfamiliar slipperiness to my thoughts, a kind of unpredictability that was both frightening and freeing at the same time. I thought of Jimmy Stewart in *Vertigo*, how he believed he was going crazy when he saw Kim Novak die and then he saw another woman on the street who looked exactly like her, how it was all a big conspiracy and Judy Barton was really Madeleine Elster all along and she never fell out of the bell tower, how it was easy to manipulate a man's mind when he was desperate and in love, how Jimmy Stewart persisted in pursuing what he knew to be the truth in his own mind despite what the world presented to him—and how he solved the mystery in the end.

I smoked the pipe until the bowl was ash and felt better. The slippery feeling spread through my body, and this time I didn't fight it. I banged my pipe against the side of the tree. I saw these actions happen, but I didn't feel that I had caused them. Walk, I told the feet, and the feet walked. Stop, I said, and they stopped. Hold your hand out flat. Now slap him in the face. I saw my hand rise, the muscles tense, and then the palm connected with my right cheek. I heard the skin connect violently with skin, but I felt nothing. My head was buzzing with the drugs and my nerve endings had finally shut down. I was numb to the world, and it felt right.

It was time to shoot the end of this movie.

The file Mouth had given me listed Rebecca Kint's old address, and I found the trailer at the back of the park, a long rectangular box painted in chipped, headache-inducing turquoise with burnt-orange doors and shutters. Inside someone was listening to Edith Piaf singing "La Vie en Rose" at full volume. I ascended the rickety porch and knocked on the door. There was a thud on the other side but no one came. I turned my fist to the side and used the meat of the hand, shaking the whole trailer with my pounding. The music died down, and the door was soon opened by the stripper I'd met at the Pink Door several days ago. What was her name?

"Hey, Columbo," she said, leaning coquettishly in the doorframe. "You here about Rebecca?"

I blinked. "How did you know?"

She shrugged. "What else? Come in. Good to see you again. I'll be ready in ten minutes, and we can all walk over together."

"Wait? Walk where?"

I had no idea what she was talking about, but I followed her into the trailer anyhow. She had thick ankles and a wide, flat backside, and when she walked, it swung like the pendulum on a sexy grandfather clock. On the back of her right calf was a tattoo of Marilyn Monroe doing the skirt-blowing-up pose from *Seven Year Itch* and on the left James Dean doing that leaning-back-thumbs-hooked-through-belt-loops thing from *Rebel Without a Cause*. I preferred Newman to Dean, but I took it as a good omen anyhow.

"We're drinking mimosas," she said. "You want?"

I said I did.

"There's champagne and orange juice in the fridge. Make one for me too, honey." She walked her grandfather clock through the oblong living room, and then Marilyn and James disappeared into a bedroom at the back. Edith Piaf started singing again.

The refrigerator was practically bare, aside from an open bottle of cheap champagne and a carton of orange juice, sans pulp. I pulled them out. I glanced at the bedroom door and then opened the freezer, where I found a half-empty bottle of Smirnoff in the back on top of a stack of green popsicles that had been frozen together in a large, frosty clump. I opened the bottle and tipped it to my lips. Three long gulps, one short shudder. I took out my flask and refilled it, spilling only a little on the table in the process. I put the vodka back and wiped up the spill with the sleeve of my coat. I pulled two long-stemmed glasses out of the dishwasher and filled them with champagne, splashed in a bit of juice.

I thought about sitting at the table and waiting, but it felt like the scene required more action. With the mimosa in my right hand, I took a tour around the trailer, purely for investigative-reporting reasons, poking my head into cabinets, digging in drawers, peeking through keyholes. I found a box of Corn Flakes in the bathroom and a doll head in the silverware drawer. On a hunch, I took the baby torso from my pocket that I found in the alley behind the Pink Door and put the doll head on it. A perfect fit. What were the chances? I put them both in my pocket.

On the door of the refrigerator, there was one of those magnetic poetry sets, a series of white rectangles with random words on them in black lettering. Someone had arranged some of them to spell out, "rub the magic clown belly" and "poisoned flowers grow in her mouth." The first sentence meant nothing, but the second caught my attention. Poisoned flowers? What did that mean? Poppies were flowers. Drugs? And mouth? Did Rebecca try to leave a message before she died? Something to do with Mouth Larkman and drugs? I took out my notepad and wrote it down. There were several magnets holding up an old grocery list, and next to that was a set of photographs, the kind taken in one of those booths where you put in money and the camera clicks every fifteen seconds. The pictures were of two young women making a series of goofy faces. One of them was the woman who opened the door for me, and I assumed the other was Rebecca Kint. She was a petite bottle blonde with freckles on her nose and dimples so deep they looked like sinkholes in her cherubic cheeks. Her eyes were blue and innocent, and her smile made my heart skip. She looked like a cute neighborhood girl who had seen too many glamour magazines. The magnets holding up the photos said "classy girl fun." I put the pictures in my pocket.

The bedroom door opened, and I tried to nonchalantly lean against the side of the fridge to demonstrate my innocence, but I misjudged the distance and banged my shoulder instead, spilling mimosa down the front of my coat. V. laughed when she saw me wiping juice off myself. She had changed out of the glamorous ball gown, and the fabulous hair structure had finally succumbed to gravity, falling in lovely brushed waves down to the middle of her back. I had no idea where she procured new clothes, but she was now wearing a long conservative black dress, black flats, and a red scarf. Her makeup was perfect and understated. She looked at me and shook her head.

"Whatcha doing here, kid? You got a crush on me or something?"

I smiled. "Of course I do, but that's not why I'm here. The police came to my door this morning."

She grabbed the mimosa out of my hand and took a long drink. "The police? You in some kind of trouble? Because Mama's a little too old to pull a *Thelma and Louise*."

"I doubt that. But they weren't looking for me. Your granddaughter is on the warpath. She saw that award at my place and nearly clawed my eyeballs out."

She handed the mimosa back. "Aw, that's sweet. The little monster's worried about her meal ticket. She didn't file charges on you, did she?"

"Not yet. I think the police chief talked her down. But she's threatening to go to the press and tell everyone you've been kidnapped. Something about Twitter and a bunch of true-crime podcasts."

V. groaned. "That sounds like her alright. Never passes up an opportunity to plaster her puss all over the web."

"What are you doing here anyhow?"

She shook a cigarette from a pack on the kitchen counter, fired up the gas stove, and leaned down to light it on the blue flame. She exhaled and squinted at me.

"Do I really have to explain it to you? Two women meet at a strip club, they spend the night together, and you have to ask what they were doing?"

"But that's not... I mean, you're not..."

"Not what? Gay? Homosexual? Lesbian? A dike? You're goddamn right I am." She opened the fridge and took a drink straight from the bottle of champagne. "Probably bisexual, actually, but we didn't really know about that when I was younger. Definitely prefer the ladies though. Can you blame me?"

"But you're so old," I said.

"Thanks, kid. I needed that." She took another drink. "That's where the money comes in."

"You paid her?"

"Jesus, you're such a fucking prude. How am I gonna get a hot piece of ass like that at my age without paying for it?"

"You might have just asked."

From the bedroom, Kate walked towards us, putting on a pair of long silver earrings along the way. I might have been mistaken, but it seemed as though her hips were swinging even more provocatively than before.

V. turned and smiled. "Does that mean I get my two hundred dollars back?"

"I'm sure I have no idea what you're talking about." She finished with the earrings and picked up the full mimosa on the table. She looked into my eyes, and my heart raced. "Is this for me?"

I nodded, dumbstruck

She held the glass by the stem, pinky out, and put it daintily to her lips so as not to smear her lipstick. She drank half the glass, made a face, and said, "It needs something."

She opened the freezer. I cringed when she took out the vodka, but she didn't seem to notice it was depleted. She filled the rest of her glass with it and drank again.

"Better. Are you guys ready?"

"Ready for what?" I said.

"The funeral, of course. It's a short walk, but we should leave soon. I don't like to be late."

I thought about the text from Mouth. Damnit.

"No, I can't go there," I said. "That's not possible."

"Why not? You're writing a story for the paper about her, right?"

"No, not really. I mean, maybe, sort of. Anyhow I can't go to that cemetery…because…I can't. And that's not why I came here." I widened my stance and nodded toward V. "I'm supposed to bring her in."

V. snorted. "Right. And how did you plan on doing that?"

"Well…" I fidgeted with my sleeve. "I, um, was going to, you know… Damnit, I told Henry I'd find you. What if your granddaughter goes to the media?"

"Are the police after you?" Kate asked V. She didn't seem upset by the news. If anything, her voice held a note of amusement and wonder.

"The police aren't after anyone," said V. "My granddaughter is just a pain in the ass, that's all." She picked up a jacket off the back of the kitchen chair and put it on. "Nina ain't gonna do jackrabbit squat. If she tells anyone I'm missing, my asshole son-in-law will find out that she lost me *again*, and he'll stop funding her so-called acting career *again* and she'll have to go back to community college *again*. So shut your yap, get your ass out the door, and let's go pay our respects to… Sorry, honey, what was your friend's name?"

"Rebecca," said Kate. For the first time, there was a hint of sadness in her voice, and she turned away. "We really must be going now. Entombment is no occasion for tardiness."

Those were not the kind of words you argued with.

"Alright," I said. "But I'm going to tell Henry where you are."

"Fine by me," said V. "I could use a ride home."

I took out my phone and sent a text.

"Maybe I'll just wait here," I said.

Kate shook her head. "In my house? I don't think so."

"What kind of reporter are you?" V. added. "This is supposed to be your story. Get your ass out that door now, kid, before I toss it out for you."

Chapter 20: Laura

THE BLUE MOUNTAIN CEMETERY WAS THE ORIGINAL GRAVEYARD when the town was first founded in 1861. It was a sad hilly little patch of land with far too many trees to be a proper burial ground. Over the decades, the pines and cottonwoods had grown tall, stretching their branches until they blocked the sun, and underneath the ground, the roots had also grown and spread, thrusting through the dirt, twisting and curling around the sleeping corpses, pushing coffins back toward the surface and forcing tombstones off-kilter, until the monuments looked like rows of crooked teeth in the mossy mouth of an ancient witch. In the 1940s, a new cemetery was built on the west end of town facing the rising sun. It was large and flat and treeless, and the headstones were lined up in perfect rows separated by a meticulously maintained carpet of green grass. Blue Mountain had been all but forgotten by the more affluent citizens of Mountainview, but it was still the primary resting ground for the less fortunate, as well as those with family plots that could not be moved.

There was a black wrought-iron fence surrounding the property, each post resembling the stem of some exotic petrified plant that had, at its crown, bloomed a spear-like flower. The gate opened with a satisfying horror-movie creek, and then banged shut like a shotgun blast behind us. We made our way toward the northwest corner, where a gathering of approximately a dozen people dressed in dark tones awaited our arrival. Mouth was among the mourners, along with multiple employees of the Pink Door, wobbly and squint-eyed from dehydration. At the front of the group was a tired middle-aged couple whose faces were frozen in stoic masks of small-town grief. The father was a stout fireplug of a man with a thick head of wiry, salt-and-pepper hair and a round meat-and-potatoes potbelly. His arms were an inch too short for the black wool suit he wore, and his leathery reddish-brown face clashed with his powder-white forehead, the mark of a man who worked outside all day with a hat on. The mother was several inches taller than her spouse and attractive in a wholesome Doris Day kind of way. She wore a thick workman's coat over a navy-blue dress with a gray flower print. They appeared somewhat unsettled by the crowd around them but also thankful for the company.

We took a spot at the foot of the casket, which was an unadorned black box with a closed lid. V. gave me a sharp poke in the ribs with her elbow, and I took my hat off.

Facing the group was a young minister, barely in his thirties, dressed in an oversized black pea coat and blue scarf, the downy blonde hair on his upper lip struggling desperately to join its cousin on his chin. He kept looking around, smiling, realizing where he was, then casting his eyes down and frowning. Two things were clear. One, he had not officiated many funerals, and two, he had never met Rebecca Kint. I assumed the family wanted a Christian burial but couldn't imagine inviting the minister of their Kansas congregation to cross state lines in order to bury their fallen daughter, so they contacted a local parishioner. He was obviously out of his depth. He clutched a small, black Bible in both hands, and kept looking down at it, as though something inside was going to save him.

"Dearly beloved," he began before realizing this wasn't a wedding. "Oh, God. I'm sorry. It was the wrong..." He shook his head and took a deep breath. I thought he was going to cry.

"We are gathered here today to celebrate the life of Rebecca Kint." He gritted his teeth. "Not that this is a celebration, of course. That's just something they tell you to say. To, you know, remember the life instead of... Oh, God. I'm sorry."

He glanced at the Bible again, and seemed to make a final decision. He put the Bible in his pocket and finally looked out at the assembled group, making specific eye contact with the parents.

"I...I lost a sister when I was very young, and I know there is no consolation in times like these." There was a long, pregnant silence that only ended with the mother gave the preacher a slight nod of encouragement.

"In seminary, they tell you to be positive, make it sound like you should be happy the deceased is in a better place, but that just makes you feel guilty about your own grief. That's not fair, is it? I didn't think so. There are numerous quotes in the Bible about death and resurrection, as you know, but the only thing that helped me through my sister's death was the movie *Four Weddings and a Funeral*. It's silly, I know, but it was her favorite movie and I must have watched it thirty times after... After..."

"I'm sorry. I don't want to make this about me or my grief. I'm not very good at this. Obviously. But there is a scene towards the end when John Hanna recites that Auden poem at his lover's funeral. Do you remember that? It's kind of depressing, but with your permission, it's...well, it's all I have."

And in a hesitant, cracked voice, he recited the poem.

> *Stop all the clocks, cut off the telephone,*
> *Prevent the dog from barking with a juicy bone,*
> *Silence the pianos and with muffled drum*
> *Bring out the coffin, let the mourners come.*
>
> *Let aeroplanes circle moaning overhead*
> *Scribbling on the sky the message 'He is Dead.'*
> *Put crepe bows round the white necks of the public doves,*
> *Let the traffic policemen wear black cotton gloves.*

He was my North, my South, my East and West,
My working week and my Sunday rest,
My noon, my midnight, my talk, my song;
I thought that love would last forever: I was wrong.

The stars are not wanted now; put out every one,
Pack up the moon and dismantle the sun,
Pour away the ocean and sweep up the wood;
For nothing now can ever come to any good

WHEN HE FINISHED, EVERYONE STOOD IN SILENCE and listened to the wind rustle the tree branches. The coffin was suspended above the grave on wires attached to a pulley system, and the preacher reached down to flip a switch, causing the box to be slowly lowered into the rectangular hole. Afterward, the preacher embraced Rebecca's parents, and the mourners lined up to shake their hands, each one pausing to share their condolences.

And then suddenly, out of nowhere, I began to cry. It wasn't one of those soft, clean cries where the tears flow down silently. This was a loud, gross, sobbing cry with lots of snot involved. People turned to look at me, and I tried to reign it in but a damn had broken loose inside and several decades of emotions had been released. The sobs increased, taking control of my entire body, each one convulsing me with an electric shock of sorrow. If someone had asked me at that moment why I was crying, I could not have said. Inside my head, I just kept repeating one word, "Why? Why? Why?"

I was still in the midst of it when a strong hand grabbed me by the shoulder. I looked up and saw Henry Moss, wearing plain clothes, a thin book tucked under his right arm.

"You okay?" he asked.

I didn't trust myself to speak, so I just nodded.

"How long has it been since you've been back here?"

I shrugged.

"Where are they?"

"I don't know," I croaked. "It was a long time ago."

Henry pulled me to my feet. "Let's see if we can find them."

We wandered through the cemetery until we reached the north middle, two rows off the walking path, my feet finding their way despite the screaming voice in my head telling them to stop. The willow tree that had been green and healthy when we buried my parents was now a dead husk, its palsied black branches pointing toward their graves. My mother's was a plain rectangular tombstone with the words EMILY DRIFT carved onto it over BELOVED WIFE AND MOTHER. One of the willow roots had found its way under it, and there was a hairline crack at the base of the white stone that would no doubt work its way to the top in the decades to come. My father was next to her, where he'd always wanted to be. My grandparents' gravestones were on the right, as well as a small stone for my uncle, who drowned at the local reservoir when he was only six years old.

"How did you know she was here?" I asked.

Henry reached down and brushed a dead leaf off my mother's headstone. "I figured her parents would want to bring her back home. My dad is buried here too." He pointed to the north corner. "Your mom was a nice girl," he said. "I didn't know her well, but I remember that she was very sweet. She had a great laugh."

"I guess," I said. "I really don't know much about her."

"She was in a lot of plays." He took out the item under his arm, and I saw it was a yearbook, half-a-dozen pages marked with colored tabs. Henry opened to a page with a title at the top that said Drama Club, and I saw my eighteen-year-old mother, slim, shy, wearing a fluffy yellow dress on the set of *Oklahoma!* Henry turned to another page, and there was my mother again, sitting at a desk in a Bauhaus t-shirt, using her hands to hide her face like a geisha fan. "And she was in student council. She was nominated for homecoming queen, but she didn't win. Her yearbook quote was, 'You mustn't give your heart to a wild thing.' Kind of a strange thing for an eighteen-year-old girl to be thinking about."

I smiled. "It's from *Breakfast at Tiffany's*."

"I thought it was something like that."

He handed me the yearbook, and we stood there for several long minutes flipping back and forth through the pages. The dark wall of clouds was practically on top of us now, blocking out the setting sun and turning the air deathly cold. I shivered. Henry squeezed my shoulder, and I wanted to scream.

"I'm going to collect our actress friend before she manages another escape," he said. "Are you okay here?"

I nodded. The yearbook was too big to fit in any of my coat pockets, but there was a tear in the plaid lining on the left side. I managed to rip the seam until the opening was large enough, then I slipped the book inside, feeling it fall to the bottom of the lining with a significant tug.

He left and I reached inside my coat for my pills. I was shocked to find the Oxy empty and only a sad rattle inside the Valium bottle. I took out my flask, raised it in salute to my mother's tombstone, and swallowed the Valium. I felt like I should say something. Whenever someone visited a loved one's grave in the movies, they always spoke to it as though the person was standing in front of them. Grave monologues provided closure for the character and narrative subtext for the audience.

"Hey, Mom. Seen any good movies lately?"

No, too jokey. This wasn't a comedic moment. I cleared my throat and tried to work up some more tears.

"How could you do that? How…how could you do that to your own son?

I was just a child. You left us…"

But that fizzled out too. It wasn't my fault. I didn't even have a script. I considered trying again with anger or hatred or even forgiveness, but in the end, I didn't have any of these feelings. In fact, if I was completely honest, I had to admit that I didn't feel anything at all. I was numb, and I had been for a very long time. I looked up into the sky and watched a tiny speck emerge from the clouds, dancing and fluttering, growing larger, until a single snowflake landed on my forehead. I waited for others to follow, but that was it.

I took another drink from my flask and headed back to the site of Rebecca Kint's grave. The ceremony was over, and the coffin had been lowered into the ground. Most of the strippers had formed a loose semicircle around the minister, who was quoting Bible verses in quick succession and blushing like a schoolgirl at her first dance. Mouth was talking to the parents. The mother was nodding politely and the father looked like he was going to run for the car. Mouth motioned for me to come over, but I pretended I didn't see her and turned away, sending me directly into V.'s perfumed cleavage.

"Hold it right there," she said. Out of the corner of my eye, I saw Henry watching us. I hoped he would intervene, but he stayed put. "I can't believe you called the cops on me, you little narc."

I stepped back in case she decided to take a swing. "But…I told you I was going to."

"I always knew you were a rat, kid." She grinned and I let out a relieved sigh. "I guess I had a pretty good run. This town turned out to be a lot more interesting than I thought." She looked at the mountains and inhaled deeply. "How did you land here anyhow? You don't seem to fit this place."

I glanced over at my mother's grave. "I went to college here," I said. "And then, I guess I just couldn't bring myself to leave. I don't know. I lost something here, and I can't seem to get it back."

She gave me a long look and seemed to decide something. "Yeah, I lost something like that before."

"What did you do?"

She didn't answer for a long time. I thought maybe she was having a senior moment, and I started to say something else.

"Same as you," she finally said. "I got lost in something else." She looked around again. "Wasn't as pretty as this place though. If you're gonna get lost, kid, might as well be here."

I looked up at the sky again. It was almost black now, and the snow was falling in slow dreamlike swirls. Henry finally approached us.

"There he is," said V., the rasping taunt returning to her voice. "The man who's going to lock me up." She put her wrists out. "I won't go quietly, copper. You'll never take me alive."

Henry rolled his eyes. "Oh, I think we can do without the handcuffs."

"I wouldn't bet on that," I said. "This one's a runner, Henry. Don't turn your back on her for a minute. She'll gun you down in cold blood."

Henry gave me a look. "*She's* the runner? That's the pot calling the kettle ugly."

V. barked. "You tell him, honey." She hooked her arm through Henry's. "This is my new man right here. We're going to drive off into the sunset."

Henry straightened his shoulders and patted her hand. "That's right, darling. We're going to drive off into the sunset…and then right back to your pain-in-the-ass granddaughter. Because that woman has been making my life a living hell for the past twelve hours. How did a beautiful, talented woman like you produce a horrific fame monger like that?"

V. batted her eyelashes. "I don't care what Sam says about you, I think you're a peach."

"A peach?"

"Or maybe a plumb. A big dark juicy plumb. I'd like to take a bite out of you."

Henry shook his head and fought back a smile. "Maybe we do need the handcuffs."

V. did a Groucho Marx with her eyebrows. "I love it when you talk dirty."

Henry finally raised his hands in surrender. "I give up. Can we get in the car now? I do have other duties besides escorting supposedly kidnapped movie stars back to their hotel rooms."

"Lead the way, plumb."

"Just a second," said Mouth, slipping into the conversation. "I need to borrow Sam here for a minute."

"Sure," said Henry. "He's got a story to file, but I don't need him for anything."

I looked at V. in a panic. "But your granddaughter did ask me to find you, so I should probably…"

"And I've been found," said V. giving me a sadistic wink. "You'd just be a third wheel. And besides, you don't want to see Nina again. She might decapitate you just for sport. You go with your friend here, and let me be alone with my plumb."

They walked away before I could protest further, and Mouth dug her claws in my arm.

"There's someone I want you to meet."

She pulled me over to the Kints and introduced me as the reporter who was writing a story about their daughter.

"Sam, this is Stan and Clara Kint. Stan and Clara, this is Sam Drift. He's the guy I was telling out about. He's been asking questions all over town about your daughter? He wants to get the story just right. Don't you, Sam?"

"Well, um, yes. I think…"

"But he doesn't have any stories about Rebecca's childhood. Do you, Sam?"

"No, I didn't think…"

"So I was thinking you could share some of your favorite stories about Rebecca."

"Of course," said Clara, a tearful shimmer in her eye. "What kind of stories?"

"Just a second, honey," said Mouth. "Sam, you forgetting something?"

"What?"

"Get out your notebook," she hissed.

So I dug around inside my coat one last time until I found my notebook and pen.

"Sam wants to know what kind of person your daughter was," said Mouth. "He needs to get some perspective."

The father cleared his throat. "She was…so small." He held out one of his large, calloused hands. "She fit right in the palm…" But that was as far as he could go. His leathery face turned even redder and he began to blink rapidly. The mother put her arm on his shoulder and he grabbed her wrist as though he was a drowning man grasping at a lifeboat. "The spiders…" That was all he said, and his wife nodded.

"Rebecca was a sensitive girl," the mother said, looking into the father's eyes. "Too sensitive for a country girl perhaps. You see a lot on the farm. Life and death. There's a certain reality that, no offense, people in the city don't see on a daily basis.

"She was six years old when I first read *Charlotte's Web* to her, and the night we finished it, she snuck out of the house and set loose every pig and chicken we had. It's a small farm, understand, so it wasn't all that much, but still quite a hullabaloo. The pigs didn't get far. We found them in a cornfield less than a mile away. But most of the chickens were killed by coyotes. Feathers everywhere. Rebecca cried about it for days. We had a long talk with her about how farms work and why farm animals had to stay locked up. I thought she understood. About a week later, she was getting ready for a bath, and I saw that her entire body was covered in red welts. I asked her where she got them but she wouldn't tell me. She could be so stubborn. I thought she had chickenpox. But when I searched her room, I found…" She stopped and squeezed her husband's hand. Her body shook, and I couldn't tell if she was crying or laughing.

"Fifty-seven spiders," he said. "You have any idea how long it would take to catch fifty-seven spiders? She couldn't save the chickens and pigs, so she went around the farm saving spiders. At least five were poisonous species. It's a miracle she didn't…"

"Thank you," said Mouth. "That's perfect. Thank you."

She pulled me away before I could ruin the moment. The snow was really coming down now, and I pulled up the collar on my coat. Mouth offered to give me a ride, and I accepted. We drove in silence across the city, and when we finally pulled into the *Mountainview Chronicle* parking lot, Mouth spoke.

"So you're going to show that notebook to your editor, right?"

"Sure," I said. "I mean, I'll talk to her about it. But there are some things you don't know about."

"No," Mouth said firmly. "Show her the notebook and the paperwork I gave you. Give it to her directly. That's all I want."

I sat up and adjusted my hat. "Let me tell you something about the newspaper business. Reporters like to have autonomy. You don't want your editor poking their nose in before have a chance to write it down. We need freedom. When I run the paper..."

Mouth reached between my legs and grabbed my balls, causing wave of nausea to wash over me.

"What the hell."

"It wasn't a request," Mouth said calmly. "You will show the notebook and paperwork to your editor. Do you understand?"

"But it's my story," I gasped.

In response, she dug in her fingernails. "It's not your story. It's Rebecca's story. Now, say the words."

"Yes," I cried. "I'll show it to Victoria. I will. I promise."

She released my manhood and I groaned with relief.

"I'm glad we had this talk," she said. "Now get the hell out of my car."

Chapter 21: The Treasure of the Sierra Madre

THE *MOUNTAINVIEW CHRONICLE* WAS DARK WHEN I ARRIVED except for a single rectangle of yellow light emanating from Victoria's office window. I ascended the stairs gingerly, the ache in my groin still pulsating along with Mouth's final words. Inside, Reyna and Victoria were hunched over long sheets of copy paper containing the contents of the upcoming edition, which had to be sent to the printer by noon tomorrow. Victoria was marking her pages in red ink and Reyna in green, each using some sort of cryptic code system that made the pages look like they'd been doodled on by an obsessed Christmas elf.

"You're late," said Victoria without looking up from her page. The headline of the article she was working on read, "Drought Bad for Local Business."

"I'm sorry," I said. "It's been a long day."

I sighed heavily and waited for someone to ask me why I was so exhausted, but both women continued to scratch away. I sat down on the couch with deliberate heaviness but still no reaction.

"Do you have the story?" asked Victoria.

"Right," I said. "About that. I think I'm going to need, like, an extension or something."

It was Victoria's turn to sigh. "I just need five hundred words, Sam. You said you interviewed the owner of the club…what's her name?…one of the Larkmans."

"Mouth, yeah, I talked to her, but she wasn't exactly forthcoming, if you know what I mean. I think she's hiding something. But she's about to crack."

"Oh, yeah," said Reyna. "How do you know that?"

"I can just feel it," I said. "You know, in my gut."

"Your gut?"

"Yeah, you know that feeling you have when something's not quite right."

"Sure," said Reyna, giving me a meaningful look. "I know that feeling."

"It's a simple article," said Victoria. "Woman exits strip club, slips on ice, hits her head. You do a little color about the club, provide some quotes from the owner, talk to the police, maybe interview the family if you can find them. Wrap it up with a quote from the city about salting the sidewalks in winter. Ta-dah!"

"Grease," I mumbled.

"What's that?"

"She didn't slip on ice. It was spa grease."

Victoria looked up for the first time.

"See there," said Reyna. "You have some details already. You should just type it up on my computer while you're here, and then you can forget about it.

Go back and party at the film festival."

"How do you know it was spa grease?" asked Victoria.

"What?"

"That's very specific. How do you know this young woman didn't slip on mechanical grease or hamburger grease?"

"Because I slipped on it when I was, you know, investigating the crime scene. It smelled weird. And then Mouth told me later that the spa next door was dumping this weird massage grease in the alley. She filed a report about it I think. Just a second." I rummaged around in my coat searching for the envelope Mouth had given me. I pulled out my notebook and the envelope Henry gave me. I dropped them on the chair beside me while I looked for the file from Mouth. Finally, I found it and handed it to Victoria. "Personally, I think she was just trying to throw me off the track. There's a deeper story here, I just know it. I think the Larkmans are involved in drug trafficking. If I had more time, I could…"

"This inspection request was filed with the city more than four months ago," said Victoria.

"Let me see that," Reyna said.

Victoria handed her the document and picked up the letter from Henry.

"When did the police department follow up on it?" asked Victoria.

"On what?" I said

"This," said Reyna, slapping the document on her lap emphatically. "This is an inspection request. The city has to send someone to check on it within three months. When did they do that?"

"Mouth said they didn't."

"Why not?"

"I don't know." This was starting to feel interrogative.

"Did you talk to the police department at all?"

"Of course I did. But I think Henry might be in on it. Get this—he told me I should give the story to a different reporter."

"You don't say."

"Um, right, exactly. And why would he do that?"

Reyna leaned forward, but I beat her to it.

"Because he's afraid of me, that's why. He knows I'm onto something, and he wants to take me off the case. That's how the bulls do it."

"The bulls?"

"Right. And the thing about Henry is I don't think you can trust the guy. I mean, he's probably on the Larkmans' payroll already. He's just a…"

"Bastard!" said Victoria.

"Well, I wouldn't necessarily go that far," I said. "He was actually very nice to me. I was going to say he's a dirty cop. He probably doesn't even know what the Larkmans are doing. He's paid to be quiet."

Reyna ignored me and nodded toward the letter in Victoria's hand. Victoria passed her the envelope, then turned to her computer and started typing furiously.

I looked from Reyna to Victoria and back again, waiting for someone to explain what was happening.

"Bastard," Victoria said again, although it was a whisper this time. I leaned over to look at her computer screen and saw that she was on the city's website looking at some documents. "I can't believe he did that."

"Did what?" I said. "What did Henry do?"

"Bastard," said Reyna, still looking at the letter.

"I know. Right under our goddamn noses, too."

I grabbed the paper from Reyna and tried to make sense of it, but it was just some document that said something about a deadline extension.

"And we can't even nail him on it," said Victoria.

"Not directly," Reyna replied. "But we can still go after the story."

Victoria rocked back in her chair and stared at the ceiling. "Maybe," she said. "But not without corroboration. All we have here is a bureaucratic loophole."

"Who's the bastard?" I asked, hoping it wasn't me.

"Gerald, of course," said Reyna.

Victoria rolled her eyes. "We should have known."

Reyna pointed to the documents in my hand. "How did you get those?"

"Henry gave them to me."

"He just gave them to you out of the blue?"

"Well, no. I was talking to him the other day, and I guess I requested them?"

"You guess?"

I rubbed the back of my head. "Yeah, it was weird. I don't actually remember asking for them, but he said I should get them. Then he showed up at my apartment this morning, like super early, and told me to bring this envelope to you right away. But I guess I sort of forgot I had it."

A rare smile spread across Victoria's face. "That sneaky son of a bitch."

"Will someone please tell me what's going on?" I said.

Reyna shook her head and hit my leg with the paperwork she was holding.

"You broke the story," she said. "I'll be damned if I know how you did it, but it's all here. The inspection request, the deferral from the city. Monica Larkman reported the dumping of illegal hazardous material months ago, and the city ignored it. The Kint family has a major lawsuit on their hands if they want to file one." She was flipping through my notebook now, and she hit me on the leg again. "You even have background on the victim and quotes from the parents. I take back everything I ever said about you. You are one hell of a journalist, Sam Drift."

"Thanks," I said, rubbing the spot on my leg where Reyna kept hitting me.

"What's that got to do with Gerald?"

Victoria frowned and pointed to her computer. "According to city records, Gerald owns the Nirvana & You building. He has plenty of pull on city council, too. Nothing in the paperwork points to him directly, but he's been trying to undermine this story since it came in."

"Hold on," I said. "That's just not true. He was very encouraging to me. If he didn't want this story to get out, why would he tell me to stay on it?"

Both women looked at me, Reyna with her mouth open in disbelief and Victoria with an expression of genuine concern.

"What?"

"You really don't know?" said Reyna. "I couldn't tell at first, but you don't."

"Don't what?"

Victoria leaned in. "Sam, he kept you on the story because he didn't think you would figure it out. The headline was too good to pass up. It would have looked suspicious if we didn't write about it at all. but he needed the reporter to fail."

I shook my head.

"You were a distraction," Reyna said. "The blog posts, the conspiracy theories. He figured you'd be so caught up in your fantasy world that the real story would just sort of pass you by."

"What fantasy world?"

The women looked at me with pity, and I felt my body shrink.

"But you still brought in the story," said Reyna. "It doesn't matter what Gerald thought, right? You're here with all this information. You have notes. We'll need to help you out, of course, but this is still your story, Sam. We have everything we need."

"Almost everything," said Victoria. We turned to look at her. "This paperwork shows that someone reported oil being illegally dumped in an alley, and that report was never investigated. However, at the moment, we have no real evidence that Nirvana & You was the culprit. I mean, it makes sense. It was happening behind their store, and I'm sure they use that oil in their spa, but without some sort of corroboration, accusing them would be libel." She turned to Reyna. "Do you have any connections over there?"

Reyna snorted. "Don't look at me. I can't afford five hundred dollar mud baths."

Victoria arched an eyebrow at me. I shook my head. There was a sudden drop in barometric pressure in the room as everyone took stock of the situation—so close and yet so impossibly far.

"They don't have *mud* baths."

We all turned to stare at River leaning against the doorframe in a casual slouch, looking like Garbo and Bacall all rolled into one. Rothko poked his head out of her purse and growled at me for good measure.

"I mean, mud baths are *so* twentieth century. *May*be you'd do a mud mask and a mineral bath if you were, *you* know, all old and gross or something, but don't pay more than a hundred for it, honey. *Total* rip-off."

"River," said Victoria, sliding the damning paperwork off her desk as she leaned back in her chair. "What are you doing here?"

River made a waving motion toward the ceiling. "I came here to see if Gerald was still tinkering around his office, but of course, the bastard's *never* around when you need him, is he?"

Everyone held their breath, not knowing exactly how much of the conversation she might have overheard or what she would do with the information if she had it.

"I think he went to one of those VIP parties for the film festival," said Reyna. "You might still be able to catch him. Sam probably knows where the parties are tonight."

River sighed and took a step into the room, indicating she was not going to leave immediately.

"Yes, he loves a good VIP party."

Her shoulders sagged and her face fell. For a moment, I thought she was going to cry. I had seldom seen River cry, or even display a hint of self-doubt when her father was not present, and the possibility of it was sort of alarming.

Suddenly, as though reading my thoughts, River snapped upright and glared at me.

"*So,*" she said with such force Rothko let out a little yelp, "you need to speak with someone at Nirvana & You."

Victoria looked at Reyna, who shrugged her shoulders as if to say, "Why not?"

"It's for a newspaper article," Victoria said, choosing her words carefully. "The story might get a little messy. You don't have to get involved, River."

River shrugged and rummaged around in her purse until she found a tube of lip gloss.

"Let's say I want to get involved," she said. She opened her mouth and pulled her lips over her teeth in preparation. When she was done applying it, she popped her glistening lips and smiled. "Let's say I *insist* on getting involved."

"We would need more than just hearsay," said Reyna. "The information would need to come from someone who has actually seen an employee dumping oil in the alley."

River cocked her head and smiled. "I have a friend, a *sorority* sister named Bethany. God, she's awful. Wears these *ridi*culous American Indian necklaces and *pretends* she's part Apache or something. I mean, girl, *please*, your parents are Dutch-Irish. But whatever. She took, like, one of those internship thingies there for a semester. That bitch owner worked her *full* time for *no* pay and then wouldn't even write her a recommendation letter. God, baby boomers are the *worst,* am I right? *Any*how, I went to visit her after hours to, you know, steal some facial creams and stuff, and I totally saw her dump that coconut shit in the alley. She said they did it every night. I was like, 'Ew, that's so not good for the environment.' And Bethany was like, 'I know, right.' "

Reyna pulled out a notepad from her back pocket and started scribbling furiously.

"This is great," she said. "So you saw her dump the oil in the alley. Was she doing it on her own volition or did the owner specifically tell her to dispose of the waste in that manner?"

"Wait a second," I said. I grabbed Reyna's notebook and pulled it away. "I don't think you understand, River. They're talking about going after your dad in his own newspaper. They want to write a hit piece about one of Gerald's businesses."

River gave me her most bored expression. "And?"

I sputtered. "And? *And*?" I started listing the possible repercussions. "He's going to be pissed. He's going to yell. He's going to throw shit. He might take away your apartment and your tuition. Have you thought about that? He might even disown you. No more credit cards, no more free clothes. And he's definitely going to fire someone." I turned to Victoria and Reyna, who were watching me with bemused concern. "Have the rest of you thought about that? Your jobs. Your health insurance. Victoria doesn't care because she's leaving us, but Reyna, it's not like journalism jobs are growing on trees these days. What will you do? Where will you go?"

"Okay," said Victoria quietly. "We get it, Sam. If you don't want to be involved, you don't have to be. We can leave your name out of it."

I didn't want to be involved, that was true, but I also didn't want them to be involved. I was scared and I wanted them to be scared with me. I wanted everything to go back to the way it was before all this started. Back to writing about movies and drinking alcohol and sleeping in late. What had happened? Bogart never had to go through anything like this. He'd just say some clever lines, punch the bad guy, and kiss the girl. Why was everything so complicated?

"He's right, you know," Victoria said to River. "Gerald is going to be livid. He'll view this as a betrayal and he will not take it lightly. All he can do is fire us, but I'm not sure what he might do to you personally and financially."

"Listen, I *appreciate* the concern," said River, casting a pinched smile in my direction. "But you all have something of an *elevated* opinion of Gerald. He has his little investments, sure, but most of our money is Mother's. Gerald is really a very poor businessman. *Further*more, my father does *not* buy my clothes or pay the rent on my apartment, thank *you* very much. The apartment is an asset owned by Mother, and it *must* have a permanent occupant for various tax reasons. I make money from selling art at *several* galleries here and in Denver, and I represent a variety of local artists, musicians, *and* film personalities, as Sam knows. Finally, I am a professional model. Nothing *lewd*, of course. Mostly local fashion magazines."

"Listen," I said. "You're just not getting it. This is your father, and your boss. This is his newspaper. We can't just go behind his back like this. He's going to kill you."

"Sam, you don't have to do anything you don't want to do," said Victoria. "This is your story. You brought it in. I have some issues with your methods, but the results speak for themselves. We can't ignore the story. We're journalists. This is what we do. It doesn't matter if the story is problematic for our boss. Gerald owns the newspaper but he does not own journalism. River is an adult. I'll walk her through the process and make sure she wants to go through with it, but in the end it's her decision to make. You have to make your own choice."

They all looked at me, Victoria, Reyna, River, and Rothko. I stared back at them in amazement, waiting for someone to laugh and say, "Just kidding!" or, "We really had you going!" No one spoke, and the silence grew uncomfortable.

"I really wish I could help you out here," I said, cringing even as the words tumbled out of my mouth. I stood up and crept toward the door, hoping someone, anyone, would follow. "Unfortunately, I have a prior engagement this evening. I'm...I didn't tell you about this, I'm sorry, but I'm going to be moving. To California. Probably. I was approached by several, you know, Hollywood people during the festival. They like my writing. I can't pass up an opportunity like that. And my friends are begging me to move there with them. He owns a movie studio, and he needs me to write scripts. So I'd love to stick around and finish this, but it looks like you have it covered. You've got the paperwork and the notebook—you don't need me."

Chapter 22: In a Lonely Place

OUTSIDE, THE SKY WAS BLACK, AND A HARSH WIND TRANSFORMED the fluffy crystalline snowflakes into a billion frozen pinpricks. The yearbook kept bumping against my knee while I walked. As I made my way to the deserted bus stop, I fished the pipe out of my pocket and lit my final thimble of marijuana. The street was dead except for the occasional blurred swish of a passing car. I kept replaying the scene in the office, trying to edit it in a way that would present me in a positive light, but there simply was nothing there. I saw the faces of the three women as they watched me back out of the office, a mixture of disappointment and pity that had come to represent all of my relationships with the opposite sex. I pulled up the collar on my trench coat and shoved my hands deep in my pockets. Fuck it, I thought. I'm going to Hollywood. Why not? Who needed this town or this job? No one here appreciated me. In California, things would be different. No snow for one thing. I wouldn't be freezing my ass off; I would be sunbathing at the beach. And the people were my kind of people, dreamers, believers, people who fantasized a better life for themselves and then made that life a reality, people who lived in a world of fantasies and didn't have to apologize for it. I would be welcomed there with open arms. They would recognize me for who I really was. A hero. A leading man.

I felt the energy returning to my body. I was smart. I was talented. I was special.

"I'm going to Hollywood!" I screamed into the cold wind. I clenched my fists and raised my arms in the air. "I'm going to be famous!"

I stayed like this until I felt silly, which did not take long, and then I put my hands back in my pockets. The wind picked up and the snow flurries increased to a blinding rate. I turned my back to the deluge and pulled my hat down. The air was so cold my eyes teared up and my nose began to run, the tears and snot freezing on my face. The wall of snow reduced visibility, and I didn't see the coyote until it was practically in my lap. It was gray and gaunt, its belly sucked up against its spine. Coyotes weren't an uncommon sight in Mountainview, especially during the winter. They came into the city when they were starving, looking for trash cans to pick through or stray cats to eat. Not often, but sometimes, they were also rabid. I knew very little about coyotes or rabies, but this one had a manic look in its eye I did not like.

It stopped when it saw me and did a little sideways dance, making like it was going to run away with its tail tucked between its legs but then quickly turning around and snapping. I took a step back and squeaked, which was probably not the correct protocol for handling wild coyotes. The animal took my reaction for weakness, which it was, and regained its courage. It yipped at me several times and bared its teeth, and then it continued on to its destination, which was a nearby park next to a row of gray condominiums. It glanced at me one more time over its shoulder and then broke into a run, loping gracefully through the park, passing by a children's playground before disappearing through a fence surrounding the condos.

The bus pulled up and I boarded. The snow was blinding now, swirling up around the vehicle in roiling waves. The driver was a young man with a dishwater-blonde ponytail and a maroon uniform that was damp in the armpits despite the cold weather. He gripped the wheel with both hands, leaning toward the windshield with unblinking eyes, as though he could push the bus through the onslaught by sheer force of will. The night was pitch-black and the windshield wipers were frantic but useless. The headlights barely penetrated five feet. There were three other people on the bus, a mother and her elementary-school child and a wide-eyed college student. We all sat mute watching the front window.

The temperature dropped another twenty degrees, and the wind increased. The pavement had soaked up the sunshine earlier in the day, retaining the heat and causing the snowflakes to melt on impact, and now that water was freezing, forming a thin sheet of slick ice over the entire road. When the driver tapped on the breaks at the next stop, the vehicle went into a slow skid, causing the student to moan and the mother to clutch her child to her breast.

It was no longer a snowstorm but a full-blown blizzard, the type of natural force that blocks out all rational thought and reduces humans to their most animalistic instincts. Businesses would close their doors and schools would cancel classes. The MIFF would be forced to end early.

Finally, the driver inched his way to my stop. "Stay safe," he said as the door hissed closed.

I nodded. The bus pulled away, and I was more alone than I had ever been in my life. The streets were deserted, and I couldn't see more than an arm's length in front of my face. My eyes burned with the cold, and I blinked back tears. It was now well below freezing, and even with my coat buttoned to the collar and my hands in my pockets, my extremities went numb in seconds. Crossing the street was difficult. There was a crosswalk but no light, and I couldn't see oncoming traffic. In the end, I bit the bullet and stepped off the curb into oblivion. My dress shoes were like roller skates, and I fell twice, each time expecting a vehicle to plow into my head. It was only six blocks to The Trap, but it took me almost twenty minutes to get there. I fell twice more, the last time twisting my ankle in such a manner that it would have hobbled me with pain if I had any feeling in my legs. As it was, I managed to stand up and limp along, completely disoriented by the blizzard. When I finally found the front door of my building, my fingers were so frozen that I couldn't get a solid grip on the icy doorknob. My hand kept sliding off. Finally, I gave up and began pounding on the door.

After a few minutes, the Mayor arrived wearing what can only be described as a tropical muumuu. It was hot pink, covered in yellow flowers, and hung loosely over his gut and all the way down to his bare feet. He poked his head outside and said, "Whoa. Kind of chilly out here?"

I tried to tell him to shut up, but my teeth were chattering too hard to speak. Instead, I pushed past him and began climbing the stairs on all fours, the sudden heat from the building causing a painful tingling in my fingers and toes and inducing tears of relief. The Mayor followed behind me, talking the entire goddamn time.

"So I've been contemplating your story, and I believe the problem here is that we're thinking too small. It's the classic mistake, man. Like, okay, so look here, okay, so there's drugs being sold in that strip club, right? There's drugs being sold and the police are in on it, right? I mean, look here, they have to be. Because Moss, right, look here, Moss is corrupt, we already know that, but they're not processing heroin in Mountainview, no way, man. So it has to be happening somewhere else in the state, and how could they be doing that without help from political figures in the state capital? They couldn't. So this reaches all the way to the top, right? I've been saying this for years. And rent is due in ten days. That makes fourteen-thirty-five you owe me, as per our previous arrangement. I'll come by to collect it first of the month."

I made it to the top of the stairs. My fingers were burning now, and I was struggling to put my hands in my pocket to retrieve my keys. After a long battle, I managed to pull them out, but they fell to the floor. I picked them up and tried to jam them into the lock. Meanwhile, the Mayor was still going a mile a minute.

"I knew it, man! I knew it! I was telling everyone...look here, I was telling people the election was rigged. They wanted to keep me down, man. They want to keep us all down. They want to silence us, man!"

I got the door open, ran inside, and slammed it in the Mayor's face. This did not deter him in the least. He kept shouting from the other side of the door.

"They want to silence us, Sam, but we can't let them. If we expose the mayor, we can get a recall, and then I can elected again. Sam! This is perfect. When I get back in office, the first thing I'll do is fire Moss and make you... um...secretary of state...or whatever. We'll expose the ugly underbelly of this city, Sam! You and me, man! You and me!"

I cupped my hands together and blew warm air into them. I plugged in a space heater and cranked the hot plate up to high. I rubbed my palms together and placed them over the hot plate until my fingers began to scream with pain as the warmth reinvigorated the numb nerve endings. I fumbled through the army of empty alcohol bottles standing at attention on the coffee table until I found one with three inches of brown liquid at the bottom. I fell back into the couch with a heavy sigh. The Mayor was still babbling.

"And, look here, and if we take what happened to Bobby Kennedy and Malcolm, man, and we have to ask ourselves where Henry Moss was when the CIA injected autism into baby vaccines…"

I put the bottle to my lips and tipped it back. The room was already warming up. I took off my hat and coat and tossed them on the bed. I fished the yearbook out of the jacket and set it on the coffee table. It had been a long day, and I was glad it was over. I had made the right decision. Victoria and Reyna could handle the story without me. I was back where I belonged.

But something didn't feel quite right. I had my alcohol and my weed and my movies, but something was missing.

"Audrey!" I cried.

I ripped the blanket off the wall and yanked open the window. My bones cried out when the blast of cold air hit me. The night was dark and silent, and there was no movement on the tree. I called Audrey's name several times, but there was no reaction. The tree was covered in snow, and there was a large white lump where she usually slept.

I had to lean halfway out the window to reach it. It was so far out that I almost slipped and fell several times. Finally I reached the patch of snow. I grabbed it and pulled it to my chest. Nothing. It was nothing but a handful of snow. I screamed Audrey's name several more times, but there was no answer. I sat back on the couch, the snowball that was not Audrey melting in my hand.

I picked out a movie and fed it into the DVD player. I took a drink from the bottle. My mind was racing with a million worries and questions. Should I go out and try to find Audrey? Should I catch the flight to California with Eric and Maggie? Should I accept the editor job at the Mountainview Chronicle?

And then the movie started and my mind went blank.

It is early morning on Fifth Avenue in New York City, and a yellow taxi pulls up to the curb. Audrey Hepburn steps out in an elegant black evening gown, a pearl necklace, and sunglasses. She's eating a pastry and drinking a cup of coffee. She looks through the window at Tiffany & Co. and cocks her head in that adorable Audrey Hepburn way. An orchestra plays "Moon River" in the background.

The wind blows cold air and snow through the open window, but I feel nothing. Audrey is here. Audrey will never leave me. Everything is perfect.

Acknowlegments

Authors write alone, but they don't complain, drink, cry, edit, or rewrite alone. At least, I don't. My wife, Michelle, is always my first and last reader, and I never would have finished this book without her. Megan and Chris have been with me from the beginning.

Thanks to Nicole, Beki, Max, Laura, Beau, Lupe, Travis, Kirk, Dru and Beth for reading early drafts. Paul and Lucas made me laugh when I wanted to cry. Zach and Michael fed me and listened to me rant. My mom, Lois, and my sister, Cheri, have always supported me. I am grateful for my family, both the one I was born into and the one I have chosen.

Pamela, Vince, Grace, Erica, Josie, and Dana—you know why. Thanks to Half Price Books and the Austin Public Library for paying me to be a nerd. And finally, deep gratitude to Katherine Noble, Kimberly Verhines, and the staff at Stephen F. Austin State University Press.

Photo by Zach Nash

DALE BRIDGES is a writer and painter living in Austin with his wife, two cats, a tarantula, a corn snake, and far too many old movies. His short story collection, *Justice, Inc.*, was published in 2014. This is his first novel.

CPSIA information can be obtained
at www.ICGtesting.com
Printed in the USA
LVHW100808300123
738071LV00003B/12